Sophia Creswell

Born in Paris in 1969, Sophia Creswell was brought up in Dorset and now lives in Oxford. She has lived in St Petersburg, where she worked as an English language teacher and an art publisher, and has travelled extensively in the Far East and Africa. She has published one previous novel, *Sam Golod*, and in 1998 won the Southern Arts' Writer's Award.

Also by Sophia Creswell

Sam Golod

Sophia Creswell

RED
TAPE

SCEPTRE

"Jerusalem" words and music by Alpha Blondy © 1986,
EMI Music Pub France SA, France.
Reproduced by permission of EMI Music Publishing Limited,
London WC2H 0EA.

First published in 1998 by Hodder and Stoughton
A division of Hodder Headline PLC
A Sceptre Paperback

10 9 8 7 6 5 4 3 2 1

A CIP catalogue record for this title is available from the British Library
ISBN 0 340 66658 7

Typeset by
Palimpsest Book Production Limited, Polmont, Stirlingshire
Printed and bound in Great Britain by
Mackays of Chatham PLC, Chatham, Kent

Hodder and Stoughton
A division of Hodder Headline PLC
338 Euston Road
London NW1 3BH

Thank you to Southern Arts and to Katie
(a gratuitous way to slip in a Higginbottom at the
beginning of my book)

Chapter One

It had to be morning soon. Not even a February night could last forever. The room was dark and stuffy and thick with used breath. Lydia stared at the raised pattern of the wallpaper on the ceiling. Maybe, she thought, if she stared at it for too long the pattern would leave an impression on her retina, like furniture leaving dimples on a carpet, then whatever she looked at afterwards would always have the faint ghost of this ceiling overlaid on top of it like tracing paper. Lydia blinked, Seriozha's white arm slumped heavy and dead across her shoulder. The base of his thumb pushed at her nipple and she could feel his stomach against her bottom. Wherever his body contacted hers it provoked a residue of sweat. On the bedside table lay his wife's pots of expensive French face cream and the latest copy of Russian *Cosmopolitan* magazine.

Slowly she lifted Seriozha's arm and slipped out from beneath the blanket and sheet. Somewhere in his dreams he sensed her absence and clutched at the pillow. Lydia stood by the window, her thin white body as luminescent as birch bark in the dark. Waves of heat rose from the radiator beneath the sill over her belly and breasts.

Seriozha's flat was on the seventh floor of a fifteen floor concrete tower block in the far south of St Petersburg. The darkness outside was punctured by squares of light from the windows of the other tower blocks. On the ground the padded figure of an old woman with her head wrapped in a scarf moved along the black line of a path that ran through the snow and the twiggy trees. Further away by the road Lydia saw the electric spark of a trolley bus. If the buses were running, it was morning.

Lydia walked through to the kitchen. Two smeared glasses and a bottle of Bison Grass vodka stood on the table beside a large jar of plum compote, a saucer of pickled gherkins and two slices of curling black bread. The sweet herbal smell of the vodka filled the room. It smells like medicine, thought Lydia. She ran a finger along the edge of the formica table and; picking up one of the glasses, filled it with plum compote. The clock, painted onto a plate on the wall, read eight o'clock.

When she had finished drinking Lydia returned down the corridor to the bedroom and took up her watch by the window once more. Seriozha was now lying on his back beneath the pink satin headboard, his arms spanning the entire bed. In this position he snored, his white body juddering as the breath left it. She could see where the more weathered skin of his neck joined his soft white chest. I will miss the times like this, she thought, when I can stay the whole night and not have to get dressed and walk through the freezing night to the stink of Kupchina Metro when I am drowsy and sex drugged. But the opposite was also true. Nights like these when she could fall asleep after sex were rare and welcome but not really as relished as the cold privacy of her own sheets. Nevertheless when he had gone with his wife and child to the Crimea the previous summer she had from time to time speculated about what he was doing at that particular moment. She imagined him swimming in the sea and tried to conjure up the smell and the taste of salt. She imagined him eating caviar, popping the little eggs between his teeth, and hoped his wife wasn't being too difficult otherwise he would be unbearable when he returned. At the same time she had felt quite happy on her own, free from his demands, and found that she didn't really want him to return. She had a daydream in which he stayed with his wife by the sea. But in reality he was coming back and she couldn't stop him. He was her lover. It was pointless to dream of things that wouldn't happen and it only made her life more complicated. So she'd banished the daydream and when he had walked through the door of her office at Lenfilm she had felt a rush of relief and discovered that after all she was quite pleased that he had come back. But this time it was she who was going away and for much longer. Would she miss him? Probably not, she thought, it's those left behind who do the missing.

Lydia looked again out of the window. Two more figures, men this time, were walking down the path. She wondered about the snow. When the British crew had come to Lenfilm to film *Orlando* Seriozha had assigned her to help them and translate for them. She remembered asking one of the set designers whether it snowed in London. He'd replied that it did but not every year. Lydia hoped that it would snow this year. Winter was bad enough but it must be terrible without snow to brighten it up.

Seriozha grunted. 'What time is it?'

She told him.

'And when's your flight again?'

She told him that too. He frowned with concentration. 'Then if we're quick we have time to do it once more before we have to leave for your mother's office. Come here,' he said, 'this is my last chance for a long time.' He stretched out his arm towards her from the bed. She didn't say, 'it's also my last chance' and she didn't ask, 'what about your wife'. She walked over and bending down like a mother kissing a child goodnight she pressed her lips quite tenderly to his forehead. He pulled her onto the bed and began pushing his tongue into her mouth. She felt the weight of him as he manoeuvred himself on top of her. She stroked her hands down either side of his spine, over his buttocks and down the backs of his thighs in order to encourage him. He pushed himself inside her and she pulled apart her knees to make it easier for him. She looked up past the white rounded rock of his shoulder to the ceiling. She thought, I know this view so well, is this what I will miss?

Seriozha wasn't hard enough and he soon slipped out of her. She squeezed her hand·between their bodies and stroked him until he was erect again and then he tried two more times to enter her before rolling onto his back and sighing angrily. She covered his body with hers hooking her knee across his thighs, and with her forefinger she gently played with the hairs on his chest. 'It doesn't matter,' she said sooth-ingly but his sigh irritated her. It was the precise tone of it. Seriozha was making her feel guilty. The sigh said; if only you were softer and more giving (and more feminine) then I wouldn't have this problem. 'It really doesn't matter,' she said again.

'It does! I want to.'

'That's why. You can't force it. We did it last night. It's enough and we don't have so much time now anyway.'

Seriozha sighed one more time and, pushing Lydia off him, got out of bed and went to the toilet. He didn't close the door and the sound of him peeing echoed down the corridor. Lydia picked up her knickers from the pile of clothes on the floor and began to get dressed.

Neither of them talked in the car and they drove through the city with only the sound of sludge splattering against the side windows to accompany them. He parked outside the Marble Palace and leant forwards with his forearms on the steering wheel. 'I'll wait for you,' he said, jerking his head towards the black iron gates. She nodded, got out of the car and slipped through the gates into the courtyard. She passed the great marble plinth which had until recently displayed Lenin's armoured car and, walking carefully so as not to slip on the compacted snow, pushed through a side door into the right-hand wing of the palace. Inside the walls were covered in deep red flock wallpaper that had begun to curl where it joined the picture rail. The polish on the parquet floor had worn away and the frosted glass in the door to Academia Publishing had a long crack running diagonally across one corner. The offices smelt of carbon paper and cheap *papperossi* cigarettes. Lydia nodded at the receptionist and crossed the hallway to her mother's office.

Olga was on the telephone when her daughter entered the room. She continued her conversation, making no sign that she had noticed Lydia's arrival. From the office window Lydia looked out across the crusted jumble of the river ice to the gold splinter of the Peter and Paul fort. The sky had turned a charcoal grey that grew paler in the east. Dawn was on its way. In another hour it would be light and the city's short day would begin. When Olga eventually finished her call she replaced the heavy Bakelite receiver on its rocker, handling it carefully as if it was an instrument of great delicacy, and pushing back her wooden chair she circumnavigated her desk and slowly made her way towards her daughter.

'I've come to say goodbye Mama,' said Lydia.

Olga planted her hands on her solid hips. 'Well I suppose I must wish you a good voyage. I don't suppose you will be gone for long. You'll soon grow tired of it all in the West. They always do. And then you'll come back to Russia and you'll probably appreciate it much more then. So I suppose it's for the best.'

Lydia blocked her ears to the edges of blackmail and hysteria in her mother's homily. Olga had said all this before and now this speech was just a formula, a string of remembered phrases that grew increasingly fast and wavering. She knew it was a waste of energy to try and change her mother's point of view so she just stood and waited while the stream of words poured over her. When Olga finally stopped Lydia held out her arms and, hugging her mother's reproachful lanolin-scented shoulders, said goodbye. She left quickly before Olga had time to deliver another lecture.

It was light by the time they reached the airport. A dishrag grey sky promised more snow. Seriozha took her suitcase from the boot but Lydia carried her portfolio and cameras herself. She was impatient; she wanted to be gone. She was bored with all these goodbyes that seemed to be dragging on forever. After she had checked in, Seriozha insisted on buying her a glass of tea from the cafeteria and she accepted, knowing she couldn't be cruel just as she was leaving him for another country. He looked ridiculous entangled in the spindly metal table with a delicate glass of tea in his fist, like a circus bear. She switched on a smile for him, 'Cheer up, I'll soon be gone!'

Seriozha grunted, 'Sasha will take care of you. He has friends.'

Lydia nodded, 'If I move I'll let you know.'

'It won't be long.'

'No,' she agreed but knew that she was lying or at least hoped she was. She hoped that it would be a very long time.

Seriozha pulled an envelope from his coat pocket and slid it across the table towards her, 'A little insurance money,' he said. She looked at it for a minute while playing scales across the back of her teeth with her tongue and then with a minute twitch of her nose covered the envelope with her palm and dropped it into her handbag next to her new external passport.

'I should go now,' she said, 'there's no point in waiting any longer.'

Seriozha nodded lugubriously and after extricating himself from the limbs of the table escorted her to the barrier. She smiled, kissed him with closed lips, turned and walked briskly away.

Chapter Two

Lydia found London disorienting. It was too warm for the beginning of February and the light was peculiar: it shone from smooth white clouds that seemed to sit on top of the buildings. Every day it rained and the stone pavements and the black tarmac glistened a slick orange under street lights as big as sunbeds. It was a strange city, everything out of proportion, the buildings either large or tiny and squashed together in long, long rows. The roads were crowded with primary-coloured cars and curiously flimsy-looking lorries. Lydia had noticed the incongruity from the moment she landed. The airport was big and brightly lit, everywhere she turned there were shops framed in illuminated plastic and decorated for a festival with lurid pink hearts and fat angels. The metro, by contrast, was small, dark and labyrinthine. Trains shot out of foul-smelling tunnels like worms. Outside, huge garish advertising hoardings leered over narrow roads. Everything was like this, the scale was either too large or too small.

She had thought that life would be very difficult and complicated. She had braced herself for problems but to begin with everything seemed to happen so smoothly that Lydia had felt as if she were in a trance; as if there were a pattern that you followed and then it all unfurled before you. She had rented a room from Sasha. He lived in Kennington in a house with six rooms. He let them all out (and all the other people living there were Russians). A doctor lived next door to Lydia. He wore brown cardigans, hunched his shoulders and smiled very shyly at her if he met her outside the safety of his door. There was a light bulb that hung on a long flex in the hallway and the wallpaper, which was covered in large orange daisies, was peeling from the walls at the edge of each strip. The plaster beneath was so old that it had hairs in it.

Sasha lived in a room on the first floor. He had been kind and welcoming. He'd met her at the airport and been full of information about the English national character. He had seemed lonely and anxious. He had kept on asking her about Seriozha and Lydia had got the impression that he was in awe of him. She'd deflected his questions and hadn't asked him how he knew Seriozha. He'd invited her to his room and given her a drink of beer and she'd sat on the edge of his large, new, brown velveteen sofa and watched the red and green lights flicker across a large stack of matt black electronic equipment. He wants a friend, or maybe a lover, she'd thought and determined to evade him as kindly as possible.

He had sniffed and shown her to her room. It was like a small piece of corridor. A huge old-fashioned wardrobe hid the bed and blocked out the light from a pair of barred french windows that seemed to lead directly out into a brick wall. 'It's cheap,' he'd said peering around the room as if he had never seen it before. 'You'd have to look a long time before you found a better deal than this. London prices.' He'd shaken his head sadly and pointed to the corner, 'Look, you've even got your own basin. I'm only doing it because you're a friend of Seriozha's. I could get a lot more for it if I advertised.'

He had hovered in the doorway and waited for her gratitude.

'I'll take it,' she'd said simply.

He'd sniffed again. 'You'll be wanting work?' he had asked. Lydia had shrugged. He'd pulled a card from a shiny new gilt and leather wallet. 'Go to this restaurant. They are Russian and they don't ask about your visa. Tell Slava I sent you. He's a personal friend of mine. Here's your key,' he'd said, pulling it from the door and tossing it on the bed. And then he had mumbled, 'I'll be upstairs,' and left her to her two neatly packed plastic suitcases.

Lydia started work at Russki's the following week. The restaurant was on the King's Road in Chelsea. The walls were lined with dark wood panelling decorated with small Palik enamels of *boyars* in troikas dashing through snowscapes. The proprietor was a man called Slava who had defected from a touring dance troupe in the sixties while they played at the Albert Hall. It was the defining moment in his life and he was proud of it. He felt it gave him distinction, a superiority over the wave of Russians now coming West but it also made him sad and occasionally cruel; nothing as monumental would happen to him again.

'You can't appreciate it in the way that I do,' he said to Lydia, as he perched by the cash desk just inside the door and tapped his carefully manicured fingers on the edge of the till, 'it's too easy for you all. It means nothing. In my day it was dangerous. We risked our lives: we didn't just fill in pieces of paper.'

Lydia nodded unenthusiastically. She wasn't interested in how it used to be before the changes. She was in England now and she didn't want to listen to tedious comparisons with the old days. She looked around the room. In the window was an ornate dusty samovar. Little brass lamps with red fringed shades stood on each wooden table. Lydia thought, this is the most 'Russian' room I have ever seen and that is how I know that I am not in Russia.

A fat untidy man came through the door. Slava introduced him as Igor. It seemed that he was the other waiter. Slava ordered him to show her what to do. She had to write down the customer's order and push it through the hatch to Dimitri, the Serb chef who made lots of obscene jokes. When the food was ready she took it back out to the table and when the customer had finished eating she gave the plate to Volodya, the kitchen hand, another Serb who hardly seemed to speak at all. It was not difficult work and quite soon she became irritated with Igor telling her what to do the whole time and began to ignore him.

One day Igor cornered her while she was making coffee by the plain stainless-steel samovar underneath the stairs. He came up close behind her and pinched her bottom so hard that it hurt. She was angry. She turned off the tap and wheeling around gave him an icy glare. 'I know how you got this job,' he leered.

'How did I get this job?' she retorted in her most superior voice.

He smirked, 'You're a friend of Seriozha's aren't you?' He laid all his emphasis on the word 'friend' making it sound as obscene as one of Dimitri's jokes.

'So?'

'Nothing, nothing. There is nothing wrong with having friends.'

'Precisely,' said Lydia injecting as much menace as she could into her voice, 'in fact I've always found it very useful.' She watched his pupils flinch and with the satisfactory feeling of having hit her target she turned back to making the coffee. She was not, she hissed furiously to herself, going to let some creep like Igor have a hold on her.

Lydia liked the strangeness of the West. She found it intoxicating. It kept her eyes hooked wide open and she could feel the air intensely on her skin. The sensation reminded her of using menthol creams or wearing a summer dress for the first time after the winter. She placed the camera between herself and the city, recorded the images she saw and then meticulously filed them away. Lydia, who was normally very frugal, was shocked by how much film she used during her first month. Then she shrugged and told herself that she didn't care. She had come to England to be free and to take photographs and to try to sell them and that was what she was doing. This is what she'd dreamed of as she'd stared through the windows of her mother's flat in St Petersburg. Now it was actually happening. She was working and she could spend her wages on what she liked. There was no one to tell her what to do – no mother to disapprove, no Seriozha to sneer.

Lydia smiled to herself and, following the (coloured, glossy) *A to Z*, walked across South London to Battersea Park to take more photographs. The things she saw were extraordinary: the shape of the road signs, the colours of crisp packets, the clothes that people wore and the parks with their stern, discreet iron railings. She thought, it's a great privilege to be a foreigner in a city. For a foreigner everything is strange and peculiar and notable, nothing has become sullied or mundane.

Each day Lydia walked a little further with her camera. At the beginning of April she crossed a pretty pink and white bridge near Battersea Park and wandered north along Chelsea Embankment. She looked at the map. She was very close to Russki's but it was several hours before her shift started. It was a day out of a child's storybook. The air was soft, white lamblike clouds drifted shadows across the water and in the plane trees sharp little green tongues licked out from the dead winter branches. Nobody, thought Lydia, knows where I am. A jogger passed her, red-faced and panting, concentrating earnestly on the rhythm of his thumping shoes. I'm invisible, she thought, I've evaporated and I'm drifting through London on a small spring wind. The idea made her very happy and she smiled. After a while she noticed a tower in front of her built on a bend in the river. It was topped by a pyramid and a curious spike with a ball half way up it. She crossed a busy junction and over the wall she saw the jostling roofs of a colony of houseboats. There appeared to be about a hundred of them rising and falling on the smooth swell of the river. Each one was a different shape and size but all of them were painted the colours of sweets; peppermint green, winegum red, bubblegum and marshmallow pink. The decks were fringed with striped awnings, flowers spilled from pots and climbed along railings. On one of the boats by the bridge somebody wearing turquoise trousers was lying on a pale-blue sun lounger reading a book. Lydia leaned over the wall enchanted. It looked as if someone had transported one of the Black Sea holiday villages to the centre of London. Who lived here, she wondered enviously and then, as an automatic reaction, she picked up her camera and fired off a volley of photographs. But for once her heart wasn't in it and she let the camera go and her eyes rambled unbound across the scene in front of her.

After a while Lydia pushed through a gate marked 'Private, Chelsea Yacht and Boat Company' and walked down a ridged wooden gangplank to a line of green pontoons that separated an outer row of boats from an inner one. At the bottom of the gangplank was a notice board with a sun-faded map of all the boats. Two pieces of paper had been stuck to the side: one was for a lost cat and the second, written in green crayon on the back of a telephone bill, read, 'Wanted. Lodger for *Toadhall*, £75 a week plus bills, ring Richard 352 9876'. Lydia looked out across the river. £75 a week. That was £25 more than Sasha charged but there would be no Russians and she could walk to work so she wouldn't have to pay for a travel pass. She consulted the map. *Toadhall* was eight boats from the bridge on the outside row. An elderly man in faded blue overalls came past and started loading black plastic rubbish bags onto a little hand-pushed trolley. He showed her the way and she stood at the end of *Toadhall*'s gangplank and surveyed it. An orange-and-white lifebuoy leant against a coal scuttle on the back deck, next to it a mountain bike was chained to the railing, a piece of Indian cloth filled a porthole, sun-bright waves chattered around the seaweed floating from the black hull and green paint peeled from the door. Oh yes, thought Lydia, definitely, I could live here.

Chapter Three

Sally had given her the car and Marjory drove it very cautiously. Approaching the turning she indicated right, changed down from fourth gear to third, second to first and held the car on the clutch in the middle of the road. She turned her head left, right and left again and seeing the nose of a yellow car bonnet peep around the corner of the bridge she dithered and then pulled at the handbrake until the car had passed and the road was clear for her to turn into the lane that led to the station.

Alex was phantom driving: foot slammed down on the accelerator – screeech – cutting straight in front of the yellow car. He could see the driver, another middle-aged woman, blench but they'd got away with it, they were gone, shooting down the lane. Except they weren't, they were still sitting in the middle of the road. *Go, go, go! What are you waiting for? The road's fucking clear! Christ!* His mother's liver-spotted hand hovered over the handbrake. Alex raked his fingers through his long curly black hair and leaning his head back on the headrest dreamt of London. He'd go to every play that was on, he'd get student tickets, he'd sit in the aisles. He could smell the plush and the print of glossy programmes – the cosy agreeable sensation of being an insider. Actors – maybe he'd know them, they might be friends – under hot lights. He'd know the scene, man. There wouldn't be anything he didn't know. Pubs; high after performances, smoking. Bottles of wine and spliffs in breeze block dressing rooms but this time it would be real. He'd have a right to be there. Not like university when they were all playing a game – Mark Dryden becoming an accountant and Jasper, Jasper of all people, leaving his band to be a tour guide.

Alex untangled his legs and propped them up on the plastic dashboard. His big feet pressed against the windscreen, his thighs squashed against his chest and his knees stuck up around his ears like a cricket. The car was imprisoned by two walls of banks. The hedges that grew on top of them were too high for Alex see into the fields beyond. Hanging on a five bar gate at the corner was a hand-written sign advertising free range eggs. Marjory glanced at her son and pressed her lips together.

'What if we had a crash?' She said, her tone disapproving but reasonable.

Alex shrugged, threw his hands in the air and putting on a mock-Jewish accent played to an imaginary audience. 'You see what I have to deal with huh? Is it surprising I'm going crazy? Out of my mind. Mother-smother. You donna understand what it's like when you have to live with legs like these and you have to squeeze them into a space like this. I tell you it's cruelty, cruelty to long-legged people. There should be laws against this kind of thing. I tell you what I'm going to do. I'm going to write a letter about it!'

'Stop fooling around and just put the seat back.'

Alex switched his accent to phoney Cockney, 'But I have guv'nor, honest, far as it will go.'

His mother huffed and gave in and Alex turned his attention back to the dreary green hedges that blurred on either side of them and tried to contain his excitement. He was going to London. At last. He was really, really going.

They passed a garage with a green-and-yellow plastic lid over the forecourt. A sign listed the prices of leaded and unleaded petrol, diesel and MOT tests. The sign was broken, a hole in the plastic showed a white gap and a neon tube. On their left-hand side the turf had been skinned from a field, exposing pale grey clay mud. A hoarding announced the arrival of sixteen new Barratt homes.

'Why don't you try and get a job in one of the theatre box-offices?' ventured Marjory. Her voice still terribly reasonable. 'I'm sure it's not very well paid but it would give you a much clearer idea of what the theatrical world is like and you could ask around and find out what the best way in is.'

He was mock-theatrical now. He pressed the back of his hand against his forehead: a young Laurence Olivier. Genius, misunderstood, unrecognised. 'But darling, I must to go to RADA.'

'If you could be serious for just one minute, darling. This is your future that we're talking about. You never know you might just find that acting isn't what you want to do after all. It's not much fun waiting around on the dole you know and there are lots of other jobs in the theatre.'

Alex groaned and stared out of the window, 'I know that Mum, but if I'm good enough I won't be on the dole will I?'

The corners of Marjory's mouth compressed into two down-turning grooves that wrinkled her dark-pink lipstick. Alex knew that his mother was wondering what would happen if he wasn't good enough. It wasn't a question he allowed himself to think about. This wasn't arrogance, it was fear. It didn't do to think about failure: it wasn't helpful.

They turned past some light industrial units next to a herd of Frisian cows grazing under some ash trees. Marjory parked by a fence in the station car-park.

It was August and the summer had exhausted the trees around the car-park. The air that moved sluggishly around the drab green leaves smelt of dust and hot metal. Alex stretched his legs and pulled his rucksack from the boot. His mother hitched the thin navy-blue strap of her handbag up her shoulder. Alex's heart sank, he wanted to be gone now, he wanted to leave her behind. 'Don't bother waiting Mum, I'll be fine, you go on to the hospital.'

'I've left plenty of time. I don't have to see the specialist until twelve.'

Of course, she would have organized the appointment to allow for traffic jams, late trains, mechanical breakdowns and acts of God. He nodded and fastening the buckle of his rucksack waited for her to lock up the car before they made their way towards the painted wooden walkway that led over the tracks to the platform. Damn, he thought to himself, I'll have to wait another ten minutes before I can have a fag.

They sat side by side on a bench and peered down the tracks towards Exeter until their eyes grew sore from the glare and the warped jellied heat. Marjory admonished Alex to be thoughtful and tidy while he was staying with his sister. 'It's very kind of her to have you and she's a busy woman.'

Alex made vague but agreeable noises but he wasn't paying any attention now because at last, at last, at last, at last he could see the nose of the train coming around the corner by the industrial units. An old man in a peaked cap disappeared inside the ticket office. The tannoy croaked, 'The train now arriving at platform one is the two fifteen to London Waterloo, calling at Sherborne, Templecombe, Gillingham, Salisbury . . .' Alex hugged his mother awkwardly, wished her luck at the hospital and found himself a seat opposite an old bird in a crimplene dress who was unwrapping a tinfoil packet of home-made sandwiches. As the train pulled out from underneath the flaking wooden awning Alex opened a tin of Old Holborn tobacco and rolled himself a cigarette. He left his bags in the care of the old lady and went to the area between the carriages. The wind boomed and roared through a half-open window as the train picked up speed. Alex lit his cigarette and inhaled deeply. He felt the cold sweat and dizziness of a nicotine rush and had to lean his head back against the scuffed yellow plastic of the lavatory door to steady himself.

Chapter Four

Sally checked her watch for the second time in a minute. Twenty to six. Alex's train had arrived at Waterloo just over ten minutes ago. She was going to be late. He'd have to wait outside the boat until she got back. Damn. She'd promised her mother that she would take care of him. Sally leant forward and scanned the words on the screen looking for mistakes then pressed 'Print' and, swivelling her chair around towards the tinted-glass window, picked up the individual sheets of the document the moment they emerged from the printer. She swept a packet of Silk Cut cigarettes into her handbag, clicked it shut and, armed with the newly printed document and her briefcase, headed for the door. Sally's assistant, Hannah, had a desk in the neighbouring office. Sally checked her watch once more. Thirteen minutes to. 'I'm off now,' she said to Hannah, 'but this has *got* to go by courier to the printers *tonight*. It's *vital* okay? Don't just leave it at reception. I want *you* to make sure that the guy gets it yourself. Okay?'

The phone was ringing. Hannah, who'd been picking her nails, nodded at Sally and then turned to pick up the receiver. 'Can I ask who's calling?' she said in a bored, prim voice and then covering the phone with her hand mouthed 'Flavia?'

Sally stretched across Hannah's desk and took the receiver from her. 'Hi, how was it? Did you see him?'

'Yeah, no it was fine. He took it very well. To be honest with you I think he knew it was coming. He must have done. Listen, what time do you think you're going to be finished?'

'I'm actually on my way out now. I'd love to have a drink but I really can't. My brother's arriving from Dorset. I'm already late as it is. The poor boy will be sitting on my doorstep waiting for me.'

'Boatstep.'

Sally smiled, 'All right boatstep then but whatever I can't chat. I'll ring you tomorrow.'

Sally passed the phone back to Hannah and, holding her hand up as if she were stopping traffic, fled through the door. A minute later she was back. 'If my brother rings tell him I'm on my way.'

'Go!' demanded Hannah.

'I am. Don't forget about the courier. It's got to be your signature on the slip. I'll see you tomorrow.' Sally closed the door, checked her watch once more, exhaled in a short jet of breath, pushed out her chin and marched towards the lift, straightening her jacket as she walked.

Outside the air-conditioned offices of Matteson Smith, London was baking in the late afternoon sun. The pavements and the great buildings were as hot as firebricks and Sally fought to pull the thick dry leaded air in and out of her lungs. The tarmac blistered like the skin of a Sunday roast and the bubbles popped as they were skewered by Sally's heels. Traffic was gridlocked down High Holborn. On either side a tight-packed mass of pedestrains filled the pavements and moved in unison towards the tube station. Sally crossed the road weaving in between the cars, their exhausts scorching her nylon tights. She bought an *Evening Standard* from the vendor on the corner of Kingsway, bodies colliding off her as she scrabbled for her change in a small pouch purse.

She marched down the escalator past chewing gum-spotted advertisements and, ignoring the busker who was blowing an electronic version of 'Summertime' into the echoing corridors, pushed through the crowds and took up position at the edge of the platform to wait for the train. Stale diesel-stinking air blasted from the mouth of the tunnel. The train was crammed, the passengers squeezed tight up against the glass. 'Let's wait for the next one,' said the blonde next to Sally, her companion nodded and in less than a second Sally had manoeuvred in front of them, placed her shoe in a small space just inside the door of the train and, with her briefcase positioned in front of her crotch, pushed her body forward and bent her head so that the door didn't close on her hair. The train stank of sweat and brake fluid, swelling feet and newspaper ink. Bodies pushed in on all sides as she clung to the railing that ran along the ceiling with slipping fingers. Sally could feel her armpits growing sticky and foetid. The waistband of her tights bit into her belly and sweat dribbled down the backs of her knees and in between her breasts until it was trapped by the base of her bra. At Covent Garden station Sally was forced out of the train backwards by people struggling to get out. She ruthlessly repositioned herself further inside the train, changed at Embankment and finally got out at Sloane Square.

She waited at the bus stop next to the flower stall at the base of the Duke of York barracks. It was twenty past six. She could see the top deck of the number nineteen bus stuck in traffic halfway around Sloane Square. She banged her brief-case against her legs and hummed impatiently under her breath.

> The Grand old Duke of York,
> He had ten thousand men,
> He marched them up to the top of the hill
> And he marched them down again.

And when they were up, they were up,
And when they were down, they were down,
And when they were only halfway up,
they were neither up nor down.

The bus still hadn't moved. Bugger this, thought Sally. She wheeled around and collided straight into a couple of Italian tourists. She apologised hastily and slaloming through the King's Road trawlers hurried up towards the next bus stop. What have I got in the fridge? There's some taramasalata and that salad I made on Monday night but that's probably off by now. I think I've got some pasta left. Oh shit, I'll buy some fizz from the offie and I'll take him out, it's a lot less hassle in the end.

The backs of Sally's calves ached, there was a sharp pain in her bunions and her shoes were rubbing the backs of her heels raw. She swung her briefcase like a pendulum for momentum. She caught sight of her reflection in a shop window, her bottom and her neck were stuck out like a jerking chicken. Straighten yourself up Sally. But it slowed her down and within a block her neck was poking forward again.

When Sally reached Battersea Bridge she walked down the Embankment. Over the wall she could see the boats. She slowed her pace and smiled as she stepped away from the choking traffic onto the swinging gangplanks. She altered her grip on the hard handle of her briefcase and hooked her thumb over the strap of her handbag as she felt her shoulders relax. Sally had been renting her boat, the *Beagle*, for a year and every day as she arrived back from work and stepped onto the moorings she felt a little kick of pleasure. There was a breeze coming off the river. She breathed it in. *Ah this is what makes it all worthwhile*, she said to herself. It was her catch phrase, she said the same thing every day, till it had been worn pebble smooth by use. The boat was her eccentricity, the thing that made her different, it was the thing that signified her. Her friends would describe her as 'the girl that lives on the boat' and Sally loved that. Better than 'Sally the management consultant'. There was something bohemian about living on a boat.

Alex was on the front deck. He was sitting like a traveller on his rucksack with his long gangly legs stuck up around his ears, smoking a cigarette. He felt the boat move as Sally stepped off the gangplank. He looked around quickly to make sure that she really was there. He was secretly relieved that she had come back. He had begun to think that something might have happened to her but now he was embarrassed with himself for worrying. He slumped his back and gazed with what he hoped was a dreamy expression into the far distance, to the dirty yellow smudge of pollution that marked the point at which the sky met the river. The *Beagle* oscillated on waves warmed by the vanilla light of the low sun. A train inched like a caterpillar across Wandsworth Bridge and on the far bank a small church spire peeked out from behind the bulk of the Hovis factory.

Alex pretended to be too absorbed in the view to notice his sister until she was standing right over him and casting a shadow across his face. Then he gave a little jump. She gushed apologies for giving him a fright, 'and I'm really sorry I'm late,' she continued, 'I just couldn't seem to get away from the office.' She stood silhouetted against the sun and he had to strain his head right back onto his shoulders to look at her. 'I didn't have time to get anything to eat either but I picked up a bottle of cheap fizz and I'll treat you to a meal at the Italian around the corner. Is that all right?'

Alex flicked the wet end of his cigarette into the river and frowned, his thick black eyebrows crumpling over his hooded blue eyes like a geological fault. 'Don't worry about it Sally,' he said gruffly, 'I'm fine, I can look after myself.'

'Don't be stupid Alex,' she said impatiently, she wasn't going to let him go off on one of his stupid moods now that she'd planned it all out, 'I'm hardly going to let you starve your first night in London am I? I'm going to go and get some glasses.'

The Blue Circle Cement barge emerged between the piles of Battersea Bridge and Alex watched as it chugged upriver, streamers of white wash flowing out behind it like ribbons. He sighed, she was as bad as his mother, they didn't understand, either of them, they didn't have a clue. He flicked his lighter. He saw Peter O'Toole in *Lawrence of Arabia* coolly putting his hand in the flame. He bought the lighter up against his palm and pulled it sharply away again as soon as he could feel it burn and then stuffed it in his pocket. 'Thanks Sal, that's kind of you. I appreciate it. I just don't want to be a bother right?'

'Of course you're not a bother. You're my brother.'

'Yeah, right.'

Sally went inside and reappeared ten minutes later dressed in a pair of jeans and a bright orange tee-shirt. She carried a bottle and two wine glasses. 'So how's Mum then?' she asked, tearing the foil of the bottle and calling 'Hi' to a dark-haired man in a deckchair on the next-door boat.

He shaded his eyes like a captain searching the sea for signs of land, 'It's a miracle. She's back from the brink. Two months ago I just wouldn't have believed it was possible. I mean they're keeping an eye on her but her T-cell count, or whatever you call it, is zero. Basically she's cured.'

'Let's drink to that then,' and Sally braced the bottle against her thighs and popped the cork into the Thames. 'Here's to Mum's good health,' she toasted and then added as an afterthought, 'and life in London.'

Alex gulped at the wine and the bubbles spat and stung up his nose. 'How about you Sal? How you been?' he asked politely. She's an alien race, he thought, you've got to treat her like a foreigner and keep it simple then it'll all be fine. The sun, fat and orange, slid down behind the Hovis factory. Shaky red neon fingers stretched across the water towards them. Sally smiled secretly, he seemed so young, she'd forgotten how young he was. The cars and buses queued over Battersea Bridge and she wondered whether they could see the boats beneath them and whether they were envious. 'Not bad, not bad,' she said looking back to her glass as if it could divine the secrets of the future, 'the boat's great, work's hectic, but then it always is and they gave me a pay rise last month so I can't be doing it all wrong.'

'That's good,' he said encouragingly.

'Yeah it is. I suppose my only real blackspot is my love life which is as barren as ever. Hardly surprising as all my friends are getting married and I never meet single men anymore, but, you know, I keep on thinking that I'm going to meet Mr Right one day and it'll all turn out how it's meant to in the end.'

Alex finished his glass. She's too hard, she scares them off, he thought, I'd run a mile if I wasn't her brother. 'There's got to be someone out there who thinks you're the woman for him. I mean look at you. You're pretty, you're fun, you're bright, you've got a good job. What more could a man want?'

'I don't know Alex, I really don't but I wish I did.'

Chapter Five

The trees on London Fields are large and venerable and most have been there for a century or so longer than any of the buildings around them. They swing like huge bells over the ground; the last echoes of the country the city enclosed and a welcome patch of green in the grime of the East End. On the afternoon that Alex arrived in London Igor lay with his friend Max in the shade of one of these London Fields behemoths. Behind them a group of shaggy-haired boys played football, crouching down to catch the ball, taunting and challenging each other with sharp cries. A concrete playground in the corner had been colonised by two tramps, who sat on the merry-go-round passing a plastic bottle of extra-strong cider between them. A young mother in laddered leggings manoeuvred her pram through a slalom of bicycle bars and trundled across the park on a thin tarmac path.

Max was slightly more sober than Igor. He had wedged his narrow bum into a depression between two roots and was leaning against the broad trunk of the tree. Igor lay flat on the ground beside him, balancing on his exposed and hairy belly a three-quarters empty bottle of cheap vodka. Max burped quietly, leant over and removed it. Igor pushed himself up onto one elbow and waited for Max to finish his turn. His hand weaved through the air in the direction of his friend and after a while Max handed the bottle back to him. Dead leaves and earth coated the back of a tee shirt that had been washed so thin you could see the epaulettes of hair on his shoulders. He held the vodka up towards the young mother and toasted her dimpled bum as she passed them. Then shakily he began to sing in a strong Eastern European accent. 'Daisy, Daisy give me your answer do. I'm half crazy all for the love of you.' The young woman looked around with a snooty expression and, hitching her shopping bags further up the handles of her pram, marched on with her hips in a pronounced and officious swagger. Igor smirked, pleased with his effect. He swung the bottle up to his mouth and then wiped his lips with the back of his hand.

'Has she got big tits?' he asked.

'Who?'

'Your wife, dickbrain.'

'Oh right. Her. Well as a matter of fact she has. Got some of the best tits in the club actually.'

Igor's stomach began to wobble with laughter. He snorted and snuffled and wheezed.

'What's so funny?' asked Max irritably but Igor was laughing so much that he couldn't answer.

'What?' asked Max for a second time.

Igor rolled over onto his stomach, tears squeezing out from his eyes and his shoulders still shaking, 'Maybe you'll fall in love with her,' he tittered.

Max grinned and let out a harsh cynical bark of a laugh. 'Yeah and *maybe* in Moscow they'll start milking hens.' He picked up a small twig and began digging a little hole in the earth. 'Shit, I might do. I don't see why not, she's not just your average hooker, you know. She's a nice girl and she's a student and she'll get me my passport.' He returned to his digging and then added as an afterthought, 'I've always had a soft spot for students.'

For some reason Igor found this hysterically funny. He hooted wildly and then collapsed back spitting out bubbles of laughter.

When the vodka was finished Igor and Max strolled down to the Dove on Broadway Market and sat outside with pints of lager. The three tower blocks of the Blackstone Estate leant over the two-storey buildings of the market street and blocked out the sun. The air was hot and heavy. Opposite the pub a man in a white jelaba squatted beside the open door of a shop selling cheap electrical goods. Next to him was an empty café with green plastic banquettes and brown formica tables bearing little yellow and red plastic bottles of ketchup and salad cream. On the other side was a shop that took up two buildings and sold remaindered carpets. A sun-faded advert in the window showed what had once been a brilliant aquamarine swimming pool surrounded by brightly coloured parasols beside which was written 'Miramand; carpets that last a lifetime at a price that you can afford'. Most of the top-floor sash windows were open and a medley of sounds wandered into the street: the agitated wail of Asian pop music, dogs barking, the banging of a hammer, the shrill protest of an electric drill and a woman shouting someone's name. On the street itself numbers and yellow lines had been painted across the cobbles indicating where the market stalls had stood that morning. Crushed cardboard boxes and the discarded outer leaves of cabbages lay in the gutter.

Max dipped his forefinger into his lager and squeaked it around the rim of his glass. 'How's Slava?' he asked.

'Still the same tight fisted bastard that he ever was,' grumbled Igor, 'you did the right thing. I swear if I don't get out of that place soon I'm going to go completely mad. I really have had enough of it now. It just makes me sick you know. I mean Jesus if you think of the amount of money that man makes. That place is full every fucking day and he's charging eight quid for a plate of blini that's costing him one quid, maybe two quid max. And then he has the nerve to turn around to us and say that he can't afford to pay us and all we're getting is tips. I mean shit, I don't know anyone else who would put up with that kind of stuff. He's just taking advantage of us because he knows that most of us can't go anywhere else. It's bloody criminal, that's what it is. I tell you the moment I find something else I'm out of there. I've had it you know. I've just had enough. If you hear of anything, anything at all where they don't ask too many questions . . .'

'Sure,' said Max laconically, 'I'll let you know. Hell I've been there, I know what it's like.'

'This new girl. Did I tell you about her?'

Max shook his head.

'She's driving me mad. I'm far and away the longest serving waiter but the moment this girl waltzes in she acts like she bloody owns the place. She's such a princess you wouldn't believe it. She's fucking some "friend" of Slava's in Petersburg and Dimitri fancies her skinny little arse so she can do what she likes. It's all "yes Lydia this" and "no Lydia that". It makes me want to vomit. It's not like she's some shit-hot superwaitress or anything, she just knows the right people doesn't she.'

'What about another drink?' offered Max who had, for some time, been etching noughts and crosses grids with his thumbnail in a polystyrene take-away box. Igor handed Max his glass.

Max came out of the pub concentrating hard on the shivering surfaces of the two pints of liquid. A strand of hair was tickling his cheek and the urge to push it away was almost unbearable, but with the two glasses in his hands he couldn't do anything about it. He stepped forward too jerkily and a wave of cold lager spilled from the side of the glass and over his thumb. Small silver bubbles beaded his knuckle. Max swore and looked up to see a posse of five bikes with their owners and two female passengers roaring down the street.

He listened as the sounds of their unsilenced engines gargled and jolted over the cobbles.

Max handed Igor his pint and watched the bikers park up beside them and disappear inside. At his feet Igor was making soft engine noises.

'I had a bike once in Warsaw,' said Max.

'I had one in Leningrad,' retorted Igor. 'Huh,' said Max scornfully, 'bet yours was some Soviet piece of shit. I had a proper bike. A Honda like that.'

Igor got defensive. 'I had a proper bike too. Bet you paid thousands of dollars for yours. I found this old Dnieper, took the sidecar off it, souped up the engine a bit and the thing went like a bat out of hell better than any plastic Japanese crap.' Igor staggered to his feet. His head was swinging from side to side but he kept his focus fixed on the nearest motorbike. 'Fall apart in a couple of years,' he said pointing a shaking finger at the bike, 'don't last at all.'

He swung his right foot over the seat of the bike, swayed dangerously and then collapsed hugging the petrol tank. 'Brm Brm, Brm, Brm Brm,' he purred.

Max suddenly felt very drunk, the sky moved backwards and forwards above his head making him dizzy. He let his eyes drop to his friend. 'That's not a good idea,' he slurred and then he sat down on the pavement, slumped his head between his knees and let the cobbles dance in front of his eyes like a giant kaleidoscope.

A woman shouted. Max heard it from a neighbouring world. The sound was ugly and aggressive. He lifted his head to find out where it was coming from. The sturdy healthy face of a female biker was pointing at Igor with outrage. Igor sat up very suddenly. He put his foot out to steady himself and the bike overbalanced on top of him with a nasty screech of metal on concrete. Max scrabbled to his feet and tried to haul the machine off his friend but within seconds he was surrounded by five angry bikers. 'We didn't mean to . . .' he started but before he could get further a fist bulldozed into his right temple and he found himself sprawled face-down on the pavement with grit sugaring his tongue and lips.

He was winded, the breath knocked out of him by the impact of the pavement. The air in front of his eyes dissolved into dizzying multi-coloured pixels and behind him he was dimly aware of the dull sound of heavy leather boots thudding into Igor's body. Max scratched his fingernails across the concrete and managed to push himself upright on his limp arms and totter towards the pub. He gripped the brass handle of the door to stop himself from collapsing. His dirt-smeared mouth hung slackly open. In the dark interior of the pub the landlord fixed a silent clammy eye on him across the bar. Then he heard the high-pitched seesawing whine of a police siren and his stomach dropped. No, he thought, please not the pigs and then he slithered to the ground and blacked out.

He was only out for a second. He came round and was sick on the ribbed black rubber doormat. When he looked up the landlord was still eyeballing him. Bastard. Max wondered whether he was even breathing. Max had a deep hard headache. He stumbled outside and winced at the sun. The glare made him want to cry. In front of him three policemen were questioning the bikers. A fourth stood over Igor who was curled up like a sleeping child on the ground.

Max heard a second siren and soon an ambulance drew up beside the white Vauxhall Sierra police car. One of the bikers seemed to be doing all the talking. He wore a torn sleeveless Megadeth tee-shirt and his snake thin hips were encased in jeans that must once have been black but had faded to a greasy grey with even paler streaks where creases ran across the back of his knees and radiated out from the small lump of his crotch. When the biker saw Max his face twisted up with venom and he began to talk very fast. The three policemen looked up at Max and then one of them broke away and came towards him. Max looked at him balefully and choked out a splattering of vomit. The acid from his stomach seared at the back of his throat and the regurgitated fumes of vodka steamed up through his nose and eyes.

The policeman regarded the dribble in front of his feet with distaste and then he turned and shouted something to the men who were lifting Igor into the back of the ambulance. Max felt very tired. He wanted more than anything to lie down. The policeman angled his pen to stab the pad of paper he was holding. He asked Max for his name and address. 'And your friend?' he added. Max was just aware of a small warning shiver deep down inside his brain – it wasn't good to give information about a friend. 'Your friend?' repeated the policeman.

Max stared at him stupidly. He tried to run his hand through his blonde floppy hair but his fingers were obstructed by a sticky mass that he knew instinctively was blood. He rocked on his baggy knees. All he wanted to do was sleep. 'Igor Mazukin,' he said in a faint voice, 'Flat 2, 13 Wilton Way.'

'Right,' said the cop putting the notepad away into the inside pocket of his jacket. 'You'd better let them take you down to casualty but sometime in the next couple of days you and your mate are to come into the Bethnal Green station to make a statement.'

Chapter Six

Alex's first morning in London: the tide was out and the *Beagle* lounged at a twenty degree angle on the sloping mud banks. He lay very still and listened to his sister's shoes clack officiously across the wooden floor. He waited for the click of the door and the slight bark as it shut behind her then, with a flourish, he threw back his duvet and, naked and white like an uncooked fish, he soaked in the sunlight that oozed over him from his high cabin window. It was unbelievably quiet. No sound. Nobody there. No voices from his mother's radio, no telephones, no barking dogs, no horns, no knocks on the door, 'Coooee, anyone at home?', no horses hooves, no cars racing through the village. Alex was on his own. He listened to the silence and then let out a whoop and listened to it echo down the boat.

Presently the incoming tide crept close enough for the waves to tap their warnings on the iron hull of the boat and Alex, taking this as a signal, levered himself out of bed, dressed, made himself a cup of coffee and slopped out onto the deck in a pair of disintegrating espadrilles. He had to blink against the light that flashed off the water and mud in silver-backed shoals. The horizon beyond Wandsworth bridge was still misty but the fat sun now sitting over the trees of Battersea Park was sharpening and shrinking as it rose. It was going to be a very hot day.

Three rotting black stumps stuck out of the water in front of the boat. A mallard duck circumnavigated them and then picking up its belly waddled inland between the *Beagle* and its neighbour. 'What shall I do today?' Alex asked himself, running his hand up and down the metal railing. 'Who shall I be today?' He shouted at the river. 'What shall I do?' he whispered and shivered and thrilled with the pleasure and luxury of the question.

He found a café on the corner of the Kings Road and Beaufort Street and, using the addresses that the career's office at Durham had given him nearly three months earlier, he wrote off to five drama schools asking for their prospectuses. He'd been saving up this moment for when he arrived in London. Somehow in Dorset he hadn't been able to do even this simple thing. This is the first step, he thought as he pressed the stamps onto the envelopes with his thumb. He leant forward on his elbows and watched girls with smooth brown skin and coils of honey hair prance past the window while he frowned and crunched the end of his biro in his teeth and pretended he was in Paris with a notebook or a nascent novel in front of him. After his second cup of coffee he left and went to a greasy spoon café by the World's End council estate. Here he ate sausage, bacon, egg, tomato and chips and ostentatiously read a copy of the *Sun* before taking himself off to the Fulham Road cinema to watch the matinée of a Harrison Ford thriller. He was celebrating, he'd sent off for the prospectuses at last. He'd set the process in motion and now he felt he was allowed to play.

He was in a daze when he came out of the cinema, blinded by the light and with his mind left behind in the world of the film. He walked slowly down the steps, bending his knees and concentrating on making his muscles as loose and alert as a soldier tracking a fugitive through the undergrowth. He was so absorbed in this that it was some time before he heard his name being shouted across the street.

'Yo! Alex, *OVER HERE*!'

The caller was nursing a Coke at a chrome table outside a café on the other side of the road. He had short black curly hair, a prematurely receding hairline and he wore sunglasses. A blue vein wormed across his bony scalp. Steve hadn't been a close friend at university and Alex hadn't recognised him at first but he was pleased to see him. It was good to know someone in London.

'What have you been to see?'

'*The Fugitive*.'

'Any good?'

'Yeah, excellent, really fab. Fancy a pint?'

They went to Finches and Alex bought a round. The pub was empty apart from one old man crouched over the bar with a copy of the *Racing Times*. They sat at a wooden table in a little booth of etched glass and varnished wood.

'I said to myself that man looks really fucking familiar. I bet that's Alex Carmichael.'

Alex searched his memory for information about Steve. He'd been a friend of Alex's best mate, Jasper. He might even have played for a bit in Jasper's band. Steve was making the same connections. 'Heard from Jasper?' he asked. Alex got out his box of baccy and began rolling himself a cigarette. 'Got a letter from him about a week ago. He's back in Kenya working for a tour company doing safaris.'

'Lucky boy, I'll drink to that.'

They raised their pints to the absent Jasper and Steve blagged a roly on the grounds that he was only smoking ready mades these days and he wanted to remind himself what rolies tasted like.

'What you been up to this summer then?' asked Alex.

'I tell you man, it's been manic, really fucking manic. You heard of "Club Together"?' Alex looked blank.

'Parties. Good atmosphere, no aggro. Cool sounds. Thousands of people. All just getting into it. Fields, warehouses, wherever. My mate Morris runs them and I've had an excellent summer helping him out. I'm actually living with him at the moment. But,' Steve squinted as he re-lit his cigarette. He dropped his voice and made it faintly apologetic, 'I thought, this is fun but do I want to do this for ever? So I decided to get serious and started looking for a job and, man, I really fell on my feet. I had the most unbelievable luck. I met this bloke who was leaving his job as a runner, right, for quite a big production agency. So he tells me about it and I get in there as fast as I can and now I'm taking over. The pay's shit but it's a way in, you know, and you've got to start somewhere haven't you? I've got my first day tomorrow actually.' He blew his smoke out in a long stream.

Alex was impressed. He's actually doing something, he thought. Film. It wasn't acting but it was still pretty sexy. He scratched aggressively at a patch of eczema on the inside of his wrist. 'You've been busy,' he commented.

'Yeah, you could say that. How about you?'

Alex inhaled loudly and turned his pint glass around and round in his hands. 'Aaah, I've had a shit summer so far.' He began rolling himself another cigarette. His eyes lifted funereally to Steve's face, 'My mum's been really sick.' He paused. 'She's had cancer. I've been looking after her. It's been pretty tough. I thought she was going to die. We all did. But she wasn't going to let it beat her. She was so determined. I was with her every step of the way man and I tell you it was a miracle. The doctors say they've never seen anything like it. She's completely cured now. As good as new. Less hair that's all.'

'Sorry to hear about that man, sounds grim.'

Alex looked him straight in the eye and nodded. 'Yeah it was,' he said.

'So what's the plan now?'

Alex hooked his feet around the legs of his stool and

pulled himself closer to the table. 'Ah right, well, now I'm doing auditions for drama school. Fame, fortune and superstardom. At least that's the idea.'

Two girls peeled away from the bar carrying half pints of lager. Alex and Steve swivelled their heads as they passed their table. Alex pretended that he wasn't looking but the girls weren't fooled, they knew they were being watched. Alex could tell by the way they walked. He could see their knicker lines pressing against the thin material of their summer dresses. Their hips had an arrogant roll. One of them stopped and put her free hand to her lipsticked mouth. 'No!' she exclaimed with a gasp. Showing off, he thought, all promise, they love it when we watch them, and he wished he had the nerve to say something.

'So where are you living then?' he demanded, abruptly turning back to Steve.

'Just around the corner from here in Morris's place. It's actually a boat.'

'On the Chelsea moorings?'

'Yeah,'

'Battersea Bridge?'

'Do you know it?'

'What's the name of the boat?'

'The *Aku-Aku*. Why?'

'I'm your neighbour.'

'No way! That's incredible!'

'You're telling me. Cool place eh? In fact that's a serious point man. We shouldn't be here, drinking expensive beer. We should be out on deck, under the stars, quaffing wine.'

They left the pub and stepped out onto pavements full of gossiping cotton shirts and dresses and chattering heels. The sun had set and the sky was turning navy blue. Groups, couples, combinations were heading out for the night. *Where shall we go?* The question passed from mouth to mouth up and down the street. The sounds of the traffic churned and swirled around them mixing the vital question with idling engines, horns and the older grunts and pants of taxis and lumbering buses. Headlights, neon, shop lights and tail lights swam together in streaks and spots as Alex swung his head to take in all the life and confusion. Flickers as pedestrians darted across the traffic. Alex blushed; he was a fool, a fraud, a country bumpkin. He stood still for a minute and pulled himself together, full of resolution and green bravery.

But now Alex had been left behind and Steve was already half a block ahead. He ran to catch up with him and as he sprinted, dodging in and out of the oncoming people, he felt a rush of affection for Steve that was connected with this chorus, this bustle of citizens out for the night. Alex had somewhere to go too now. The affection spread to every corner of him and over everything around him so that Alex suddenly loved the traffic, the estate agents' window, the off-licence and the man in jeans coming towards him and bickering with the woman on his arm in the beige dress. He reached Steve and remembered that he was much taller than him. This triggered other memories of Steve; at the Q Ball nightclub, eating Indian takeaways in front of the gas fire with Jasper and the day they'd driven around Durham putting up posters together when the Bubble Zone had played at the Union. He was glad that he had bumped into him. It was a piece of good luck. And now he could meet Steve's friends, these people who lived their lives by cool parties with good atmosphere. 'All just getting into it.'

Alex's excitement buoyed him all the way back to the boat and then collapsed like a balloon when he walked into the *Aku-Aku*. He was disappointed. He couldn't deny it. He'd expected a student den and instead there was a floating chintz palace. It wasn't right. He wanted to walk out again and come back when Steve had got the right place. He found it hard not to blame Steve for fooling him. He'd been cheated by all the talk of raves and free living and he was angry with himself for being taken in. Steve's friend was just the same as him, another middle class boy. Of course – who else would have the cash to run parties – of course. It was a shame. Maybe the fantasy didn't really exist. Maybe it was always like this.

He clicked his shoulders back and felt sad and imagined himself rather world weary and cynical. The boat, he decided with a sneer, was like an expensive version of his mother's cottage. She and Sally would love it. Just their kind of thing. Stuff everywhere; piped sofa covers, ruched curtains, tapestried stools and a fake coal fire with a brass and red leather fender. It was an illustration from a glossy interior-decoration magazine and it was only slightly leavened by the young man debris; ashtrays piled high with stubs, old copies of lad's magazines and coagulating mugs of tea at the foot of each chair. 'It's Morris's mum's place,' explained Steve, 'she did the décor.' Through the deck doors Alex could see the neon from the factory stretch across the river. The same neon that you could see from Sally's boat. After all it was the same place, the same mooring, the same patch of city. He swallowed and stared at the river, his vision blurring slightly. Suddenly he wanted to get pissed, really pissed, so pissed that he wouldn't be able to walk and it wouldn't matter what he said or did. 'Let's open that wine then,' he demanded impatiently, 'and have you got any spliff?'

Alex and Steve sat in the dark in deckchairs clutching tumblers of wine while Steve rolled a spliff. Alex had smoked loads at university but obviously not while he'd been at home. He was excited, he smelt the scorched scent of hash and his fingers itched for the joint. Embarrassing. Definitely not cool to want it that badly. He scratched at a patch of eczema in the crook of his elbow. '*Don't scratch it!*' That's what his mother would say. '*Don't scratch it!*' Reacting to the phantom voice he speeded up, raking his fingernails across the swollen cracked flesh. Scritch, scritch scritch until there were half moons of blood and dead skin under his nails and he willed Steve to hurry up, hurry up and pass the joint along so that he could stop scratching.

Chapter Seven

Alex's second morning in London. He heard the door slam shut as Sally left for work. He opened his eyes. He was sweating. The bottom sheet had coiled itself around his legs in a rope and his mouth was dry and at the same time unpleasantly sticky. Alex had an image of the previous evening, the two of them on their deckchairs addressing the tangerine tinted London night sky while the boats clanked and wheezed on their slimy mooring chains like inhabitants of some great mediaeval dungeon. He pulled his pillow over his face. Steve's first day at work. How was he feeling?

Alex threw the pillow at the door. He couldn't possibly be feeling worse than this. Anyhow Steve was used to it. Alex was a novice *and* he'd smoked more *and* when he'd tottered shakily back to the *Beagle* he'd sniffed out a bottle of Sally's whiskey, taken it out onto the deck and drunk liberally to the black night creatures that lurked in the oily water of the shadows.

Sally had left him a note propped up against the kettle. Alex squinted at it and ran his tongue across his gummy teeth.

Dear Bro,

Hope you got in all right last night. Are you going to be around tonight? Ring me at the office and let me know. I've got some friends coming round for dinner – nothing smart, just a cosy supper – it would be nice if you could make it? Could you also do some shopping for me (see list and £20). You should be able to get everything in the King's Road Tesco's.

Lots of love Sally

P.S. If I'm not at my desk when you call, leave a message with Hannah.

Love S.

He couldn't face Sally's friends. Not with a hangover. He knew what they were like: young couples, not drinking because they came in their red and blue tin-box cars leaving baby sitters at home. Smug Oxford types who would finish each others sentences, ask him brightly what he was going to do and say 'that's interesting!' with conversational smiles. He'd ring up Steve and see if he could take refuge on *Aku-Aku* for another night. Still, at least Sally hadn't realised her whiskey was gone.

Alex went out onto the deck, this time with a mug of instant coffee. The creatures had gone, chased out by the sunlight, and Alex was ashamed of the previous night's drunken imaginings; his secret fears for the future. Fuckwit, he scolded as he lent on the deck rail staring at an iridescent film of oil on the mud. His young legs protruded awkwardly from his boxer shorts down over the knotted outgrowths of his knees to large, almost flat feet. He took a sip of his coffee but it was still too hot and it burnt his lips. He placed it on the black tarred roof of the cabin and, even though he knew it would make him feel worse, began his first cigarette of the day.

A tourist boat with a green-and-white-striped deck awning emerged from underneath the bridge. The sound of the tannoy carried across the water. Alex heard the guide point out the Chelsea Houseboats and, together, the crowd turned their heads to look. Alex waved regally at them with his cigarette lodged between his first and second finger. No one returned the wave. He gave the boat a fuck off sign. Stupid gits, he thought contemptuously, bunch of bloody lemmings. Jasper in Kenya, driving rich tourists round the Masai Mara – how does he stand it?

He thought of Lamu and the bus going up the coast from Mombasa. He'd spent the whole of last summer in Kenya with Jasper but when he looked back it wasn't the animals or the landscape that he remembered. It was being temporary, shifting through the bars, the trains, the guesthouses. It was that absolute freedom of being a traveller. No responsibility. No one expected anything from you. Weird how pleasant he'd found it, being surrounded by people he didn't know and how twitchy he'd got when they'd gone up-country to stay with friends of Jasper's parents. It had been much better by the coast. Much looser. A guy persuading him to buy mango. Women washing clothes in a stream, looking up as the bus went past. Kids jumping up and down on the beach, getting you to take their photograph, Hallo! Hallo! Present! Hallo! Casual encounters. Another foreigner, forgotten within a day. Alex hadn't minded that. He'd found the slipperiness of it hypnotic. Very unreal. A dream where friendships were instant and just as instantly gone, where you didn't really connect with anybody else and there weren't the usual rules. Jasper used to get furious about being treated like just another back-packer, a walking wallet to be bled. He'd rant about it for hours. It was different for him of course. He lived there, he was Kenyan but Alex had never felt foreign like that before and the sensation lingered with him in the way that a smell sometimes does.

The boat of tourists had bought the feeling back to him

and now it was reinforced by the high treble of a pipe. He couldn't place it for a second. When he remembered it a great white grin split his face. He waited for the choir voices to join in and then finally the great thump of a reggae beat:

> From the Bible to the Koran revelation in
> Gerusalem.
> Shalom. Salama Laikum.
> Christians, Jews, and Muslims worship together
> and pray Amen.
> Let's give thanks and presents.

West African reggae and a favourite in the coastal bars. They'd been playing it when Jasper had helped him to buy his first grass. The drug was measured in bundles that were either arm sized or finger sized. They'd bought an arm between them and smoked it with some young Rasta guys on the beach and Alex, whose idea it had been in the first place, had become paranoid that their new friends would rob them and dump their bodies into the sea. He'd dragged Jasper back to the guest house, looking over his shoulder and listening for footsteps, convinced they were being followed. It had taken ages for Jasper to calm him down. Alex had been mortified in the morning but Jasper hadn't said anything. Neither of them ever referred to the night again. Alex sometimes wondered whether it had happened at all.

Alex looked up to shake off the memory. The music was drifting over from the next door boat. It wasn't a barge like the *Beagle* but another houseboat like the *Aku-Aku* and standing in the shadow of the French windows was a woman. Her white face glowed gently in the shade and a rope of fire-red hair curled over one shoulder and down to the small swell of her left breast. She was watching Alex; watching him and not blinking.

'Alpha Blondy,' shouted Alex, 'I haven't heard it for ages.'

The woman stepped into the light. The sun sparked on her hair. She was thin and very small with a bony face and yellow eyes like a crocodile's. She blinked and looked puzzled.

'The music,' explained Alex, 'it's Alpha Blondy.'

She held a CD case in her hand and she turned it over and studied the back, running her forefinger down the list of tracks. 'Alpha Blondy,' she repeated, 'yes, you are right.'

She spoke with an accent that Alex couldn't place. It was foreign but he didn't know where it was from. 'How come you're playing music you don't know?' She was standing straight in front of the sun and in order to look at her Alex had to shield his eyes with his hand. She could have moved out of the light, but she didn't.

'It is not mine. Its Richard's, my landlord. Maybe you know him?'

Alex shook his head, 'I've only just arrived, I'm staying with my sister. My name's Alex.' He stuck his hand across the gap between the boats. It sounded too formal, he thought, but how else were you meant to introduce yourself? She shook his hand, rather limply and disdainfully. Her hands belonged to a much older woman. They were red and chapped and her nails were chewed down to below the quick.

'Lydia,' she said, 'nice to meet you.' Russian, thought Alex pleased with himself for placing her. That's where the accent's from, she's Russian.

'What do you do Lydia?' he asked and then swore at himself for coming up with such an inane question. He could have said anything else, anything else at all and it would have sounded more original.

She didn't seem to mind. 'I'm a photographer,' she told him and then tilting her head she stuck out her bottom lip in a grimace, 'and I am also a waitress but not, I hope, for long. And yourself. What do you do?'

Alex changed the hand that was shielding his eyes and splayed the fingers of the other hand out along the deck rail.

'I don't really do anything. I want to be an actor you see. I'm waiting to do my auditions for drama school.'

Lydia nodded, 'I think it must be very hard here,' she said and Alex felt a small sense of relief. A reduction in a tension that he hadn't, until that point, been aware of. It was almost as if this strange woman had absolved him.

Chapter Eight

The doorway of number 105 Berwick Street was set slightly back from the pavement making it a favourite shelter for runaways, winos and homeless punks with scraggy dogs on strings. A flattened cardboard box and a thin sleeping bag like a discarded snake skin lay in the corner. Unusually for the street there was only one intercom and the sign, in engraved brass instead of paper and peeling sellotape, read 'SEC, Special Effects Company, Reception First Floor'.

The reception was stylish and fashionable. The walls were painted burnt orange. Carefully arranged halogen lights imitated a cleaner sunlight than the one found on the street. A vast earthenware jar filled with artfully twisted twigs stood next to a reception desk made of pale ash wood and curved to look like the prow of a ship. The basement of SEC was equally hip but a lot less formal. Computer screens glowed like fish tanks in a large room as dark as a shooting gallery. There was a reason for this: some of the work SEC did was light sensitive but the darkness also pleased the people who worked there: it reminded them of raves and after hours drinking joints.

Richard came from Dublin. He had lived in London for fourteen years. He was proud of being Irish and had consciously maintained his accent. He was a big man, some would say fat. He didn't fit comfortably on the rotating office stools that SEC supplied for its programmers and he had wedged himself in a corner with his plump knees, clothed in combat trousers, jammed against the desk top. In the thin beam of the spotlight he held a copy of *Ms London*, a free magazine handed out at tube stations to female office workers. Richard studied it carefully.

'You surprise me Richard. Wouldn't have thought that that was your usual reading material.' Richard looked around to see his boss, Jill, standing behind him, her long pale fingers resting on the sharp hip bones that protruded from her jeans.

'Why not? You saying I wouldn't make a sexy secretary?'

Jill raised an eyebrow and Richard grinned lopsidedly and dropping his knees from the desk to the floor pulled his chair closer to his keyboard. 'You're right,' he said 'never read it before in my life. My new lodger's trying to get into photography. She's got some pictures in it.'

'Let me guess, it's another girl?'

Richard gave his mouse a nudge. The screen saver disintegrated to show an image of a cigarette packet floating through clouds. 'I prefer women,' he said with a smile, 'I don't like living with men. It's tiring. All that competition stuff.'

Jill scratched at the cuticle on her thumb nail. She felt a sudden flash of resentment against this new unknown lodger. Stupid, she told herself sternly. Richard's lodgers were none of her business. 'What you really mean is that you don't sleep with men.'

Richard grinned again. A dimple appeared in his freckled cheeks. 'There is that too.'

'Well if she's a photographer you won't see much of her. At the moment Barry is more married to his studio that he is to me.'

Chapter Nine

The reception area of the Bethnal Green Police Station was as small and deep as a well. A high rectangular window left a rhomboid stain of sunshine on the opposite wall. Two young women sat in a glass box operating a flashing switchboard. Worn cardboard lever arch files queued up in shelves behind them. Beside the glass box a door made of reinforced safety glass led to the rest of the police station. It was opened by pressing a code into a panel by the handle. Red plastic stackable chairs of the kind found in village halls and school assembly rooms lined the walls. Two teenage boys nervously fingered some documents next to a very short old man in a brown shirt and a greasy, heavily stained pair of pin-striped trousers. A monumental woman in a transparent blouse and straining skirt stared at the window. The room was hot and stuffy. Nobody talked. They examined the public information posters and read them again and again. They crossed their legs and re-crossed them. They hunched over their knees and with covert side glances tried to guess why everyone else was there.

Max and Igor pushed through the heavy wooden doors and the glass fire door that barricaded the room from the street. Igor looked bad. He had a black bloody graze that covered his right cheek. A butterfly stitch held together a gash on the bridge of his nose. He peered at the large woman's breasts but his vision was blurred by blue and yellow swelling that had reduced his left eye to a slit. He walked stiffly and his left arm was in a sling. Max had a bruise on his temple but no other visible wounds. He was laughing. 'There you were trying to grope the nurse and he was a bloke. Always knew there was something a bit funny about you Igor.' Igor groaned and Max stuck his head into the glass box, 'we're here to give a statement.'

The receptionist didn't bother to look up from her appointments book. 'Name?' 'Max Golanski and Igor Mazukin.'

'Take a seat.'

But there were no seats left to be taken so Max and Igor stood by the door like children sent to the back of the class. They spoke in Russian and Igor stood at an angle to the wall and dropped his voice to a whisper. A tall, orange blonde policeman with a red face appeared at the glass doors and shouted a name. One of the teenagers got up and looked anxiously and conspiratorially at his friend. He was dressed in a pair of baggy jeans and fat trainers and a metal dog chain was looped from his belt. Max jumped into the seat still warm from the teenager's nervous farting.

Igor whined. 'Let me have it. I need it more than you do.'

Max gave a short harsh bark of a laugh. 'Tough. I got here first.'

They waited for three quarters of an hour and then Igor was called through the glass door and ushered into a room with strip lighting, a spindly formica table and a barred window. He could see the station car-park through the window. The tarmac was a deep black and freshly laid. Sun glinted off the roofs and windscreens of the cars. An old-fashioned big-buttoned tape recorder lay on the table next to a green tinfoil disposable ashtray. Two red plastic chairs sat on either side of the table and underneath the window stood a metal wastepaper basket with R7 painted on the side. A bald fat man with alarming cherry-pink cheeks and two extra chins spilling over his shirt collar stood next to the window rubbing his palms together. Igor could hear the squeak of the man's breath as it escaped from his chest. A pair of grey suit trousers were fastened under the melon of his belly with a plastic belt. His white shirt was cheap and translucent and he wore a Mickey Mouse tie. Beside the waste paper basket he had placed a black plastic briefcase with a metal trim.

Igor shuffled into the middle of the room, closed his bad eye and picked at the fraying edge of his sling. He was uneasy. He had prepared his story with Max over a couple of pints in the gloom of a pub on the corner of Wilton Way. Igor hardly remembered the fight. He'd assumed they'd give their statements together. The separation was ominous. The presence of the fat man made it worse.

The policeman who had shown Igor into the room sat at the table with his back to the window. He introduced himself as PC Ford and asked Igor to sit down opposite him. He inserted a blank tape into the machine and pressed the Record and the Play buttons. Speaking in a flat solemn voice he leant over the tape recorder and announced the commencement of the interview of Mr Igor Mazukin of Flat Two, Thirteen Wilton Way, London East Eight on July the twenty fifth nineteen ninety three at fifteen twenty five in the presence of PC Ford and Mr John Allison from the Home Office.

'Home Office.' Igor tasted the word with gloomy satisfaction. He'd been right. His instinct always had been good. A sweat broke out across his forehead. The stitches on his nose throbbed. 'I want you to describe the events at the Dove public house on the afternoon of the twenty third of July.' The man was talking to him. Why did they bother? No one was interested in the fight. It was irrelevant now. Igor wet his lips and told the story as he had prepared it with Max. Max who, fuck him, had a valid visa. Several times he stressed his drunkenness. He weaved his head, shook his jowls and played the clown. It was a good performance, Igor thought so anyway, but it was futile and he knew it. Events had already been decided but he still playacted to the black machine of the table so that everyone present would feel satisfied that protocol had been observed, that the first course, so to speak, had been eaten. His sweat gathered in dew drops along his brow and he avoided the eyes of the man from the Home Office. Several times he forgot the English words for what he wanted to say and found himself speaking in Russian.

When he had finished there was a short silence and then PC Ford turned to his colleague. 'I believe there are a few questions that you would like to ask, Mr Allison.' The fat man smiled chirpily and stepped forward to the table. 'Have you got your passport with you Mr Mazukin?' Igor nodded. A moment ago he'd been unable to look at him but now his eyes were stuck to the glistening pink-and-white face. A magnet had locked them into position and he couldn't break the hold.

'Could I see it please?' prompted Mr Allison. He had a smug squeaky voice. The young policeman was impressed, deferential. Igor winced as he moved his sprained elbow and extracted a small red passport from his breast pocket. Mr Allison flicked through the passport with podgy fingers, he paused on a particular page and curled his wet, shell-fish mouth. 'Are you aware Mr Mazukin that your visa expired on the ninth of February this year.'

Igor didn't move.

'I'm afraid that I am forced to issue you with a notice of deportation.' He was showing off. He was very pleased. His instinct had been right as well. It was all turning out just as he had predicted. Igor shuffled forward in his chair and placed the fingernails of his right hand on the edge of the table. He thought of his flat in Kupchina and the money that he owed and he wondered how hard he would have to beg Seriozha. What would happen if he rang him from here. His swollen eyes didn't leave Mr Allison's face. 'You'll fly to Moscow as soon as we can organise it and until then I'm afraid you'll have to remain in police custody. Igor closed his bad eye again, it had become too heavy to keep open. He'd been outmanoeuvred. The game was over. He was caught. Maybe it would be all right. A fat, almost pleasurably self-pitying tear bulged in his eye, reflecting the barred window and the cars beyond. Mr Allison moved the tape recorder to one side, picked up his briefcase, placed it on the table and snapped it open. The teardrop slowly toppled over Igor's eyelashes and trickled down his face. He felt the salt water sting the graze on his cheek. Mr Allison was bent over his open briefcase. His bald head shaped itself into a squat Soviet metro station and Igor tasted the shells of sunflower seeds.

'There's no right of appeal on this one,' said Mr Allison to PC Ford. He spoke as if Igor wasn't there and his voice was professional and confiding, colleague to colleague. He signed two documents on the lid of his briefcase and handed them to PC Ford. 'If you can keep him for the moment I'll send you down a couple of men from the Alien's Deportation Squad and they can take him home to pack.'

PC Ford pushed back his chair and shook hands with Mr Allison. 'Thank you very much for coming down.' He turned to Igor. 'You come with me,' he said and gripping him tightly around the biceps of his undamaged arm he led him out.

53

Chapter Ten

Alex's room smelt of unwashed clothes, sweaty shoes, stale alcohol, sour sleepy breath and cigarette ash. The cupboard at the end of the bed was open and clothes sprawled from the shelves like strings of melted cheese. There was a pile of unread plays by the bed, an empty beer can, three mugs, a wine bottle and two overflowing ashtrays. A half-smoked cigarette was carefully propped up against the base of the bedside light.

It was probably about ten o'clock and Alex knew that outside the sun was shining again and the sky would be blue. It was like that scene from *White Mischief* when the hero opens the windows and snarls wearily that it's 'another bloody beautiful day in paradise'. The sun had been shining since Alex had arrived. For a month London had stewed in its toxic juices. Records had been broken. The hottest August since eighteen something. Ozone levels three, four, five times the World Health Organisation's safety limits. Asthma sufferers and old people couldn't breathe. Sally talked incessantly about the sailing holiday she was taking in Turkey with a group of friends.

Alex was tired of waiting for his auditions. He'd applied for them all; Guildhall, Drama Studio, RADA, Bristol Old Vic, LAMDA, as soon as the prospectuses arrived. It was about three weeks now since he'd sent the last one off and he hadn't heard anything. His life was on hold. He didn't seem to be able to do anything. He couldn't even read a play and all those resolutions about going to the theatre every night. Ha! He hadn't even been to one. He'd been on the boats a month and he'd achieved nothing. All he did was sunbathe on deck and get spliffed up with Steve on the *Aku-Aku*. It was if the boats had sucked him in and now he didn't have the energy to leave. Not that he had much choice. London was so fucking expensive that the allowance he got from his dad barely lasted a week, he could hardly afford to breathe; but there was no point in getting a job until after the auditions.

Yesterday he'd seen the Russian girl again. It was the second time he'd seen her since she'd played the Alpha Blondy song. He was on the deck when he noticed her (he always checked to see if she was there). She was sitting inside out of the sun. He waved to her and thought he saw her smile but in the gloom he couldn't be sure and she didn't come out. Maybe she was avoiding him. He'd seen her before about ten days earlier, on the pontoons. She'd been in front of him on her way out. She had a brisk little walk and she looked like she was in a hurry. Alex was sure that he heard the quick tish, tish, tish of her thighs passing against each other but she was too far ahead so he must have been imagining it.

He lay on his bed and watched the light from the blinds play on the ceiling like the end of a video before it's rewound. He talked to himself sternly: he was rotting, if he didn't get off his arse and do something soon Sally would come home to find him sliding into the mud. But still he couldn't seem to pull himself together. Part of the problem was that he couldn't stop thinking about his mother's illness. It paralysed him. From the moment he'd left Dorset it had haunted him how close to death she'd actually been. He found his imagination hovering over what would have happened if she hadn't got better and, even more frightening, what would happen if it came back. Then he felt ashamed: it wasn't his mother that he was worried about, it was himself. If the cancer recurred he'd be forced to go back to Dorset. He'd be trapped once more in the endless rotting days. The thought terrified him more than the possibility of his mother dying. He still couldn't really bring himself to believe in that. She was all right now, he told himself, so what was the point in thinking about it all the time? But he could still smell her sour sick-room breath and his dreams were full of plastic prescription bottles and lengths of rubber tubing. He frowned and turned over.

He tried to blank his mind until he heard the letter box clang and, glad of a distraction, he leapt out of bed and climbed the stairs. An envelope from RADA eyeballed him from the brown bristle of the mat. It had arrived. Finally. He circled and then, in slow motion, bent down, picked it up and slit it open with his thumb. Inside was a form letter acknowledging receipt of his application form and inviting him to an audition on fourteenth December. Shit December! That was centuries away. That was months. He'd thought that he'd get an audition straight away. He descended the stairs slowly, flipping his feet over the steps, one at a time. He let the letter fall to the table and rolled himself a cigarette. His mind whirred and clicked as his plans recalibrated. December. What the fuck was he going to do with himself until December?

He ran a bath while he shaved, clearing a smeared hole in the condensation with his fist so that he could see what he was doing. He tied his hair neatly back and scrabbling through his cupboard unearthed a clean shirt and a relatively new pair of jeans. Outside the sun glared and the heat twisted off the metal pontoons in a shimmering curtain.

It was time to get a job. He started looking in Langton Street. The first place he tried was an art gallery. A woman in her fifties wearing a caramel-coloured silk shirt and trousers sat behind an antique desk at the back of the gallery. 'I don't need anyone,' she said and then, to ensure that Alex understood, 'we don't employ casual labour.'

Fucking snooty. Silly cow, he thought viciously and he turned to leave. He stood outside on the doorstep while the woman watched suspiciously through the plate glass window and his face burned. His first rejection. Better get used to it if you want to be an actor. Try everywhere. If you try every single place you've got to come up with something. He pushed back his shoulders, breathed in and marched, puffed up with fake swagger and confidence into a smart Italian restaurant next to the gallery. Lunch was starting. A few early guests sat breaking bread sticks on white linen table cloths. Alex asked the waiter whether there was any work available and the man stared at his ponytail. He went to fetch the manager. Alex stood alone in the middle of the restaurant. The manager strode across the room from the kitchen door in a dark double-breasted suit. At ease. In control. 'We're not taking on any staff,' and before he'd even finished his sentence he was swivelling his broad well-dressed back and gliding smoothly to the kitchen. Alex tried again in the Italian restaurant next to the Oxfam shop. 'Excuse me, I'm looking for work and I wondered if you had anything available?' And again he had no luck. He crossed the road to the Water Rat pub on the corner of Milmans Street. A family was sitting at one of the tables outside; the two parents were positioned opposite each other with pints of fizzing yellow lager in their fists. Three packets of crisps, the foil ripped open, between them. A little girl in red leggings slithered up and down the bench humming to herself. A blackboard on the doorframe advertised the Wales-France Rugby International in fluorescent green-and-orange chalk. There was a mirror behind the shelves of drinks and a white strip light illuminated the spirit bottles. The manager had flesh like an uncooked potato. He was halfway through pulling a pint when Alex approached him, 'Have you got any experience in bar work?'

'I'm willing to learn,' bleated Alex, not looking at his reflection in the mirror, knowing how pathetic he sounded. The manager snorted and counted out change for his customer from the green glow of a computerised till. Why didn't I lie? thought Alex, that's what you're meant to do isn't it, why the hell didn't I lie? They didn't have any jobs in the Carphone Warehouse and the bookie's on the other side of the zebra crossing told him that there were no permanent vacancies, they did take on part-time staff for evening racing but he was too late for this year, which he could have done without knowing about.

'Excuse me,' chanted Alex, 'I wonder if you can help me? I'm looking for work and I wondered if you had anything available?' 'Excuse me I wonder if you can help me?' 'Excuse me . . .' Excuse me, excuse me, excuse me. Can you just listen to me for a second please? One small moment of your time? Oh well thank you very much. Thank you for your help. No, sadly I don't have any experience in retail work but I'm willing to learn. Thank you very much all the same. I'll fill in the form. I'll come back later then. Thank you for your time. Thank you. Yes thank you for not giving me a fucking job.

By the time he reached the Sydney Street junction Alex was sprung tight with frustration and the smarting sensation of rejection. What the fuck am I meant to do? He'd tried everything. In the antiquarian bookshop between the chocolate shop and the hairdressers he'd begged the old man who emerged from the gloom at the back to take him on as an apprentice. Full of tragedy he was, voice almost breaking, said it was his ambition to have a career in old books, said they were his passion. The old man said no.

Slava sat like a spider on a high stool behind the cash desk and observed the door speculatively. He tapped his well manicured fingers on the till and watched Lena scurrying around the half-filled restaurant. Lena came from Poland, she was learning English in a school three days a week. Slava doubted that she would stay longer than the summer. It was a month since Igor had disappeared. Slava gave a short indignant sigh. He wouldn't see that one again. It was always the same. They just went without warning. They didn't turn up for their shift and that was it. Ingratitude. It was so rude. After all I do for them they don't even have the manners to tell me when they're leaving. It wouldn't take much, just a telephone call but how often do they bother? They don't care, they don't remember. Without me they'd be on the streets, begging, picking up tricks, but they don't remember.

Alex tried to force himself to treat each place as completely new but he was tired, Alex, manager, Alex, manager, question, response, question, response, question, response. They were twisting together until the words rhymed, a chant, a song, a ditty like the ones he sang as a kid. *Yum, yum, bubble gum, stick it up your mother's bum.* Every sentence a question that he already knew the answer to. He pushed through the door of the Russian restaurant, looked around the wooden tables and the fringed red lamps and marched up to Slava at the cash desk.

'Excuse me, I was wondering if you had any work available,' he intoned. One more time. Slava ran his black glittering eyes over Alex and scratched the cleft in his chin.

'Waiter?' he asked.

Alex woke up, this was the first positive comment he'd heard since he'd started. 'I can learn,' he panted.

Slava's eyes flickered. The boy was good-looking in a billowing shirt, English angst kind of way. 'Tomorrow at six o'clock' said Slava, 'I'll give you a trial shift.'

'Thank you, thank you very much,' gasped Alex but Slava had already lost interest in the good-looking English boy and had begun preparing the bill for table sixteen.

Alex floated to the door. Boys and girls, young and beautiful, paraded the King's Road, flaunting, chattering, strutting, catching their reflections in shop windows with coy eyes blanked by dark glasses. Alex lingered by the door of the restaurant and, tipping his head back, closed his eyes. He could hear the panting traffic and the confident tap, tap, tap of high heels on a pavement, there was the birdcall of mobile phones, clothes rustled and a cabbie leaned indignantly on his horn. Alex opened his eyes and watched the sky swim over the buildings above him. I've got a job, got a job, got a job, got a job. He drank a cappuccino outside Café Picasso's and poured three sugar sachets into the white foam for celebration. The cruisers carried on stalking each other, oblivious to his triumph. On they went; up to the World's End, down to Sloane Square, up and down, one side of the street and then the other. That old, continuous dance that had been played out every day and every week for all the decades that Chelsea had been a place. And behind the cruisers middle-aged businessmen and girls from private schools panted in pursuit of whatever it was that was still cool in the King's Road. Tourists strolled, ignorant of the chase, blocking the way for old Chelsea ladies, hunchbacked in tailored cream suits and tottering determinedly along with their corns bulging from patent-leather court shoes. Alex leant back and smiled.

Chapter Eleven

The day that he started work at Russki's the weather broke, which Alex decided was prophetic. Things were going to change in his life. No more waiting for things to happen. The weather didn't break as dramatically as Alex felt that it should have done. He would have liked to have seen a real autumn thunderstorm with lightning cracking over the Thames. Instead there were two hours of heavy drizzle at midday but it left the air noticeably cooler and fresher and to Alex, excited about his new job, it seemed significant.

He arrived at the restaurant five minutes early to find the door locked. He pressed his nose against the glass. The lights were out. Maybe they'd gone bankrupt overnight? His heart flumped. He balanced the tips of his teeth against each other. Oh God, please no.

He cringed at the thought of what he'd have to say to Sally and his mum. They'd both been so jolly about this job. So *pleased* for him. That morning Sally had left him a good luck card. This had irritated him which was mean and he knew it. Sally meant well but he was only going to be a waiter. Not such a big fucking deal. (Only he was allowed to be triumphant about it, only he was allowed to have fantasies about all the film stars and famous writers who'd been waiters; when Sally got excited it was patronising.) Sally had even told his mum, she'd rung up just before he'd left.

'Everyone's got to start somewhere,' Marjory had said and when he reminded her that he wanted to be an actor she'd ummed as if she'd forgotten and then asked him rather tartly and sarcastically whether he was now considering a career in catering. Alex sighed, dug his thumbnail under a translucent hexagon of eczema skin by the base of his thumb and flicked it off. The annoying part of it all was that if he did actually get into a play his mum would be chuffed to bits and she'd tell all her friends and completely forget all the times that she'd tried to persuade him out of it.

He rattled the door. No go. He tried again, this time more frantically, then he saw a square of light flicker on somewhere in the back. It was okay. Thank God. He watched with relief as Slava's plump, neat little figure emerged from the unlit interior of the restaurant and unlocked the door.

'Come in, come in!' He was Russian, no doubt about that, but his accent was very BBC, very genteel.

Alex looked more carefully around the room than he had the previous day. It was set out like a Shakespearean theatre. (Very suitable, he thought, I shall act my part here!) At the back of the main body of the restaurant there was a small four-table balcony beneath which was an alcove with a staff table, a coat rack and a curious-looking sand tray with Turkish coffee pots on it. Behind this was a hatch and a swing door leading to the kitchen. The walls were wooden and dotted with icons and enamel paintings and a large silver samovar stood in the window with a cap of dust on its spout.

'Sit, sit, sit,' insisted Slava patting the wooden bench by the staff table and somehow managing to introduce an extra 'z' into the word. So Alex sat and Slava promptly disappeared through the swing doors into the kitchen, leaving him alone in the dark alcove. He could hear Slava speaking rapidly in

Russian and whoever it was he was talking to replied in grunting monosyllables. The sand tray stuck out from the wall in
front of Alex. A mess of electric wires hung down below it and
next to it was another giant samovar, much plainer and made
of stainless steel, more like one of the tea urns that the dinner
ladies at school used to use. Alex squinted at it and wondered
how it worked. Slava returned carrying a menu, an apron, a
pad and a pencil. Alex considered asking him about the sand
tray but decided against it.

Slava placed the pile of objects with great precision exactly
in front of Alex and checked the time on his Rolex watch.
'Choose, choose, choose.' Did he say everything in threes?
'Then inform him,' he jerked his head in the direction of the
kitchen, 'what your desire is. And when she shows up, the girl
will tell you what to do,' and he swung theatrically on his heels
and tapped upstairs leaving Alex on his own once more.

Alex scanned the menu. He didn't realise that he was
going to get food. He didn't know what any of it was. He'd
heard of beef stroganoff and he'd heard of borsht because his
mum used to cook them but the rest sounded weird. How was
he going to serve stuff when he didn't know what it was? He
decided on piroshki: whatever they were and stuck his head
through the hatch.

The kitchen was brightly lit and smelt of bleach and
cleaning fluid. On the right side of the room a thin boy was
hunched over a huge pair of steaming stainless steel sinks with
shoulder-blades like wings sticking up under his tee-shirt. On
the opposite side of the room a man with a dead-brown
drooping moustache glared at Alex from beside a bank of gas
cookers. 'Da?'

Alex made his request and bumped his head as he extricated himself from the hatch. When he turned around he
found himself facing the Russian girl from the moorings. He
stood there stupid, his eyes adjusting from the light of the
kitchen to the gloom of the alcove, the girl like a ghost, her
pale face and hair hovering in front of him.

Blood flooded up his neck in a tide that beat red and hot. Shit! He bit his lip hard. Please go, please go, please don't blush. What the fuck is she doing here? And he shook his ears to rattle his brain.

Lydia was confused too. She recognised his face but couldn't place it and when she remembered she was suspicious. 'You the new waiter?' she demanded. He gulped and nodded; miserable because he could hear the disdain in her voice. She turned away from him, hung her jacket on a hanger in a little cupboard underneath the stairs, put her handbag underneath it and pulling up a chair changed her shoes. 'Don't leave anything out,' she advised, but it was curt cold advice and she proffered it without even looking at him, bending her rust coloured head over her knees as she neatly tied the laces of her trainers. 'It'll get stolen. The cupboard's safer.'

Alex sat down again on the bench. 'Have you told him what you want to eat?' she asked brusquely.

'Yes,' he said finding his voice for the first time and pleased that he had something to say, 'I've just done that.'

Lydia got up, smoothed down her trousers and shouted through the hatch, '*Blini c ribie pshalusta.*' Her body was centimetres from his face. 'Don't let Dimitri bully you. He's Serb and a shit. Do you want coffee?' She stood in front of him with her hands on her hips.

'How do you work that thing?' asked Alex.

Lydia's stance became less aggressive. She had expected Alex to try and impress her. A request was a relief. It was a small request but he was asking her something all the same. Alex stood up. He felt lumbering and huge above her and he had to loop his back over to see what she was doing. She touched the samovar with a chewed finger tip. 'This is for the hot water. Careful. You can burn yourself.' She flicked an electric switch on the side of the sand tray and, picking up one of the copper jars with the long handle, tipped a tablespoon of coffee into it from a large tin that sat on a table with a pile of coffee cups. She added a tablespoon of sugar and filled the copper jar with water from the samovar and the earth scent of coffee flooded the air. Then, using a pushing instrument, she made a hollow in the sand, placed the copper jug in it and piled more sand around its sides. Alex watched transfixed by the movement of her fine-boned hands. 'You wait until the water rises to just here,' she said pointing to the point at which the copper jug narrowed. 'If they ask for an expresso or a cappuccino just explain that we only do Russian coffee. Don't forget to ask them if they want sugar when you take the order. In Russia we always drink coffee with sugar.' They waited side by side in constrained silence for the sand to heat up and the crust of coffee to rise up the little jug. When it was ready Lydia tipped the tarmac-black coffee into a cup. 'This one is for me. Now you do one and I will watch.'

Alex filled a copper jug, nestled it into the sand and looked at her for approval. She nodded. Standing this close to her he could see how sharply defined the tendons in her neck were; like a gymnast's or a ballerina's. 'Careful,' she admonished, 'you must watch it. Now that the sand is hot the water will rise very fast.'

There was a knock behind them and a pair of disembodied hands delivered two steaming plates through the hatch with a rough shout. He poured his coffee and sat down in front of a plate of five white dough parcels. He broke one open with a fork and spiced meat and cabbage spilled out onto the china. He bent his head down towards his plate and shovelled it into his mouth in rapid forkfuls. Lydia, in contrast, pushed her food fastidiously around her plate with her fork, chopping up little bits and scooping them up with her spoon. When she had eaten about half of her food she grew tired of it and leant back, lighting a cigarette. She flicked her ash into the leftovers and when her cigarette was finished she stubbed it out and picking up both plates pushed through the door into the kitchen. Alex gulped the rest of his coffee and followed her. The chef had his back towards them.

'That's Dimitri,' said Lydia scraping the scraps into a dustbin. She put the plates down by the sink, 'and this is my friend Volodya,' she said more gently, 'also a Serb.'

He was scrubbing a baking tray with a disintegrating ball of wire mesh. He looked about sixteen. He was very spotty and the back of his neck was covered with large painful-looking boils. He raised his head and looked at Alex, baring his teeth and bunching his upper lip under his nose in a strained smile. He made Alex feel uncomfortable.

'You've got to be nice to Volodya,' said Lydia, talking as if Volodya wasn't there, 'he's one of the world's victims.'

'Excuse me but my English is very bad,' said Volodya shaking his head sadly.

'Better than my Serbian,' said Alex.

Alex hovered behind Lydia watching carefully while she took orders from the first two tables of guests. He didn't want to get in her way. He concentrated hard on guessing where she would step next but he wasn't fast enough, his feet were too big, limbs weren't knotted tightly enough to his body and whenever she turned he was in her path trying to move backwards.

When it came to taking his first order on his own Alex pretended he was doing it for Lydia. He imagined that she was watching him (she wasn't) and he walked up the steps from the alcove trembling and approached two girls, of about his age, at a table by the wall. He smiled at them warmly.

'What would you recommend?' asked the one sitting with her back to the window. Her hair was cut into a brown bob and her matter-of-fact face was decorated with a large amount of red lipstick. She puckered her lips into a tight circle and pointed them at Alex while she waited for him to answer.

'It's my first day here,' he apologised, 'so I don't know the menu very well but I had *piroshki* earlier on and they were very nice.'

'They're like dumplings' said the girl's shaggy blonde companion.

'Oh! I don't know about that.'

'They were delicious,' enthused Alex. 'Yes okay,' said the girl and then she changed her mind. 'On second thoughts I'll have the stroganoff. No, I'll have the *pirosh*-things. Forget that I'll just leave it as it is.'

Alex wrote down *piroshki* and blini for the other girl. He pushed the order through the hatch to Dimitri and then opened a bottle of wine and a bottle of mineral water. He could do this. It was easy. He hummed the Stereo MC's 'get yourself connected' under his breath as he worked.

He brought their food to the table and the girl with the bob looked at her plate with disgust. Keeping her arms firmly down by her sides she said crossly, 'No. That's not what I ordered. I wanted the other one, the stroganoff. I don't want dumplings.'

Alex clenched his teeth. He snatched the plate away. Stuff her silly face in it. 'I'll ask the chef to cook you another one,' he said failing to keep the anger out of his voice.

'I ordered the other one,' she whined defensively.

Alex pushed through the door into the kitchen. Slava was talking to Dimitri. He wanted to go away again. He wished he hadn't got the job. Silly cow. Why couldn't she have made up her mind. His stomach felt heavy. He made a sham cough to attract Slava's attention. His thick eyebrows peaking anxiously into a pyramid in the centre of his face. 'This woman kept on changing her mind. I swear she ordered *piroshki* but now she's saying she wants stroganoff. It actually wasn't my fault. She just kept on changing her mind.'

Slava twitched his nose and turned his face a fraction to the side. It was his trial shift, Alex had failed, he'd disappointed Slava. There was an echoing judgmental silence in the kitchen. The sounds of the guests rattled through the door. 'We'll have to change it then won't we?' he said sarcastically. He might have been talking to a primary school pupil. He turned to Dimitri and started talking in Russian and Alex knew that they were talking about him and that he had just exemplified some fault in the English national character. Dimitri rolled his eyeballs sighed and faced the stove. Alex disconsolately tipped the dish into the dustbin. 'What do you think you're doing?' squawked Slava, 'Never, ever, ever let me catch you wasting food like that again. That could have gone to another customer or one of the staff could have had it. This is a business here you know, we don't just throw food away.'

Lydia had come through the door carrying a pile of plates halfway through Slava's tirade. Her eyes were on Alex's face and it flamed in response. 'I didn't know,' he begged. Dimitri handed Alex a plate of stroganoff. 'Take that out,' said Slava with an angry flick of his hand, 'and it better be right this time.' Alex said nothing. He pushed past Lydia with the blood drumming in his ears.

When he returned to the alcove Lydia was standing by the staff table watching a middle-aged man and woman come through the door. 'Do you want to take it or shall I?' she asked softly.

'You'd better,' he said despondently, 'I really fucked up the last one.' Lydia placed her hand on Alex's forearm. She had a very cool touch. It earthed his anger. He felt it flow out of him through her arm. 'Slava is that kind of man. You didn't know. How could you? It's your first day. You'll get used to Slava's ways.' Her clear yellow eyes regarded him.

'I'll do this table then,' he said.

Chapter Twelve

At the beginning of August Seriozha had taken his reluctant wife, Yelena, and his seven-year old-daughter, Katya, to their dacha north of the city not far from Lake Ladoga. He stayed for a month and then returned to St Petersburg early in September to take possession of his new Volkswagen. Yelena protested, she hated the countryside, it bored her. Seriozha was firm with her, she was to stay, it was good for Katya, a child shouldn't be in the city all the time. There was at least another month of good weather, it was time to dig up the garden and he had business to do in the city. Yelena was not convinced and she whined and clawed at him all the way to the station, pleading with him to stay. When the train pulled away from the station Seriozha brushed his wife's face powder from his shoulders and leant out of the window and waved at his wife and daughter as they stood forlornly under the scalloped wooden shelter of the platform.

Seriozha met up with the car courier in a courtyard off the Fontanka and handed over the rest of his dollars. The courier was a little weaselly man and Seriozha immediately felt pleasantly superior towards him, a feeling that intensified when he saw the gleaming red car, newly washed after its long drive from Berlin. He savoured the sensation as he slipped into the driver's seat. He sat running his stubby hands sensuously around the steering wheel and stared without focusing through the windscreen. After a while he turned the key slowly in the ignition, let the engine idle and nodding curtly at the courier as if he were a gopher on a film set, drove the car through the soft dusty summer streets. He played Queen on the stereo, wound down the windows, hung his elbow over the side and watched other drivers turn to look at him. He was now the owner of a foreign car. He cruised it over the bridge from Lenfilm to Vasilievsky Island and ringed the island, driving down to the port and back past the Sphinx and the Kunstkamera and over another bridge to the Winter Palace, the mainland and through the heart of the city to the southern suburbs and his block of flats. Then he switched off the stereo and sat for a while with his arms across the steering wheel, watching a group of children younger than Katya playing on a metal climbing frame amongst the straggling silver birch trees.

His flat was hot and stuffy. He opened all the windows as wide as he could but the air outside seemed to be trapped between the huge grey tower blocks and there was no breeze. He listened to the messages on his answer phone and booked a call through to Lydia for the following day. Maybe he'd send a telegram to make sure that she was there but he preferred to take her by surprise. He stared out of the window. The blocks were flagged by lines of washing. Shadows moved behind the open windows. He could hear the shrieks of the children playing below and the sound of someone hammering. A caravan had set up in front of the next-door block of flats selling *kvas*. He thumped the aluminium window-sill with his fist. Why wasn't Lydia here? With Yelena and Katya in the dacha it would have been perfect. He didn't understand this London business. What was the point in her being so far away? He snatched the keys from where he had chucked them on the sofa and leaving the flat with the windows wide open he went back downstairs and slipped back into the driver's seat of his shiny new car.

As he hugged the black leather steering wheel he saw Lydia, with her hair piled high on her head, make up and jewellery, high heels and a silk dress, walking into a restaurant on the arm of a man in a dark suit who turned out, when he looked closely, to be himself. Then the picture changed and she was standing on the steps of a palace and there was a garden of fountains and yew hedges and there was a horse, yes there was a horse with gleaming brown flanks and a servant at its head. Seriozha closed his eyes and opened them again. In front of him was a concrete tower block and a tubular climbing frame with three children clambering over it like spiders. He shifted his bottom in the black leather seat, and thrusting the car into reverse, roared out of the parking space.

The avenue from Kupchina into the centre of the city was wide and there was little traffic. The blocks of flats on either side of the road were set well back from the road. The sun was soft and low and the sky was lavender coloured. Seriozha drove past a large gap on either side of a line of pylons. The city seemed very empty. He drove to Nevsky Prospect and parked on Canal Griboyedova. In the back of the car was produce from the dacha garden that his neighbour had given him. It embarrassed him that it had to be his neighbour that gave them this sort of thing. It should have been made by Yelena, that's what he'd tell the old woman anyhow. He took a jar of home-pickled mushrooms and some fresh raspberries carefully wrapped in newspaper and slamming the boot marched under an arch and up a staircase in the corner of the courtyard beyond.

Lydia's mother was shocked to see Seriozha. She had brooded resentfully over him for many months. In her mind he had become a hate figure, caricatured and grotesquely swollen by her imagination and now suddenly he was standing in the doorway and she found that she had forgotten that for all his size he was a reasonably good-looking man. She watched him warily. No one had ever told her but she'd known from the beginning that Lydia was having an affair with him and she'd known too that he was married and had a child and that he was a director at Lenfilm and it was this last fact that had held her in check. Seriozha was a powerful man and this had made Olga reverential. She hadn't approved of her daughter's behaviour but she had said nothing. It wasn't wise to make enemies of powerful men. Olga had begun to treat her daughter with new respect. After all it was not unheard of for a child to turn against its parent. They used to give medals to young Komsomolets who unearthed conspiracies in their families. And then Seriozha had proved the extent of his influence by sending Lydia to the West and Olga knew that she had been right to be so cautious. That Seriozha was behind the journey was obvious to her. Olga had never accepted her daughter's explanations of career opportunity and independence. She was not, she congratulated herself such a fool. She hadn't believed her because she hadn't understood the explanations. They were foreign to her. Of course it had to be a man she reasoned as she shuffled around her kitchen at night. Women were always fool for a man, she told herself.

Olga stood in front of Seriozha. Without making a greeting of any kind, she stepped back and allowed him into the hallway of the little flat. At the end of a deep narrow corridor was a sitting room. Every thing in it was fragile and worn. The wallpaper was a faded pink and in places it had been rubbed away altogether. A sofa-bed dominated the middle of the room. Olga directed him to a wooden chair at a table with a white lace tablecloth. There was a mirror on the wall, spotted and blurred with age. A black-and-white studio photograph of a man proud in his army uniform stared placidly at Seriozha from inside a cabinet between two windows. The surfaces of the room were covered in lace; the cabinet was filled with delicate glass; tiny china figures crowded onto the mantel-

piece and window-sills. Seriozha sat down cautiously, afraid
that he would knock against something and all the little bits of
glass and porcelain would shatter into a million tinkling splinters. It had not occurred to him to wonder what Lydia's home
looked like before and this was the first time he had come
further than the hall. Now that he was in the heart of the flat
he found it easy to imagine Lydia surrounded by all these
delicate hard-edged little objects. A silent self-contained girl
growing up in imaginary worlds of china ornaments.

Olga offered Seriozha some juice and he accepted,
politely. 'I have been away in the country,' he said and he
made it sound as if he was in the habit of visiting her and he
was explaining an unforeseen absence.

'It is good to be in the country in the summer,' she said
abstractly, 'when we were children after the Great War we
used to leave the city from spring until autumn.'

'I thought you might like these . . . My wife . . .' He
pushed the mushrooms and the paper packet of raspberries
across the table like a bribe. Maybe he shouldn't have
mentioned his wife. Olga nodded but didn't look at the offer-
ings, instead she stared with blank, fixed, watering eyes that
made him feel very uncomfortable. He examined the table
and then his fingernails (always scrupulously clean) and then
because he couldn't bear this game any longer he asked her if
she had heard from Lydia.

'She writes that she is living on a boat,' she said, her voice
thick with disapproval and disbelief in the peculiar habits of
Westerners. She spoke slowly and she had a habit of pausing
after each sentence, like a badly trained actress. Seriozha
detected something in her voice. She was blaming him for her
daughter's absence. Your mistress, your responsibility. She
lapsed back into silence. The woman didn't seem able to
blink. There was something not quite right about her. He
wished he hadn't come. He felt foolish now and he was going
to have to explain to Yelena how he had got through all those
mushrooms so quickly. 'Yes,' he said, shuffling his voice

uncomfortably, 'well I am sure she won't want to spend the winter on a boat.'

Olga sniffed and with pointed fingertips moved her glass an inch further away from her. 'I'm not worried. She will come back to Russia. This is where she belongs. In time she will get bored and then she will come back.'

The light refracted busily off the edges of all the hard little objects in the room. Seriozha felt acutely uneasy and out of place. The older woman's silence was a powerful tool, a protective, mirror-plated wall that reflected his discomfort back onto himself. The man in the photograph stared glassily at him. Somewhere in the room a clock was ticking. Seriozha placed his hands palm down on the lace tablecloth. 'I'd better be getting on,' he said and he had to force the words in bubbles out into the oppressive atmosphere of the room.

Olga angled her head graciously and stood up. 'Naturally,' she said and she ushered him out of the door.

Chapter Thirteen

Lydia knew that Alex was attracted to her. She'd sensed it from the very first moment, when she'd stood in the shade of the french window watching him gather the courage to call out to her. His youth disturbed her. There were three years between them but Lydia, used to older men, exaggerated the gap and in her mind Alex became *the young boy next door*. She was wary. She was worried there would be trouble. Long ago Lydia had divided the men in her life into two categories: those she should avoid and those it was necessary to sleep with. Alex came into the first category, Richard into the second.

One night, two weeks after she had moved on to *Toadhall*, she had been lying in her bed reading when Richard had walked in and leant on the door jamb. He'd looked at her straight between the eyes and said 'So, are you going to ask me in then?' His tone had made it more of a challenge than a request. She'd guessed that he was taking a gamble and that he wasn't as sure of himself as he had appeared. She'd squinted at him while she'd weighed up the situation. Richard wasn't attractive but she had slept with more unattractive men in the past. He was her landlord; annoying him would make life difficult and although he wasn't a young girl's dream he had charm. She hadn't been able to think of any strong reason not to, which had made it churlish to refuse. She'd flicked her duvet back and he had got into her bed and had made love with enthusiasm. He had been an attentive lover and Lydia had discovered that since leaving Russia she'd been missing sex. In the morning Richard been prosaic and friendly. He had brought her a mug of tea in bed and then had become flustered because he hadn't been able to find a clean pair of jeans and he had been late for work. Lydia'd been relieved that Richard wasn't going to be lovelorn and awkward. The affair had then developed in a way that had suited Lydia very well: once or twice a week Richard got into her bed rather than his but during the day he never acted as if he were her lover or referred to what they shared in any way. Very satisfactory.

Alex presented her with a more complicated problem. Lydia liked him. She liked his fierceness and his enthusiasm. She liked the extravagance of his fantasies and his dreams and she liked the way that after raging against some imagined slight he would suddenly stop and laugh a great wide melon-slice laugh. She liked watching his body as well. There was something comic in the way his long thin limbs were attached to him. It was as if his joints hadn't been tightened properly and when he got agitated she could imagine one of his arms or legs flying off into the air. She liked too the great black eyebrows that dominated his face and danced above his eyes so that she could always tell what mood he was in. It was annoying that he had a crush on her because it meant that she couldn't get to know him better. Unfair that because he wanted to go to bed with her she couldn't make friends with him. His desire made him her responsibility and part of Lydia resented that.

After his first night at Russki's Lydia was careful about how she behaved towards Alex. When his expression began to get too hangdog she'd grow deaf and not hear the whispered comments that he made to her. At the end of each evening she'd suddenly become extremely tired and make wide open-mouthed yawns as they walked down the King's Road together. When they got close to the moorings she'd slip in front and once they'd reached the pontoons she'd smile briskly at him and disappear firmly up the gangplank to *Toadhall*.

One night in October Slava let Lydia go while Volodya and Alex were still washing the floor. A table had stayed for ages so it was late, coming up to one, when Lydia set off up the King's Road. It was an autumn night with no edges: the shadows were blunt, the air damp and still relatively warm and the sky fuzzy and muffled with cloud. Occasional cars passed through like uninvited guests, hurrying on, leaving behind the subdued memory of their engine noise. As Lydia's trainers pressed down on the pavement they squeaked. Once she had noticed this the sound grew until she could hear nothing but the protest of her shoes as they were pressed between her feet and the pavement. She found a new sound by scuffing her toe against the concrete slabs and she began to walk a rhythm: *squeak, scuffle, scuffle, squeak, squeak, squeak*. She walked her song past Chelsea Town Hall. A wino wrapped in cardboard boxes and plastic bags lay asleep on a bench. The pavement here was made of yellow-brown slabs of stone and Lydia could see the lines where the different layers of sediment had compressed to form the rock. The next section was dark. There were no shops. The wide doors of Chelsea Fire Station waited on the other side of the street. A tree with small yellow segmented leaves leant over the pavement and the air smelt of earth from the private gardens behind the black wooden fence. *Squeak, squeak, squeak*. Lydia wrapped the quiet empty city night around her and smiled at the pleasure of it.

She reached a builder's wholesale merchants just beyond Bramerton Street. Then she heard the tapping of feet in hard bottomed shoes coming up behind her. The feet were moving fast. Lydia counted. To every *squeak* of her trainers there were two *taps* from behind her. *Squeak, tap, tap, squeak, tap, tap.*

'Lydia, I thought it must be you. Listen, I want to ask you a favour.' Alex spoke in short, breathy bursts. Lydia twisted her head towards him, their feet slowed and she smiled as the rhythm of the shoes changed once again. He gulped at the city air, like a fish. He knows that this is stupid, thought Lydia, and she liked him more for the self-consciousness. Alex gulped again. There must be great mouth sized bubbles of air in his stomach, thought Lydia.

'I want you to show me how you carry plates up your arm like that. I mean, I'm sure it's really easy if you know how, but I don't dare risk it in the restaurant. Are you *really* tired? Are you going to go to bed *right* now?'

Lydia shrugged, *squeak, tap, squeak*. If Alex wasn't going to let her protect him he would have to look out for his own feelings for himself. 'Okay, I'll show you. It's easy. It won't take long.'

When they reached the moorings the river was still and fat and welcoming and it gleamed like graphite, the boats lined up against the Embankment like sleeping piglets against a sow's belly. As they came down the gangplank Lydia noticed the square of light in the door of *Toadhall*: Richard was in. This could be interesting, she thought, aware of a reluctance to let Alex and Richard meet. She liked to keep the people she knew in separate compartments. It was cleaner and easier that way and if Alex found out that Richard was her lover he would probably be hurt. That wasn't her problem. He didn't need to find out. He invited himself, I can hardly turn him away, that would hurt him even more. She shrugged to herself and walked ahead without checking to see if Alex was following her.

Richard was lying on the sofa watching a video when they came in. On the floor beside him lay a dirty plate, an ashtray, a tin-foil tray containing the lurid-orange remains of an Indian take-away and another with bits of orange-and-white rice in it and two empty beer bottles. Richard held a third beer bottle in a large smooth white hand. 'Hi.' He pressed Pause on the remote control and shifted his big body around to face the door. He smiled a crooked-toothed smile and as Alex came through the door he raised an eyebrow. One of the deck doors was open. Cool metallic river air spread across the floor nosing into the other smells in the room: the mousy scent of undisturbed dust, old carpet and stale cigarette smoke, the smell of electronics and heated plastic from the television and the new warm oily smell of the take-away.

'This is Alex,' Lydia told Richard as she slipped away down the staircase. Like dogs, she thought, leave the two of them to work each other out. Downstairs she took a stack of large dinner plates from the drying-up rack and poured two cans of beer from the fridge into glasses. She waited for the head of foam in the glass to subside and listened to the jerky rhythm of the voices above her. Richard was saying something that sounded like a question. Alex replied and then there was a pause. Lydia slowly poured the rest of the beer and resting the two glasses on top of the pile of plates carried them upstairs.

Alex was examining Richard's CD collection. This was his most prized possession and it spanned a whole wall of the boat. Alex's head was tilted sideways so that he could see the titles. He fingered each case as he passed it and moved his lips in a kind of silent litany as he went through the names. Richard was rolling a spliff on his thigh and watching the television.

'Alex works at Russki's,' said Lydia. Richard poked at the joint with a matchstick, 'Yes, so he was telling me. I thought they only employed illegal immigrants at Russki's.'

Alex stopped examining the music collection and balanced on the edge of a chair. 'Well it's only temporary, I need the cash, I'm going to go to drama school you see.'

'Oh yeah, which one?'

'Well I haven't actually got into one yet. I'm applying for auditions at the moment.'

Richard nodded his head dismissively and offered the

joint to Lydia. This irritated her. He knew that she wouldn't take any and yet each time he used the stuff he persisted in offering it to her. She passed it over to Alex.

'Right!' she said after he had taken one puff, 'I thought you wanted to learn how to carry plates?'

Alex nodded and took another drag. Telling him to watch she placed a plate on her palm and secured it by hooking her thumb and little finger over the rim. 'You've got to get the first plate secure, the others you just balance.' She lined three plates up her arm and walked across the room. Then taking two of the plates she handed them to Alex. 'Try with two to begin with.'

She took his hand and with a touch as impersonal as a nurse's she bent his fingers over a plate and then placed another one on his forearm. 'Make sure this bit is level,' she instructed. Biting his lower lip with concentration, Alex set off across the room in his loose loping walk. After his second step the plate balancing on his arm came crashing to the floor. 'Don't look at them,' she told him as he bent to pick the plate up, 'look the way you're going.'

Richard squinted at Lydia through the smoke. Alex attempted to cross the room three more times. Richard began to get bored, he shifted his weight on the sofa and took a swig of beer. 'By the way Lydia' he said, 'there's a party in Dalston at the weekend. Do you want to go?' Lydia ignored him. She was concentrating on Alex. Richard's face tightened, his easy features grew petulant. He stubbed out the roach in the take-away tray, got up from the sofa and narrowly missing Alex, who promptly dropped all his plates, stepped across the room and put on a Crowded House CD.

Alex completed two successful runs and sat down. 'Enough Lydia, I'll practise at home.'

'You see it's not so hard, you could do it in the restaurant now.'

'I'm not sure about that – I think I could do with a little bit more practice.'

'Do you want to come or not?' interrupted Richard.

The interruption annoyed Lydia. What right did he have to be so proprietorial?

'What to?' she said vaguely.

'This party in the old cinema in Dalston. This Saturday. Jill, my boss, was telling me about it.'

'Can anybody come?'

'Yeah, yeah, it's an open thing.'

'Well how about inviting Alex too?'

'That sounds really cool,' said Alex.

'Okay then, I think you should come. We both have Sunday night off right? Why don't you meet us here? What time Richard?'

'Yeah, right. I'm not sure exactly. It'll probably get going quite late. Errrrm. Well I suppose, yeah, ten o'clock, something like that?'

Chapter Fourteen

Lydia had worked the lunch-time shift. She got back at five o'clock. Richard was on deck, she could smell the marijuana smoke through the open doors. I can't be bothered to say hello to him if he's stoned, she thought, and she went downstairs and ran herself a bath. Baths were one of the great havens in Lydia's life. She'd lie there and meditate on the rising coils of steam while slowly scooping handfuls of water over one breast and then the other, letting her thoughts drift through the air until there was no more steam, the water was cold and her skin had turned to felt.

But today Richard was not going to leave her in the privacy of her bath. As she slipped into the procelain tub she heard him pad down the stairs and then the door opened and he stood over her and casually flicked at one of her nipples before wandering off to do the washing up. She thought about closing the door but they were lovers and it seemed prudish, so instead she lay her head against the back of the bath and raising a leg in front of her began to soap between her toes. Next door Richard moved blearily around the kitchen tossing her comments about the party. What Jill had said, what another bloke had said, the place where it was being held and at least twice, and this was the bit that had really irritated her, that he had bought some coke for them off a colleague at work and how pure it was. Lydia cupped water over her knee and, rinsing the soap from her one washed leg, wished that Richard would go away and leave her to her thoughts until the water had gone cold. She didn't want any of their silly Western drugs. Why did he have to buy this stuff? She could see the evening stretching in front of her in cold sober isolation. She frowned crossly, it was going to be very boring and she'd have to entertain herself.

Alex hadn't thought it was at all boring. 'Excellent,' he'd exclaimed with enthusiasm, and then 'actually I had the same idea. I scored some speed off a mate of mine who lives just down the moorings here.' Richard had been superior and said that there was no point in doing speed when there was nice high-grade coke about and why didn't they save that until later. They'd laid out the powder on an album sleeve. Lydia, pressing her lips tightly together, had walked out onto the deck. She heard them sniffing and after a brief battle between curiosity and disapproval she turned around to see what they were doing. Richard was holding his finger to his nose. 'Your turn,' he'd said to her and she'd said 'No,' very firmly and at the same time wished that she'd felt brave enough to join in. Richard had glanced down at the thin lines of powder and mixing them up with his credit card had said, 'Lovely, all the more for us then.' His tone was jokey but on the edges of it Lydia could hear a burnt tinge of sourness. She knew that she had taken some of their fun away and that made her even more cross.

Richard had two vehicles, a Suzuki 550 bike and a van. The van was a sentimental relic. He didn't use it much but he kept it anyway. He'd had it since his painting and decorating days and he could never get around to selling it. It was an old white Ford Escort with mirrored back windows and a sticker in the passenger window that read 'Fuck Work, Let's Surf.'

There were spots of rust across the side where the previous owner's logo had been covered up with rough white paint. Someone had tried to hot-wire it at one point and messed up the ignition so Richard had fixed up a hanging arrangement of wires underneath the steering wheel which seemed to work well enough. They used the old van to go to the party. Richard drove with one hand on the wheel and a large, pasted grin, Alex hunched in the back balancing uncomfortably on a wheel arch and Lydia sat in the passenger seat.

She twisted around to look at Alex in the back of the van. He was disconsolately scratching a patch of eczema in the crook of his elbow. 'Are you all right?' she mouthed above the noise of the engine. He nodded lugubriously and she turned her head back to Richard, examining him carefully for signs of the drug. How are they being affected, she wondered? What is it they're feeling? She felt very separate from them. I'm like some kind of scientist, she thought, observing their lives for chains of cause and effect. I live my life here in England with my eye pressed to a microscope and in that way I can see many things and protect myself from the consequences. She fingered the small camera that lay on her lap and then taking off the lens cap held the mauve-lustred surface of the glass up against the tail lights of the car in front to inspect it for scratches.

'Why is there nobody here?' she asked. All around them the streets were empty, deserted as if some plague or poison cloud had descended.

Richard waved a hand extravagantly at the buildings that reared up on either side of the street. 'This is the belly of the beast, Lydia. This is the City.' She peered out of the window at the polished marble walls. 'It's empty,' he carried on, 'because nobody actually lives here, do they? This isn't real city, what we're in now. It's virtual city. We're inside a computer game. Welcome to Suit-land, where brave computers run small grey men on intrepid missions of great daring and bravery through the dangerous, infested jungles of the financial world. Mondays to Fridays, office hours. After that these grand edifices are closed to the public and reserved for computers alone, allowing them time to communicate with each other by a string of electric pulses incomprehensible to lesser mortals. This is POWER. Thatcher, Bush, Yeltsin, paah! Mere flesh and blood. It's here, in the markets, that it really happens. This is where the Cold War was won. Money brought the Wall down. Nothing can be done without the approval of the markets. We're the ones who complicate it. We are the ghosts in the machine. The markets rule without mercy and if you're dirt, shit, poor, the markets'll squeeze another penny out of you because your government's in debt. But that's okay because debts are good for the markets, keeps up the balance of payment et cetera, et cetera. There's force behind these walls. You can't see it and you can't buy a loaf of bread with it but it rules us all. This is what keeps us in our place. This is it. The heart of the system.' He stopped, looked sideways at Lydia and then burst out laughing, 'Shut up Richard. Stop talking a load of crap.'

Alex crawled to the front of the van. 'Where are we going?' he shouted at the back of their necks. Richard replied, tossing the words over his shoulder, 'Hackney, well Dalston really.' Lydia watched Alex's reflection in the driving mirror as he shuffled, crouching like an animal back to his perch on the cold metal wheel arch. She could tell that he was annoyed about being put in the back. He feels left out, she thought, well so do I, maybe even Richard does too, all of us sitting in this little van feeling left out from each other.

Outside the window the view began to change. The skyline shrank down to three storeys, the houses leant into each other, people appeared on the streets and shops interrupted the blank wall of buildings. There were kebab shops and newsagents, chemists, off-licences, saree shops, ironmongers, pawn shops, junk shops, charity shops, betting shops, little supermarkets, fish and chippies, cafés.

Richard parked the van in a side street and twisted round

in his seat. 'Let's do some of your speed now,' he said. Alex grinned, glad to be included again, and pulled a little plastic bag of white powder from his pocket. Lydia looked out of the window and examined a dirty brick wall with a sign saying 'No Billstickers' while they sucked their fingers and stuck them in the bag like it was sherbet. Then they got out of the van and Richard released Alex from the back. On Dalston High Street they stopped at an off-licence to buy some beers for the party. The till and the shelves of bottles were screened from the customers by a floor-to-ceiling perspex and metal grill. The man behind the till was Asian, his arms and half of his face glossy pink and puckered from severe burns. Lydia wondered if the shop had been firebombed. They bought twelve cans of lager and loaded them into a little rucksack that Richard was carrying with him. The street outside was noisy and confusing, the pavement soaked with red-and-yellow lights from the shops. Cars double-parked down the kerb, their doors open, their engines running and music thudding out into the night, and the battling smells of sweating meat, cigarettes, fried food, rotting tropical vegetables, aftershave, spilt beer and exhaust.

They followed Richard's solid silhouette up the road and cut across a floodlit garage forecourt with a small shop with barred windows, a security alarm and closed-circuit cameras. Richard squeezed through a gap in the corner of a corrugated iron wall that bordered the yard on the opposite side from the shop. Lydia hesitated and looked behind her at the bright safety of the garage. Alex had already dived through the gap after Richard. She tucked some hair behind her ear and followed him. It was very dark on the other side of the wall and the sounds from the high street were muffled. Her eyes slowly adjusted She was standing amongst some tall straggling bushes in front of an abandoned building. The windows of the building had been filled in with concrete breeze blocks. At some point there had been a fire and half the roof was missing exposing skinny charred timbers. Lydia didn't like the look of it. This seemed like a bad area of the city. After the noise of the street the quietness and darkness of the wasteland was eery. She surveyed the unfamiliar shapes, the twisted shadows and the blind-eyed deserted building. The two men were now quite a way in front of her. She stepped forward, crunching on the rubble. A searing line flashed across her knuckles. She jumped and looked down. It was only a nettle. Just a plant. Stupid, to be afraid of a plant. A hot flush of relief and a blink then she pulled her hair behind her ear again and started after the men.

She could only just see the path – a few less thistles than the rubble on either side of it. At the corner was a door that had once been bricked up. A hole had been knocked into it down to ankle height. Inside it was even darker. It smelt of powdered cement, urine, candle wax, rotten wood. Voices were coming from somewhere above them. Lydia stretched her hand forward and took a piece of Alex's shirt, lightly holding it between her thumb and forefinger. He turned his head back and she saw the blue night light catch the angles of his eager face. 'You all right?' She nodded curtly in reply but all the same she was grateful that he'd noticed she was nervous and then she realised that he hadn't noticed at all and that the words were only a formula to communicate his excitement. This is an adventure for him, she thought, he is as excited as a boy playing dens.

'Up these stairs,' hissed Richard and they followed him up a narrow rickety wooden staircase into a room as big as the building itself.

The room was full of people and they were standing on a carpet of a hundred night lights flickering in small tin foil containers. The sound of their voices was diluted by the size of the space making the place strangely quiet. Above the people the sky glowed blue behind bars of blackened and charred beams. Richard turned to her at the top of the stairs and grinned smugly and then moved his tongue around his mouth as if he was shifting around a piece of chewing gum. 'Glad you came? Told you it would be good eh?'

'All these candles,' said Lydia, 'they make the people look like they are walking in flames.'

'Jill said something about a sculpture,' Richard said, pushing through the back-to-back people until in the middle of the room they reached a huge fish. It was so high Lydia couldn't see over it and it was as much as twenty-five foot long. It had been welded together from pieces of engines, gear cogs, radiators, wheel rims, spark plugs, radios, copper piping, a watch, the grill from a fridge and part of a window frame. Alex posed in front of it, weight on one hip, squinting critically and rolled himself a cigarette. 'What d'you reckon?' said Richard boastfully.

'It's interesting,' said Lydia but she didn't want to say anything more because he was too triumphant and she was still cross with him about the drugs. Now he's pleased that Alex is here. It gives him an audience to show off to, she thought cynically.

Richard put his rucksack on the floor and while he was bottom up Jill arrived and tapped him on the shoulder. 'Jill,' he said with all the blood in his face, 'want a beer?'

'Of course.'

Richard straightened up and waved a fist with a beer in it at the fish. 'Good call. You weren't wrong.'

'I never am,' she said.

'Jill, this is Lydia, my lodger, and Alex who's our neighbour.

'A right little Chelsea gathering.'

Lydia drifted away to have a closer look at the rest of the fish. An outline of nightlights marked its place on the concrete floor, which Lydia had to step over to look at it more closely. It was clever, all the bits blended into the whole. She really had to stare to work out where they came from. The tail looked like a metal chimney from a wood-burning stove. There'd been one exactly the same in her grandmother's dacha.

The room grew crowded and the conversation became louder. People strained and jostled to look at the fish. A band started playing, they were very loud but not very good. A few people cheered, they must be their friends, thought Lydia.

She began to take photographs, squeezing through the crowd, fixing a stranger's face in the square of her lens. She was invisible; a clicking button and the guillotine chop of a shutter, carving the scene into slices. The room changed, it became a pattern, a combination of shapes, a balance of dark and light: black beams, light sky, flames, black legs, pale tendrils of smoke issuing from pale faces. Richard was still talking to Jill. He was animated, persuading her of something. His hands went wide, describing a ball, his elbows on a level with his rounded shoulders. Jill pouted sceptically. He is trying to get her into bed, mused Lydia. She watched the pictures their bodies made. She was detached and interested in a clinical way. It didn't occur to her to be jealous. She remembered that Jill was married to a photographer. It's a complication, thought Lydia, but Jill is not as firm as she would like to be, maybe he'll succeed but then she'll be angry with herself. She framed Richard and Jill, pushing up onto her toes to get the angle right and was about to take the photograph when a hissing voice prickled across the back of her neck. 'Pigs.'

Lydia straightened up, three punks standing next to her were staring across the room. She followed their gaze. Two police helmets were cutting through the crowd. Lydia was afraid. Max had come into Russki's and told them what happened to Igor. She changed her film, drumming her finger tips on the barrel of the lens. Alex appeared beside her. 'Have you seen them?' he said putting his mouth close to her ear and shouting above the music. She could see that for him it had not stopped being an adventure. 'I don't understand it,' he yelled, his hands dancing excitedly up and down, 'why aren't they doing anything? There are enough drugs to arrest us all several times over.'

Richard and Jill joined them. Richard was laconic. 'There's nothing in it,' he bellowed confidently, 'they're just checking us out. We're not causing anyone any trouble.'

'They've already gone,' pointed out Jill and then mimed to Richard that she wanted another beer.

Lydia searched the room again. Jill was right, no blue helmets. She ran her finger across the top of her camera leaving a smooth smeared line on the black plastic. 'Beer, Lydia?' offered Richard. She let the camera fall against her chest and it banged painfully against her breasts. She took the can and opened it, sucking the froth from the surface. Her teeth collided with the metal and set off a nerve inside her gums.

Jill and Richard started talking about crime films. Lydia kept watch from behind her camera while Alex hovered beside her and explained his theory of acting. 'If you're going to be any good at all,' he shouted, 'you've *got to* believe in your character. If you're playing a heroin addict then you've *got to* try heroin. I mean obviously you don't want to become a junkie but you've got to try it once otherwise how do you know? Okay that's a pretty extreme example. But the point is you've got to live haven't you? Otherwise how can you act?'

'What if you have to play a murderer?'

'Well obviously you can't go out and stab somebody but you can get in touch with some of the feelings of a murderer. I mean we've all thought about killing somebody. I don't think that there is anybody in the world who hasn't had that thought once, even if it was just for a second. Okay we don't do it because we are in control of ourselves. So if I was going to act a murderer I'd have to think about what it would be like not to have those kind of controls. Pretty frightening I'd imagine.'

'If you know all this, why are you going to drama school?'

'Well, yes I know about it in *theory*. But it's not easy to actually do. I mean at drama school they teach you lots of stuff but they also teach the *method*.'

'You mean there is a technique necessary to make you believe you are somebody else?'

'Well yes, and anyhow nobody will give you a part unless you go to a good drama school.'

'Why not?'

'Because you haven't come from the right place and so they don't know what you're like.'

Lydia held up her hand. Her eyes were as alert as a hare scenting a predator. A strange deep vibration was coming from beneath them. Alex frowned and cocked his head. Jill and Richard broke from their conversation. All around the room people looked up and sniffed the air.

By the staircase two helmets appeared amongst the heads of the crowd and then rapidly began to multiply, four then six then nine then twelve, more and more spreading out around the walls of the room, their helmets making grotesque shimmering shadows in the candlelight. The band faltered and stopped. There was a whine and a hiss from the speakers. Smoke whirled uneasily around the room. More and more feet pounding up the staircase and then they stopped and all that Lydia could hear was the shuffling of boots on the gritty floor. She held her camera like a shield in front of her neck. Nobody moved, they were caught, mesmerised. What would happen next? What would they do?

A voice, harsh with static, grated out through the speakers. 'Time to go home. Let's clear it up now. Nice and easy. Out now, nice and easy, out now.' The policeman stood with his legs braced next to the drums behind an electronic keyboard. The band looked on, hands hanging limp by their sides. A long line of helmets like wallflowers around the edges of the room. Lydia could feel a vein trembling in the hollow of her temple. She looked at Alex. His shoulders were pushed back and he was standing very upright and stiff as if someone had pumped air into his chest. She looked down at her hands, her knuckles were white on her camera. She hardly recognised them, they were another person's hands. Something touched her and she jumped. It was Alex. He took hold of her upper arm. She made a miniscule nod and accepted the protective grip of his bony hand.

The crowd behind her pushed forward and the two of

them were propelled towards the staircase. Alex shifted his hand to Lydia's forearm and in the brief moment that he loosened his grasp she felt ice brush across her forehead. She turned and took a photograph of Alex's concerned chivalrous face. She felt the palm of another hand push between her shoulders. She heard Richard's voice. She became confused. Bodies were pushing in on them from every side. It was close and hot. She tasted tobacco. She'd had her last cigarette ages ago but suddenly now she could taste the sharp residue of it on her bottom lip. Her fingers were hot and greasy on her camera, she smelt sweat and fear. Alex became obsessed with keeping hold of Lydia. Whatever happens I mustn't let go of her, he thought. He hauled her towards the staircase his fingernails cutting a line of sharp crescents into the dip between the muscles of her forearm. The floorboards underneath them sank and swayed with the crowd. How's the staircase going to hold? It can't, it can't possibly. She pressed her eye closer to the viewfinder, clicked and rewound, clicked and rewound, the hard case clashing painfully with the cartilage of her nose.

At the bottom of the stairs the policemen made a funnel forcing them through the door. 'Out! Out! Out!' Uniforms and caps, young faces canine with aggression. They reached the bottom of the stairs. There was a surge of people from above them. Lydia lurched forwards. Alex's hand snatched at her, she felt the fluttering of his finger tips but she was falling away from him, he couldn't hold her. She cried out like a bird. She was falling. Her stomach rose in her throat. A thigh, a stomach, the little finger of a hand. Fast, fast, warm thick bodies pressing on her. She couldn't breathe. Acid in her mouth. Camera strap cutting her neck. She had to get upright. Something soft against her shins. It's a body, horror, it's a body, it could be mine. She was nothing, nobody, part of the mass. She shot out a hand and gripped with monkey fingers. What was it? There was a bone. A shoulder? A hip? Doesn't matter. The smell of crotches and dust, the seam of your jeans. Hold on tight. 'Out! Out! Out!' chanted the police. Rubble under her feet and somewhere nearby the thud of a truncheon on a body. Very deadened. Near the entrance now. Cooler air fingered her hair. Air stinging on her dry gums, etching into the cracks. There was a high circular whining of sirens. Her jeans snagged on the jagged edge of a brick and then she was out, standing upright, gasping as if after a five mile run, air harsh in her lungs, sandpapering the back of her throat. Oxygen. More. She scrabbled for her camera, sausage fingered, changing the film. A reflex. Time to pause.

The corrugated iron barrier had been flattened and the wasteland surrounding the ruined building was flooded with a pulsing blue, x-ray light from the police cars. Black shapes ran towards the pavement. A bull shouldered policeman pushed her and she looked at him, her mouth blowing bubbles like a fish. 'Shift it. Get a move on. You can't stay around here.' He looked like Igor. She was surprised that he spoke English not Russian.

'All right, all right, keep your shirt on. We're out of here, there's no need to be so fucking aggressive,' shouted Alex all bristle and defence. Where did he come from? Now his arm was around Lydia's shoulder shepherding her up the street. She was shivering and her heart was pounding at her ribs like a prisoner. People still poured from the derelict building. Police radios crackled in the air. There were shouts, she could still hear the police chanting inside the building. Igor, Igor, Igor! No, no it was something else. Car doors opened and slammed shut again. The breeze blew cool on Lydia's damp forehead. An engine started. Some wheels span. A passing car flared music briefly and was gone. Alex, taut and upright, continued to escort her silently up the pavement. She wanted to sit down. She wanted to stop and she wanted to cry. Past the garage forecourt, customers staring, past the off-licence and a chippie where a man leaned on the glass and steel door while he waited for his kebab. Alex's stride was much longer than hers and he slowed it so that she could keep up with him.

They stopped at the corner of the side street where they had left the van. Lydia stood in front of him and rocked her insteps on the kerb. 'What the fuck did they think they were doing in there?' ranted Alex. 'Somebody could have been killed. I wouldn't be fucking surprised.' Lydia felt very shaky. She wanted someone to hug her but Alex was flailing his arms indignantly in the air. He was fired up with adrenalin and righteousness. Tears seeped from her eyes. The street refracted through them as if they were lenses. Lydia looked at the pavement and blinked, one tear, catching the light like a crystal, fell to the ground. She blinked again, brought her head upright and looked at him.

She eased a squashed packet of cigarettes from her back pocket. 'I think I took some good photographs,' she said tremulously and in the back of her mind she heard her mother telling once again the story of her father's arrest. When she was a child Olga had related it over and over again until Lydia had shut her ears and screwed up her eyes at the sound of it. Always the same words, the same phrases, a horrible mournful chant. Particular details fixated Olga, not least that it had happened under Brezhnev. Not during the purges when everyone else was arrested but under Brezhnev, and she implied that somehow, because of this, it was a shoddier job. In Stalin's time, when they knew how to do things, they'd come at night but they came for her husband in the morning, while he had been getting ready to leave for his job in the Department of Public Transport. Lydia's mother found this particularly humiliating. He was dressing, she would tell her daughter with outrage. No one had been safe, not even her, a former Young Communist and the daughter of respected Party officials. Lydia didn't remember the arrest but she remembered her father coming back. She'd been about five at the time. His cough had frightened her and she still had a very clear image of him staring out of the window into the courtyard. He looked grey and collapsed and when he talked to Lydia it was with a false cheeriness that ill people use in the presence of children. Lydia had found it creepy that someone so sick should have such a chirpy voice and at night she had prayed that this scary stranger who was her father would go away again. He didn't leave the flat for days at a time. Eventually she accepted his presence, she grew used to him. A year after he returned from the camps he went to bed. Six months later he died of a chest disease in the same bed, because he refused to go to hospital. He was too afraid of the officials. Lydia never found out whether what he had was curable or not. From time to time she still heard his death rattle in her sleep.

Chapter Fifteen

Lydia's pulse was accelerating, driving her blood at breakneck speed around the switch-back corners of her veins and arteries. Images, thoughts, voices, potentials, possibilities; this could have happened . . . what if? . . . swirling faster and faster. If these things inside her didn't slow down she would break, shatter. She could hear the scream she would make. She tried to force herself to calm down. Tried to make her mind blank. Ignore the faces – you don't do this (which makes it more frightening). You're a cool character. You're calm, unemotional, this isn't you.

Lydia fixed her eyes on the road in the way that someone who is seasick will fix their eyes on the horizon. What was going on around her? She forced herself to concentrate on the scenery. The London Wall roundabout. A sign to Cambridge and a large yellow lorry heading east. No people. Crash barriers crusted thick with grey mud and exhaust. A building of red plastic and concrete. A sign to Tower Bridge and a brief glimpse of the Tower itself lit like a cathedral against the sky. Empty drink cans and a triangular-shaped sandwich packet. The van shaking, a slight scorching smell from the electrics. A purple plastic lighter. Richard ranting at the wheel; steering with one hand and remonstrating with the other. Alex smoking a spliff in the back. The sweet smoke filled the van. Lydia lit a cigarette of her own. She wanted some of the spliff; maybe it would help, but she never smoked and they'd remark on it if she asked for some now and she didn't want that. If they turned their attention on her there was a danger she might cry. She sucked hard at her Rothmans and stared out of the side window at the yellow streets.

They pulled out of a multi-lane traffic flow system and Richard stiffened at the wheel 'Alex, kill the spliff, man. Police,' and with his eyes still on the road he leant across Lydia's lap and wound down her window. He pulled the van to a stop and three large policemen in black bullet-proof vests approached them. Richard got out of the door and closed it firmly behind him. Alex hissed from the back of the van, 'Shit, it stinks in here.' Lydia held her breath. She thought, now Alex is scared, he wasn't scared in the building but he is now. Outside Richard was speaking to the policemen. One of them walked over to a large white van with a sliding side door that was parked near by. Lydia sat on her hands. It was strange, now she felt alert. The hysteria in her head had cleared. There is nothing I can do, she thought, but all the same I am prepared. But another side of her mind prayed: Please God, but I don't believe in God – well please Fate, don't let them take me. Not yet. Give me more time. I will make good use of it. On the other side of the glass Richard was nodding his head. His face was as blank as a schoolboy in front of a teacher. Lydia watched the wing mirrors. Two policemen were approaching the back of the van. They opened it and stared at Alex huddled on the cold wheel arch like an animal in the zoo. One of them sniffed loudly so Lydia and Alex knew that he must have smelt the spliff. He prodded into an old sleeping bag and barrel bag that Richard kept in the back. 'All clear,' he said over his shoulder and he banged the two back doors shut letting the noise reverberate against the cold metal doors of the van.

Two minutes later Richard got back into the van. 'Right,' he said as he fiddled with the ignition system underneath the steering wheel, 'let's get out of here.' They moved forward. Alex started unlacing his shoe. 'Fucking hell!' he gasped, 'I've got half an ounce and a bag of speed on me. That's the closest I've ever been. We were fucking lucky that copper said nothing about the spliff.' He stops being afraid so quickly, thought Lydia, the nightmare has finished for him and turned itself into a story that he will tell with extravagant and not very English flourishes of his arms. With her head twisted around over her shoulder she watched him pull off one shoe, tip a Clingfilm wrapped brown block of hash on to the rusting floor of the van and then begin to unlace the other shoe. 'They weren't interested,' shouted Richard over the noise of the engine, 'and once they'd heard my accent you were safe. All they wanted to do was run a check on me. I mean drug takers are one kind of sinner but Irishmen, well they're in league with Satan aren't they?'

And immigrants, thought Lydia, and although her mind remained calm her hands started shaking so she turned her attention back to the road and squeezed them under her thighs. They drove through the empty streets of the city and then down into a tunnel that ran along the embankment. Richard was driving very fast and the old van rattled in protest. 'As those nice British bobbies have left you with your stash do you want to roll us a big fat one to calm my nerves?' shouted Richard. Alex, who'd just retrieved his bag of speed from the other trainer, grinned and got to work.

When they got into *Toadhall* Alex peered through the curtains to the *Beagle* next door. 'Oh fuck, my sister's having one of her bloody dinner parties,' he groaned. He flopped down on the sofa and fishing out his papers from his pocket began to roll another joint. Richard pulled a bottle of Famous Grouse out from behind a dusty-looking Buddha that stood by an old yucca plant in the corner. Lydia wanted to get away from them. 'I'm going to make some tea,' she announced and as she went down the stairs Richard shouted after her to bring up some glasses.

Lydia didn't turn the light on downstairs and through the window she could clearly see Sally's dinner party. They were sitting around the remains of a meal with wine glasses and candles. Lydia felt like she was watching a scene from a film. The girl at the far end of the table was talking. She was bright and animated. She wore round gold earrings that reflected the candle flames. Her neck was very straight and long and as she talked she showed her wide white teeth. Next to her a man with short clean hair rested his chin on his hand and listened to her intently. Lydia looked away. She wished that she could go to a place where there was wine and candles and people sat around a table and talked and listened to each other.

Her hands were still shaking too much to be able to fill the kettle from the tap so she put it in the sink and let the water flow over it. Her mind and her body seemed to have separated themselves completely. She remembered the feeling she had had in the disused cinema when she had looked at her hands and felt like they belonged to someone else and, she thought, in one respect this was right, her body didn't belong to her; it belonged to Seriozha and Richard and the other lovers she had known and it belonged to Slava and her mother and her country and when they had all had their part there was very little of it left to belong to her. She thought of her father and how so much of his body had been taken away from him in the camps that there wasn't enough left to keep going on its own. Then the kettle boiled and the noise broke her train of thought so she poured the water into the teapot and returned upstairs with a tray bearing milk and sugar and glasses and mugs. The boat rocked slowly on the river. The men talked rapidly. They were outraged, they said so again and again. Alex kept on looking at her and then diving back into the conversation. He was searching for her reaction but she felt too tired to understand English. She was living in a foreign language. Its strange noises filled the air around her and seemed, at that moment, as curious and unintelligible as birdsong. She had a sudden deep pang of longing for Seriozha: she yearned to speak her language, to lie down, to be near his solid presence, the feeling of safety that he brought, the feeling that if you were with him everything in the crazy world was under control. Tomorrow, she thought, I will ring him.

Lydia stood up. 'I can't finish it,' she said pointing at the whiskey glass they had given her. The men's white faces were turned up to her like studio lights. 'I must go to sleep.'

Her bed was on a level with the window. She folded her clothes into a neat pile on the chair by her bedside table, clambered up onto the mattress and flipped the duvet over her body. She curled up on her side, like a child, and placed her hands on either side of her cheeks. She had left the curtains open and she could see her reflection in the dark glass of the window. A small face framed by hands and behind her the hanging clothes on the back of her door, her tripod and the skin lotions on her bedside table. She could also see through the reflection over the oily water to the black back of the pontoon. Tubes, cables and mooring chains looped through the air like aerial intestines.

She heard Alex leave. Heard the tramp of his footsteps as he walked the gangplank above the window. Not long afterwards a long column of yellow light appeared in her reflection. Richard was silhouetted in the doorway. 'Are you awake?' he whispered. She rolled over onto her back and watched him standing there. 'Lydia, are you awake,' he said again. She waited for a moment letting the dark air fizz heavily above her and then because she felt lonely and sad she propped herself up on one elbow and said that yes, she was.

He took his clothes off and got into the bed and she made room for him by shuffling up towards the window. He kissed her and held her bottom in his hands. She felt his fingers at the join of her legs. She slipped her hands under his arms which was awkward because they were both lying on their sides. She wriggled down so that her head was level with his chest. She rubbed her face against the side of his rib cage. He lifted her up the bed and rolled in between her legs. He began to make small grunting sounds that slowly turned to whimpers. A warm sticky layer of sweat covered his body. He dropped down to her right nipple. The sensation made her curl her knees upwards. She turned her head to the window. The reflection of her face glistened with either sweat or tears. She glared at herself rudely as if she was letting the reflection know that she was none of its business. Later, as she was falling asleep, she thought, well if it's not my body that's fine because then I can just enjoy it and I don't have to think about it and it leaves me alone to be free.

The following afternoon Lydia rang Seriozha at Lenfilm.

'It's me,' she said.

He grunted, 'The English girl.'

'How's your car?'

'Very good. They make good cars.'

'Don't be like this Seriozha. I wanted to hear your voice but if you're going to be like this I won't bother calling you again.'

'What are you wearing?'

'My jeans and my blue-and-green jumper with the gold buttons.'

'And under that?'

'The black lace underwear that you gave me.'

There was a pause. The static crackled. Lydia could hear the faint murmur of a conversation on another line.

'I might have sold another photograph,' said Lydia.

'What's it this time? Flowers in the Park?'

'No this is for a newspaper. I saw the police raid an illegal party and I took photographs.'

'Jesus Christ Lydia. Don't be a fool. Are you *trying* to get yourself into trouble? You're not safe to let out on your own. Really you're not.'

'Calm down Seriozha. It's fine I promise you. I'm not going to do anything stupid. I know what the situation is here. Believe me.'

'When are you coming back? I thought you were only going for six months?'

'I thought you'd be pleased for me. I can stay. I've got work so I can afford to stay and if I sell this picture it will be really good for me. It's what I came for.'

There was another pause.

'I miss you. Yesterday I really wanted to speak to you,' she said.

'And the other days?'

'Those too. Of course.'

'I want you to come home.'

'I'm coming, I'm coming, I promise. I just need a little bit more time.'

Chapter Sixteen

Alex's mother was dressed in a surgical apron in a field hospital at the front. The ground rocked as shells exploded around the tent. Blood and mud splattered over the walls staining the original canvas with blossoming brown trees and clouds. The tent was empty, there was only his mother and the body of a man that she was operating on. Alex had come to rescue her and he was pleading with her to leave. There were no knives for some reason, only his mother's white fingers dipping in and out of the slippery intestines. She kept on repeating that she couldn't find it, she couldn't find it and then her hand would plunge once more into the white bloody guts. There were shadows on the side of the tent. They were being surrounded. The troops wore dinner jackets and black bowties like bouncers. It wasn't just her hand now, her arm up to her elbow was immersed in the man's belly. Alex was reminded of a vet pulling a calf out of a cow. She pulled out a gold Rolex watch and held it up to the dim gas light before placing it carefully on the bedside table. For an awful moment Alex thought he saw the man's legs twitch. His mother began slowly and methodically soaping her hands. There wasn't time for this. Alex decided to act; she doesn't understand, he said to himself, but it is for her own good. I am doing it for her. He pushed his mother aside and picking up the man with his split-open belly and green surgical tunic, tucked him under his arm and with his free hand pushed his mother towards the door. Now his mother had changed into Lydia and she wasn't so heavy to pull. He ran with her through the flaps of the tent. Outside two goons blocked out the sun. They were enormous, Alex's head reached their hips. They were like tower blocks in front of him and they were chanting, 'Out! Out! Out!' Shells were exploding to the same rhythm as the chant. Alex suddenly became worried that he had got the wrong word: they can't be called shells, shells are a woman's vulva, shells are for listening to the sea. But the goons were still there, he had no time to think about shells, his mission was to rescue Lydia. The man under his arm had disappeared. He made a signal to Lydia and she understood his plan. Together they ran between the goons' legs. There was a shout. They'd been discovered. Lydia was still with him. He was gripping her forearm. Now they were running up a hill. Alex's feet and legs were bare. There were thistles underneath the ball of his foot, his toes dug into the chalk mud, the downland grass whipped against his legs. The sun was warm on their backs and his breath came as clearly and easily as if he was singing. They ran like this for some time, just for the pleasure of it and then they flopped onto their backs on the grass. Lydia rolled her body towards him. He pushed himself up onto his hands and as he bent down to kiss her he smelt wild thyme.

Alex began to wake up but he didn't want to finish the dream, he kept his eyes closed and tried to conjure up again the deep-blue sky of the hillside. He lay very still but he saw nothing except the vague neon shapes on the inside of his eyelids and he knew that the dream was lost and he wouldn't be able to catch it again. He opened his eyes. It was raining and the raindrops were making kissing sounds as they landed on his window. He turned on his bedside lamp and screwed up his eyes while they adjusted to the glare. He swung his legs over the edge of the bed and leant his elbows on his knees. He felt empty. It was if the dream had stolen something from him. He rolled himself a cigarette and smoked it cross-legged on the bed, leaning against the partition wall. He plucked a hair from his leg and listened to the rain. He was wide awake now and slightly dizzy from the cigarette. It was five o'clock in the morning and he knew that he should try and get back to sleep. He turned out the light and lay on his pillow. Lydia's face gathered in the air above him. She turned slightly sideways. It seemed to Alex that she was listening to him.

'You see,' he said, 'what I really want to do is not just to become an actor. Don't get me wrong, I do really want to be an actor but for me, that's just the first stage. I mean, after I've done that for a while then I want to become a director. I think you've got to do one before you do the other. I mean, it makes sense, doesn't it, you can't tell people what to do unless you can do it yourself. If you're an actor you can do the best performance in the universe but the production might still be shit because ultimately you're not in control which you are if you're a director.'

Lydia nodded wisely. 'But it is a very hard world,' she said.

'I know that,' replied Alex, 'but if you really want something, you've got to do it haven't you, otherwise you'll always regret it. I mean, I'll fight for it. I'm not going to give up easily you know. *When the going gets tough, the tough get going* and all that. No, I'm prepared to really go all out for it.'

'I'm sure you are,' said Lydia. Her voice was very gentle. 'I'll support you all the way. You know that don't you?'

'Thank you Lydia,' he said, 'you don't know how much it means to me to hear you say that. You will be my inspiration.'

'Whatever it takes.'

'Yes, exactly, whatever it takes.'

Alex folded an entire fat blini crammed with sour cream and

mushrooms into his mouth and tapped his fork on the table as he tried to chew it. Dimitri was taunting Volodya in the kitchen. He was talking in Serbian but the bullying tone was so familiar that Alex felt he was hearing the words in English. Alex was uncomfortable. He wanted to get up and defend Volodya. He knew that was what he should do, that was the honourable thing, but how could he when he couldn't understand what Dimitri was saying? He might think that he knew what was happening but what if he was wrong? Imagine how stupid he would feel then. He was still struggling with his conscience when Lydia came in through the door. She was unusually jaunty. She was swinging her hips so hard as she weaved in between the tables that she was almost skipping. God she was beautiful. Like some fantasy animal with all that red hair and the white marble chip of her face. There was a bone halfway down her nose that looked like a knuckle. Eyelids so fine you could see the thin blue threads of her veins. She wasn't real this woman. Alex shook his head. He remembered his fantasies during the night and he was ashamed, he'd been taking liberties with her, without her permission he'd been talking to her, he'd been kissing, worse. She'd reached the staff table now and he realised that though he'd stopped chewing, he still had a mouthful of blini. Could she read the guilt on his face? She wasn't looking; she was smiling, pink lips curling up through her cheeks. What was she smiling about? Lydia never smiled. She swung her handbag on to the table; black fake leather with a large tacky gilt clasp. All her things were like that, cheap and flashy. With any other woman that would have bothered him but somehow with Lydia it was actually quite perversely sexy. She was so luminous she shone through the shoddiness of her clothing.

She was still smiling. In fact come to think of it she'd said something to him but he'd been too distracted by the sight of her to take any notice. Alex finished his mouthful. 'What?' he said. 'I've got a picture in the *Evening Standard*.

Look.' She took a neatly folded square of newspaper from the awful handbag, smoothed it out on the table and turned it around so that he could see. Meanwhile she lit herself a Rothmans.

The photograph took up a quarter of the page. Frightened party goers were spewing out of the old cinema and running towards the camera through dark wasteland, their faces lit with an eerie striated light from the police sirens. Alex ran his forefinger around the edge of the photograph. In the bottom left-hand corner PHOTOGRAPH: LYDIA GUROVA. Alex realised that he hadn't known what her surname was. His finger completed another circuit of the photograph. Alex was impressed. He didn't know what to say.

'Well what do you think?' prompted Lydia. 'Do you like it?'

'Fucking brilliant Lydia, how did you manage it?'

'It was Richard. He's got a friend who works there.'

At ten o'clock Alex took a break. He squatted on a metal staircase outside the fire escape door at the back of the kitchen and shivered over a cigarette. It would be Richard, he thought sourly. He remembered the boys who claimed the back seat of the coach on school outings and the music crowd that Jasper but not Alex had been a part of at Durham. At university music had been marginally cooler than acting which was why, he supposed, Jasper had gone for music, but he hadn't had the nerve. It's always like that isn't it? There's always a cool group that you're not part of. We never grow up. We never stop being kids; who's part of the gang, who's in, who's out? What jobs, what clothes, what music? Where have you travelled? Where do you live? What have you done? Who do you know? An air extractor chugged away beside him, blowing the smell of frying meat into the evening air. I'd never have been able to sell Lydia's pictures, he thought glumly.

It was a cloudy night and Alex could only just make out the shapes in the gardens behind the restaurant and the glowing orange squares of electric light that hovered in the houses beyond them. A staircase crossed one window and on the top floor of the house a man stood staring through the glass at Alex. The man turned his head back to the room. Somebody inside the house is calling to him, thought Alex. The man glanced out of the window once more and then pulled the curtains closed in front of him and the window was eclipsed. Alex blew on his hands and rubbed his arms. The temperature was dropping, a dew formed on the metal floor of the fire escape. There were sharp smells of earth and damp brick. Alex imagined he could see Lydia's face and body as thin as a reflection hovering like a dew mist over the jumbled shadows of the city garden. His stomach tightened. He felt as if he still had an umbilical chord and it was tugging away from him. He slipped a hand into the warmth of his groin for comfort and cradled the soft dropping fruit of his balls in his hand. He sighed. There was a pressure building up inside him that demanded some kind of release. I'll tell her, he resolved, I'll tell her how much she means to me. Pause. The decision made him feel better. Now he had a plan. He flicked the end of his roly into a fire bucket full of sand and pulled himself upright. 'I'll tell her I love her,' he proclaimed out loud to the empty staircase and the eclipsed windows of the house. '*Faint heart never won fair lady.*'

Alex avoided Lydia for the rest of the shift. If they passed each other on the way to and from the kitchen he turned his head in the opposite direction. He didn't idle by the staff table. All night he was out amongst the tables, busily clearing glasses, changing ashtrays, wiping tables or else he was in the kitchen making monosyllabic conversation with Volodya (to make up for Dimitri bullying him) as he scrubbed the big steel oven trays. Now that he had made his resolution he didn't want to have any contact with Lydia until he had carried it out. He wanted to keep it pure. He wasn't going to be weakened. He was going to do it and he wasn't going to let her deflect him. How he was going to do it he wasn't quite sure, but somehow or other he was going to try and show her how he felt. It was a concrete decision, a solid thing and he carried it with him like a piece of stone until the muscles across the back of his neck and shoulders grew as solid as a plank and the area between his neck and his jutting collar bones grew so tense that it hurt.

They walked back to the moorings along the King's Road and the burning space which her body displaced bumped into him as she walked. Empty sofas and static dummies stared at him from shop windows as they passed by. So what are you going to say then Alex, what are you going to do? 'Lydia, I want to tell you something . . . Lydia, how about . . . I know it sounds really stupid but I . . . Lydia what would you say if I was to tell you . . . I don't know how to say this but . . .' By the cinema they passed a group of three young businessmen; ties loosened, laughing in the raucous, callous way of boys out on the piss. Beside him the legs of Lydia's jeans whispered together as she walked.

He was trembling as he stepped off the solid embankment behind Lydia. The gangplanks swung underneath his feet crying and squeaking. At the notice board at the bottom of the Milmans Street entrance he made his first move. 'I've got a bottle of wine. Why don't you come round and have a drink on our deck?'

Lydia was slick in her refusal. 'I'd like to but I want to go back and say thank you.'

Alex looked over at *Toadhall*. The glass in the little grid above the door was black. He pointed, 'He's already gone to bed.'

'Not necessarily, he might not be back from work yet.'

Alex's eyebrows squeezed determinedly together. 'Then you can have a drink,' he countered.

She looked at him curiously. 'All right. A glass of wine,'

she said, uncurling her fingers and rolling her palms backwards and forwards across the metal tubing of the deck rail.

Alex swallowed and started forward, 'Good, well I'm glad that's decided then.'

He showed her around the gunwales of the boat and then left her on deck while he went inside to get the bottle and a couple of glasses. There was no wind, the sky was moonless and the city was wrapped in low cloud. Lydia looked out across the sleek water being pulled by the tide up towards Wandsworth and Putney. A light mist like smoky breath rose from the surface. Just then a white egret landed on a buoy by the bow of the *Beagle* and stood motionless like a crack in the darkness, facing the tide.

Alex watched her as he edged down the side of the boat with an opened bottle and two glasses. She's daydreaming, he thought and he was jealous. He wanted her to be here, now, with him so that he could make his move. It was wrong that she should be distracted, that she should be thinking of somewhere else. Alex nudged her shoulder with a glass of red wine. She took the glass and pointed at the egret and he stood beside her following her gaze. The tide turned and for a minute the river became as still and glossy as obsidian and the reflections of the lights from the shore grew sharp and focused. Then the current reasserted itself and the river streamed down under Battersea Bridge towards the East End and the sea. The egret rotated 180 degrees on its buoy and slowly extending its wings to their full width took off upstream, flying low over the water to the red-and-green navigation lights that wavered over the surface from Chelsea Harbour.

Alex was relieved when the bird had flown away. It would have been clumsy not to have watched it with her but he was too restless and itchy with resolve and anticipation to appreciate it. 'That was magic,' said Alex a little too quickly and not very sincerely. A trace of a frown passed across

Lydia's forehead as she turned and smiled at him. There were five feet between them. Five feet of black space that he had to launch himself across. And the moment his hand entered that air space she'd be on to him, she'd know exactly what he was doing and she'd be able to respond to it. But he had to do something. He couldn't just stand there with the whole city night whispering around them. A car's headlights came over Battersea Bridge and the black oil of the river with its soapy light-slicked surface sucked at the metal bow beneath their feet. He turned stiffly towards her. His joints seemed to have seized and locked together. He took a gulp of wine. The silence stretched between them. Okay, don't move, he told himself, but say something, anything at this point otherwise it's going to get really awkward. He took another gulp of wine and swallowed it, feeling the tannin stick like velcro to the back of his tongue. Then he opened his mouth to speak but instead he stepped forward, put his hand on her shoulder and dipped his face down to kiss her. She moved her head very quickly to one side. 'No Alex,' she said.

'Why not?' He snatched his hand from her shoulder and let it flop by his side. 'Is there someone else? Is it Richard?' He spoke too loudly and too fast. His voice was harsh against the soft black water.

She wet her lips with the tip of her tongue and looked out across the river. She made evasive noises, 'I don't think it's a good idea.'

'Well why not?' he said angrily.

She took a very small sip of wine and sucking her finger ran it around the rim of her glass making a small squeaking sound. 'Alex,' she said, 'It doesn't matter why not. I don't want to. Okay?'

Alex's face burnt with blood. He deserved that. What a stupid thing to ask. What was he thinking of?

He closed his eyes, screwed up his face and stamped his foot down hard on the metal deck. 'God I hate things like this!' he burst out violently. 'Can you just forget it? Can you pretend that the last five minutes never happened?'

'They never happened,' she said and offered him her glass for refilling.

Chapter Seventeen

It was meant to be Alex's night off on Thursday and he'd arranged to meet up with Steve in Soho but at lunchtime Slava rang him from Russki's. 'I have a small problem that I think you may be able to help me with,' said Slava. Alex, standing in his boxer shorts by the kitchen, sandwiched the receiver between his right ear and his shoulder and waited for Slava to continue. Outside a dog was barking and Alex listened to the echo as it bounced up and down on the metal pontoons. 'Both Dimitri and the young Volodya are required elsewhere tonight so I want you to come in for an extra shift.' Alex removed the telephone from his shoulder and held it to his ear with his hand, 'Slava, I've organised to go out with a friend tonight,' he protested.

'Well sadly you will have to unorganise,' said Slava with an edge to his voice, 'needs dictate and we need you tonight.'

So Alex rang up Steve, cancelled and went to work. The atmosphere in the restaurant was strained. It was the first time that Alex and Lydia had worked together since Tuesday night and Alex was convinced Lydia was trying to be especially nice and friendly towards him, which he found humiliating. In the kitchen there was an agency chef called Michael, and a kitchen hand called Darren, a small dark boy who was studying Tourism and Leisure at North London Poly. They were more cheerful than Dimitri and Volodya but they didn't know their way around the menu. Slava didn't help by being in a particularly testy mood. All night he prowled around the restaurant picking holes in people's work and constantly reminding Michael and Darren how much he was paying for them per hour. So when the two policemen came in at about eleven thirty the atmosphere was already very tense.

They were both in uniform. The first man was in his late thirties, tall and thin with two deep creases that ran from his nose to his chin like brackets around his tight straight mouth. The second man was about ten years younger and broader, with a pink soft face. The younger man pushed the door shut behind him while his colleague waited for him and together they approached Slava who was perched on the stool behind the cash desk adding up bills.

The two remaining tables of customers twisted their necks around to look at the policemen and then bending their heads together began speculating with each other. Alex was clearing a table so he was the first to see them. Lydia had just taken a pile of plates into the kitchen and was now making coffee by the sand tray underneath the staircase. Alex did a quick mental calculation of what drugs he had on him but he reckoned he was all right, he only had a blim of dope at the bottom of his baccy tin. After that it didn't occur to him that there might be anything sinister about the policemen. He didn't really think about it; he assumed they were there for some bobby-on-the-beat community policing reason.

Alex passed by Lydia laden with heavy plates on his way to the kitchen. He blushed. Again. He hated himself blushing. Why couldn't he control it? 'Have you seen we've got the fuzz through there,' he said to Darren. 'What for?' asked Darren, 'Do you reckon your man Slava's been doing something dodgy?'

He returned to the main body of the restaurant to get the rest of the plates. Lydia was hovering around a table in the opposite corner. She had her back to the policemen. Her movements were short and agitated. She fussed unnecessarily around the table; she moved a bottle holding a carnation, changed the ashtray and provided the customers with a second bowl of sugar. Alex wondered why she was paying them so much attention. She fancies one of the blokes, he thought bitterly. He watched her load five plates onto her left arm, lining them up to her elbow, letting the bases stick to the fine bluey white skin of her wrist. Five, he noticed with jealousy. What was she trying to prove? She began walking towards him and it was then that he realised that something was wrong. She was looking straight at him but it seemed as if she couldn't see him. Her eyes were fixed like a doll's, there was no movement in them at all. Her face had turned to ice, a blue cord stuck out from her neck. The plates must have been very heavy but she didn't appear to notice that she was carrying anything at all. She collided into the back of a chair, corrected her course and began moving towards the kitchen. Still nothing moved in her face. Alex picked up his plates and hurried after her.

He was just behind her as they reached the step down into the alcove. Then Slava called out from behind them, 'Lydia can you come here a minute?' She turned instantly. Alex had the impression that she had been waiting for him to call her over. As she turned she almost collided with Alex. She was like a sleepwalker. Alex wanted to stop her, put his hands on her shoulders, take the plates away from her and shake her awake but he didn't do anything. He just stared at her and watched her go and although she swerved to avoid him it seemed to Alex that she still hadn't seen him, that she was working on radar, not sight.

He dumped the plates on the side of the sink beside Darren and rushed back out through the swing door. The two policemen were asking Lydia questions while Slava grinned obsequiously beside them. What the hell was going on? He couldn't hear what they were saying. The hair on his arms stood up in goose pimples. He hesitated at the top of the step, unsure of what action to take. Lydia put the plates down on a nearby table and turned back towards him. She noticed him this time. A brave weak little smile flickered across her face.

Slava beckoned him over to the policemen. Alex didn't feel that he was there at all. His senses were warped and disconnected from each other. The air resisted him as he walked. It took him forever to reach Slava and the police. As he got nearer to them their faces shimmered in front of him as if they were in a heat haze. Their voices were divorced from their bodies. It was like watching a foreign film where the dubbing is out of sync. Lydia went away and then came back and stood behind him. The older policeman looked up. His tongue flickered out onto his dessicated lips. He took a little red book from Lydia. 'In a minute, sonny' he said and Alex had to lock his tongue over his oesophagus to stifle a hysterical giggle. Policemen didn't really call you sonny, did they? It didn't matter. It wasn't funny. This wasn't the time for laughing.

The younger policeman turned to Alex. 'You work as a waiter here?' He nodded and looked at the floor, watching Lydia out of the corner of his eye. She seemed completely composed now. Was she illegal? What were they going to do to her? Slava had called her over. He'd dumped her in this. He must've known.

'Can I have your name please?'

'Alexander Carmichael,' he said scuffing the toe of his shoe across the tiles.

'How long have you been working here?'

'Just under three months,'

'British citizen?'

Alex nodded stiffly. Slava was looking at a print of some onion-domed churches on the wall as if he'd never seen them before. He must be purposely looking away from Lydia. What a cunt. Alex felt himself vibrating with anger. He wanted to slap Slava's smug after-shaved face. Do something. You're Russian aren't you? What was all that stuff about defecting in the seventies?

The policemen were moving away from them now. The tall policeman went first, ushering Lydia out of the door as she was putting her hands into the arms of her jean jacket. He ought to tackle them, punch them and let her run free. That's what would have happened in a film. His muscles were all tensed and ready to leap but he knew that he wasn't going to move, that he wasn't going to do anything. He clenched his fists impotently. He called out to her as she reached the door. 'I'll wait for you on the *Beagle*. Call me if you need someone.' She turned around towards him but she was almost completely blocked from view by the policeman. All that Alex could see was a lock of red hair.

When the door had closed behind them one of the women from the table by the window coughed. 'Excuse me,' she said indignantly 'but can we have our bill please?' Alex was still staring at the door. Slava slipped a clammy confidential hand onto Alex's shoulder.

'Don't you worry. That sort of thing always looks worse than it is. It's because she's not English. They have to check up on these things. It'll just be a formality. Now I have a feeling that that table in the corner wants some attention.'

Chapter Eighteen

Lydia's interview room was lit by a dangling 200-watt light bulb and painted a genteel café-crème brown from the floor to a moulded ridge that ran around the room at hip height. Above this a raised patterned wallpaper had been drowned in cream gloss. The walls were dented by kick marks and around the door the plaster was blistered and crumbling.

The younger policeman sat at a wooden table that looked like an old school desk. There was a thin glaze of grease across his puffy face. He flicked his eyes from right to left and from left to right like a cockroach trapped in the bottom of a bath. His hands were like a baby's with dimples instead of knuckles. He circled them around a plastic disposable cup of tea that he had got from a vending machine in the hallway. Lydia didn't deign to look at him. She examined the plaster work with an expression of superior boredom that implied that although the policeman was the only other living creature in the stale-smelling room he wasn't worthy of her attention. It was a point of pride, this man (definitely younger than her, she decided) was not going to see that she was frightened. The two of them waited in silence while the red second hand jolted around a battery-powered clock on the wall. The policeman turned his cup of tea round and round in his plump palms. Lydia lit a cigarette. She rested her wrist on her knee so that her hand wouldn't shake and then flicked the ash onto the floor.

The tall policeman came into the room holding a sheaf of papers in his hand. 'Miss Gurova,' he said politely as he closed the plywood door behind him. Lydia turned towards him and her eyelids dropped over her eyes in a good imitation of a bored lizard. 'Your visa does not permit you to take up employment during your stay in the country so I am serving you with a decision to deport in breach of conditions. You have fourteen days in which to either leave the country or appeal against the decision.' He held up a sheet of pale blue paper with his thumb and forefinger. 'Using this form.' He handed the papers to Lydia who placed them face down on her lap, waiting for him to continue. The clock ticked through the silence.

'You are free to go now Miss Gurova.' Lydia started and then brushed her hand quickly across her face as if she was trying to get rid of a cobweb. The young policeman nodded at his colleague and pushed his chair back. For one terrifying moment Lydia thought the policemen were going to hit her. She lost all her composure, jumped up, snatched her handbag up from the floor and clasping the rolled up papers she walked very fast out of the interview room and down the corridor, her trainers screeching against the linoleum.

Once she got outside she began to run. She wasn't fit. Too many cigarettes. She felt as if she had been coiled up tight and now suddenly she had been loosened and she was springing out in a reflex. Her body parted the air. She felt a small, electric jolt every time her feet hit the pavement. She ached to be violent, to hurt someone, she wanted to be physically exhausted, spent and annihilated. Once she had started running she couldn't stop. She panted past the blank staring eyes of the houses. Her chest cracked and wheezed in pain, on and on and on she ran, not slowing down until she reached the embankment and the river. She clambered needily onto a bench as if it was somebody's lap. It was a green wooden bench raised on a concrete plinth with black wrought-iron lions' heads on its arms and claws at its feet. She hugged her legs to her chest, buried her head between her knees and gasped for breath. The wind flayed the leaves of the scaly plane trees across a sky scattered with dirty grey rags of cloud.

She bit her knees through her jeans. She could taste her sweat through the fabric and it was all mixed up with smells of the restaurant, smoke, food, sour cream and detergent. She opened her eyes and saw the muddled humps of her legs. She banged her head again and again against her knees and she crushed the roll of papers in her fist. She was trapped, trapped again. Her eyes were smarting and the wind whipped at the salt water and made them sting even more. Images flashed in her mind like a strobe. She saw her mother's flat: the worn pink wallpaper, the double glass windows, the ornaments, the squares of white linen carefully laid over piles of crockery. Nothing will have changed. It will all be exactly the same. Like walking back into a museum. She saw the police interview room and then Seriozha's palatial office at Lenfilm and the entrance hall of his flat at Kupchina, the steel inner door, the chains and locks and the worn out slippers piled beneath the overcoats.

She remembered her last conversation with Seriozha and chewed at her finger tips. He's behind this, she thought, and she shivered. It was as if she had no life of her own. He's angry. He wants me back. He could have talked to Slava. It wouldn't have been difficult. The wind cracked and sighed in the trees. The surface of the river was rough. In front of her Albert Bridge was strung with lights. She remembered crossing it the day she had stumbled on the boats. The frilliness of the bridge made her feel bleak and sad. She let her feet fall from the bench. She didn't want to rage, or think or blame any longer.

She didn't want any thought at all to pass through her mind. She stood up. The wind was strong enough to lean against. Leaves scratched against the stone as they were blown spinning down the pavement. She walked over to the embankment wall and leaned over it, tucking her hands into her armpits to stop the shaking and keep them warm. The rounded top of the wall pressed into her belly. A ridge of mud glistened beneath her and a black line of algae marked the point which the water would reach at high tide.

Chapter Nineteen

Alex pushed through the kitchen doorway blazing. 'I just don't believe I saw that. I mean how the fuck could he?'

Darren dipped the baking tray back into the hot soapy water. Behind him Michael was wiping down the stove.

'They weren't bobbies out on the fucking beat. They were Immigration Police. And what did he do? He shopped them Lydia. I mean, you just don't do that man. Your own country-man? He didn't have to. He could have brought them through here and got them to talk to you guys. He had three completely clean members of staff and one possibly dodgy one. So the minute the pigs walk through the door he calls her straight over. I mean he knows for Christ's sake. He's Russian. The bastard did it on purpose. He must have done.'

'You see some weird stuff in restaurants,' said Darren, 'only about a couple of months ago me and Michael were working in Soho and the police did over the Chinese place next door. You should have seen that. That was heavy, like some kind of paramilitary raid. They drove the entire staff off in a paddywagon.'

But Alex wasn't listening. He was thinking of Lydia.

Which police station would they have taken her too? Did they deport them straight away? How did it work? He felt like cellophane was being crushed inside him. Questions kept on popping off like flashbulbs in his brain. Slava must have known. Surely they couldn't just take her away and not inform anyone? What if he couldn't say goodbye? I'm glad that I tried to tell her how I felt about her, he thought, so what if it didn't work, at least I tried, at least she knows.

Alex stamped his way from Russki's to the boats. He didn't see the buildings around him. He wasn't aware of the shops or the cinemas, the traffic or the pubs. The wind blew his hair in his face. He hauled it back and tied it more tightly in its elastic band. He went over the things he could have done, the things he should have done. He could have hit Slava. The slimy little git deserved it. At the very least he could have walked out in protest after the police had gone. He should have helped Lydia. She could have got away, if he'd told her when he'd first seen the police, if he'd created some kind of disturbance. Then he could have helped her go on the run – he liked that idea, he could just imagine visiting her secretly in a cottage in the countryside. If only he'd thought about it they could have done something. If only he'd thought about it.

The wind was strong and bullying and when he reached the moorings the boats were banging into each other and swinging violently on their chains. It was noisy, the gangplanks squealed on rusty rollers and the mooring chains boomed against the thin steel sheeting of the pontoons.

Sally was sitting at the dinner table with her lap top and a pile of papers. Why did she have to be in tonight?

'Working?' he said as he reached the bottom of the stairs. Sally slapped a folder shut, 'Yep, trying to catch up on some of the backlog.' She rubbed her eyes and yawned, stretching out her arms and rocking on the back legs of her chair. 'I was going to have a glass of wine before I went to bed. Do you want one?'

'Thanks.'

'How's the restaurant trade.'

'Don't ask Sally. Bad, bad night.'

'Customers being difficult?'

'No nothing like that. You know Lydia, the girl who lives next door?'

Sally shook her head and handed him a glass of wine. The wind howled over the top of the cabin and the boat rocked, splashing the wine up the sides of the glass.

'Well anyway, she's one of the waitresses. She's Russian you see and tonight she was taken away by the police.'

'That's awful! Why?'

'I don't know. Something to do with her visa.'

Sally shut down her computer. She clicked her tongue across the top her mouth. 'Oh, right. Well I suppose if she doesn't have a visa it's only fair isn't it? Otherwise you get half the world coming to claim on our social security.'

A wave bashed against the side of the boat and the hull juddered. Alex winced, there was no point in trying to explain it to Sally. Alex didn't ask himself why he thought Sally would never understand while he could, to him it was a matter of category. There were people who could see it and people who couldn't and his sister belonged to the latter. 'Yeah, I suppose there's not much anyone can do about it,' he mumbled sulkily. Neither of them said anything. The silence was sodden with misunderstanding and resentment. They each listened to the sounds of the storm outside.

Eventually Sally pushed back her chair. 'I'm pretty knackered and I've got an early morning meeting tomorrow, so I think I'm just going to slip straight off to bed.'

Alex listened to Sally padding around the bathroom until her bedroom door clicked shut. The boat was cold and empty. The mooring chains banged as the wind blew them against the pontoons and the waves crashed and echoed against the metal shell of the hull. Alex got up from the table, flopped restlessly into a big armchair and immediately began rolling himself a cigarette. He regretted being so sulky to Sally. He didn't want to be alone. He could have done with her company. He thought about ringing up Steve but Steve wasn't right somehow, anyhow he'd promised Lydia that he'd be here. He must wait. He leant his head back, the circles of light from the lamp in the corner jumped around the ceiling as the boat jolted on the waves. He left his cigarette in his mouth, just holding onto it with his lips. At first it was the smoke catching in his eyes that made him cry but then the tears were real and they slithered miserably down his face. After a while he stood up and walked over to the window. Jagged waves with edges like holly leaves leapt up from the river. He pressed his face onto the cool glass. They're going to take her away and there's nothing I can do about it, he whispered in a small self-pitying voice and as he spoke he watched in fascination as an aura of condensation blossomed on the glass. On the other side of the glass there was a small white crescent on the back of each black wave. Alex imagined the same cold black waves in his lungs crashing against the red walls. It's not fair, it's not fair, he wailed to himself smearing his face across the glass. I haven't had time, I haven't been given a chance. It's not fair, it's not fair. He could hear his mother's voice saying 'Life isn't fair Alex and the sooner you learn that the better.'

He poured himself another glass of wine and went back to the armchair, crouching this time, with his knees up around his ears and the stem of the wineglass clenched in his fist. The lights were on in *Toadhall*. Richard must be there, he could wait with him. No. Did she sleep with Richard? He told himself petulantly that he didn't care, it was probably part of the rent. To torment himself he pictured them in bed together and then abruptly stopped in disgust as his dick began to twitch at the idea. He shouldn't think of her like that. She was more than that. He wasn't going to go next door. No way. He'd promised he'd be on the *Beagle* so he would be. How long would the police keep her? Maybe she'd forget his promise. Please come, he prayed, please, please come. The night gaped in front of him. He strained his ears for the sound of footsteps. Seven times he got up from his chair and opened the door to find that it was only a chain or a wet rope flapping against a wooden post.

Alex looked up when he heard footsteps on the gangplank. He wasn't sure to begin with. It could be more noises sent by the storm. He strained his ears to analyse the sound. It stopped and then he heard a scratch on the door and he sprang from the chair and bounded up the stairs. Lydia stood on the mat with a slightly lost expression on her face as if she wasn't sure that she had the right place. Her cheap handbag dangled from her right hand and she held her arms a couple of inches away from her body like a child does when it is waiting to be told what to do.

'What happened?'

Lydia stepped forwards and Alex stumbled clumsily backwards down the stairs. She stood in the middle of the room and let her handbag drop to the varnished pine floor. 'Hug me,' she said in a tight small voice. Alex wrapped himself around her. He squeezed her narrow ribs tightly, rocked her slowly from side to side and murmured her name deep into the cloud of her hair.

After a long while Alex broke the hug and led her by her finger tips to the sofa. She sat down obediently and gazed blankly into the wall. Alex stooped over her. The waves in his lungs had quickened and the weight of the imaginary water swung heavily from spine to his ribcage. 'There's some wine if you want some' he offered. She nodded and tried to light a cigarette but her hands were shaking and she couldn't hold the flame of the lighter to the end of the cigarette long enough to ignite it. 'Here, let me do that,' said Alex. He took the cigarette from her mouth, lit it for her and returned it. He fetched another glass from the kitchen, poured some wine into it and placed it on the table in front of her. Now is the time, he thought, she needs me. She's the woman I love and she needs me. If I comfort her now she won't push me away, she'll be grateful. He sat down nervously on the sofa beside her at a precise and self-conscious angle and smoothing her red hair to one side of her neck put his arm around her shoulders.

Lydia lent backwards onto his chest. The warmth of his body soothed her. 'They're going to deport me,' she said quietly.

Alex closed his eyes. No they can't, he thought, I won't let them. He squeezed his arm more tightly around her. 'When?'

'I have fourteen days. I can appeal but there is nothing I can say. I had a tourist visa. I was not allowed to work.'

'You must!' burst in Alex, shifting himself into a more upright position and forgetting his plans for a moment. 'You must appeal, even if it's only to buy you time. You have to!'

'But if I don't work I cannot afford to stay. How can I eat and pay my rent with no money?'

'Doesn't matter, we'll work something out. I'll give you a hand and I'm sure Richard will too. There'll be a way but you've got to appeal. You'd be crazy not to. You've got to do it.'

She said nothing for a while and then she whispered so quietly that he could hardly hear her, 'I do not want to go back to Russia now.' She blinked, her lips were slightly open. Alex realised with a shock that she wanted him to kiss her. That she was actually asking. He made himself breathe in and out and then he made himself breathe again. Now. Now. He bent forward. He was moving in slow motion. She'd know now, she'd know what he was up to. She hadn't moved away. Not yet. He curved his face around her neck and kissed her. She was still there. Tentatively he caressed her bottom lip with the point of his tongue. Then her mouth opened slightly and her tongue came out to meet him. Yes! Yes! Yes! And they kissed for a long time, coiling their taut tongues in the slippery wetness of each other's mouths and then Alex just held her and slowly stroked her arms. 'Lydia, do you want to stay here?' Lydia didn't say anything and he wondered if she'd heard him. 'Lydia?' he asked again.

'Yes,' she said, hesitating uncertainly on the 'Y'. She sat up and turned around so that she was looking straight at him. 'Just to be with someone would be good.' He smiled and taking her hand led her down the corridor.

Chapter Twenty

Alex woke with a hair tickling his upper lip. Sharp, fresh river light washed the room, splashing the walls and rippling in marbled patterns across the ceiling. The boat was rocking gently from side to side. Lydia was only cupped into the crook of his body but her hair spread out over his shoulder, his arms, chest and face. He squinted down past his nose and all he could see was a sunset of orange and gold refracting light that gently moved as she breathed. He set his front teeth together in a full-bar grin and a current of triumph thrilled through him. He applauded himself. Yes, yes, yes! He thought of Steve and Sally and his mother and his grin broadened even further, they just don't know me, he thought, they just don't know what I can do. Very slowly he extricated a hand from beneath Lydia's shoulder. He wanted her in a way that twisted in his gut. His swollen dick was caught between his stomach and the rise of her bottom and it throbbed with a deep bass note.

He tried to return his hand to the warm hollow under her shoulder but her body rippled and slid in his fingers. The movement was too much for Alex's self control and raising his head he stroked her awake in long waves from her shoulder to her hip. She opened her eyes, snuffled into her fist and looked at him. Without breaking her gaze he reversed his stroke bringing his hand over her sharp angular hips up her stomach to her little pointed breasts, hovering for a second over her nipple before returning again. Lydia rolled over to face him. It was a single bed and there wasn't much room. It seemed to Alex that they were going to tumble on to the floor at any second. She catlicked his chest and slipped her hand in between his legs. 'Wait, wait a second Lydia,' he stuttered, 'I've got to get a condom.'

He extricated himself from the tangle of duvet and blue-white limbs. The wardrobe smelt rank and adolescent. Alex became suddenly very conscious of his nakedness. He stroked his erection with the back of his hand. Lord please don't let me come too quickly, please, please, he prayed as he frantically fumbled amongst his clothes for a three pack that he'd bought while he was still at university.

He came back to the bed, stood in front of her and hugged her head to his belly. She linked her arms around his bottom and nuzzled against him, her hair drawing backwards and forwards over him like a net. He ran his knuckles down the bumps of her spine and spanned her ribs with splayed fingers. The rhythm of their bodies began to quicken. He tore the foil condom packet open with his teeth. Please God make this last, please make it last. He bent his head and lapped at the arch of Lydia's neck. He moved his fingers over her hips and into the wet well of her body. He panicked. I haven't got time. Kneeling on the bed he shifted himself awkwardly on top of her. His blood boomed in his ears and as he plunged into Lydia she let out a high, almost ultrasonic squeak. The landscape of her body blurred in front of him as if he was looking through a cataract. As he moved inside her she kneaded the ridges on either side of his spine, massaging with the heels of her thumbs from his shoulder blades to the small of his back. He pushed into her and she closed around him.

The warm depths of her tugged at him and sucked him further. He gripped her shoulders and swore as his hip bone clashed against hers. He had to get there. He had to finish the race. He had to leap the hurdle. He pounded into her, his breath came faster and faster and his blood howled and ululated. The crowd descending the staircase. Lydia's hand being wrenched from his. The steady thump of reggae music. Red chapped hands on the metal handle of a Russian coffee pot. The two policemen. Slava's face. A little red passport. The shaking flame of a lighter in a trembling hand. Running against the blue flashing police lights. Lydia ground the crown of her head into her pillow, pushed her breasts up to meet his chest and cried like a bird. Alex was under water. The weight pushed down on him. He had to reach the surface before his lungs burst. He scooped the water to either side of him pulling himself up until he burst through to the air and collapsed gasping for breath onto Lydia's body. He stayed inside her and she ran her hands over his back and thighs again and again and then she just held him and for a while they dozed.

Later, when Alex's energy returned, he slipped out of bed and wrapped a Kenyan kikoy around his waist. 'Do you want a cup of tea?' he asked, raining her with kisses so that she wasn't able to say yes for quite a while. Alex danced from foot to foot and did judo moves across the kitchen floor while he waited for the kettle. He poured the boiled water into two mugs and using the end of a fork dipped a tea bag in and out of the water. The sun stamped squares of light onto the kitchen floor. Outside the waves danced with the light. Alex carried the two mugs back to his bedroom and placed them on the bedside table. He lifted the upper half of Lydia's body and laid her head on his thigh. Running his fingers through her hair he combed it out across the rough black cotton of his kikoy. She smiled up at him and then rolled over onto her side and nibbled gently at the material. He felt her hot breath on his leg.

'Lydia?'

'Mmmmm'

'They can't deport you if you're married to an Englishman can they?'

She stopped nibbling. 'I don't think so,' she said.

He slipped his hand underneath her arm and covered her breast. 'Then why don't you marry me and then you can stay for as long as you want?'

Lydia rolled over onto her back again and drew her forefinger over the bristle underneath his chin. Her face was very still, a tear track glistened from the corner of her eye across the dip of her temple to her hairline. Alex could hear his heart thudding as he waited for her answer. He took his hand away from her breast and wafted his palm lightly from nipple to nipple.

'Why?' she said cautiously.

'I mean you don't want to go back to Russia, I don't want you to go back and if you marry me you won't have to. So why not? It makes sense.'

Her fingers descended to his chest and drew little circles in a line underneath his collarbone. 'But Alex you don't . . .'

'Yeah and I won't have a chance to if you get deported. Lydia, fourteen days is not very much time. I *want* to get to know you, I want to have the *chance* to at least. You don't want to go back. You told me so. This is between you and me. It's private stuff and I don't see why the fucking politicians and civil servants should have anything do to with it but the only way we can get them off our backs is to get married. If we don't they'll take you away and we'll never know what this could have been.'

'I don't love you Alex,' she said, softening the brutal words in a dreamy sing-song voice.

Alex swallowed, 'I know,' he said scratching at a scab of eczema in the crook of his elbow. 'I know. Obviously you don't, I can't expect you to. You hardly know me. That's the point. We'd be buying ourselves time. We'd be giving ourselves a chance. This would be *our* marriage, it doesn't have to be like anybody else's. We'd make up the rules. And if it doesn't work out, well fuck it, it doesn't work out but at least we won't be wondering for the rest of our lives. We will have tried, we will have had a go.

'I want to be an actor and I'm trying to get into drama school at the moment but the only parts I've ever played have been in bloody student productions. I don't know if I've got it in me to be professional. But if I don't try I'll never know. I could go into an office job and trundle along all my life and think, well I could have been an actor but unless I try, and maybe fail, I'll never know whether I had the talent or not. It's the same with you and me.

'I don't know, I'm probably talking around in circles. Do you see what I'm getting at? You don't want to go back to Russia. I don't want you to go back to Russia. So get married to me and we'll try life out together.' Alex paused and then began speaking even more quickly. 'You've got a problem and I can help you out so why don't you let me? I won't try and keep you if that's what you're worried about. I'm not trying to trap you. I just want to give you a hand.'

There was a long silence while Lydia traced her finger across his chest. She moved slowly and hypnotically. She appeared to be in some kind of trance. Eventually she stopped at the hollow at the base of his neck and rolled her finger onto its knuckle.

'Okay,' she said eking the word out over a long inward and outward breath. 'How do you get married in Britain?'

Alex grinned until all his teeth showed and then he hailed Lydia's face with little smack kisses. 'I'm not sure. I haven't done it before but I think you just make an appointment at your local registry office, pay some money for a licence and Bob's your uncle.'

She smiled, 'I don't have an uncle.'

'You know what I mean.'

'What about my visa?'

'It shouldn't make any difference. I mean they can't stop you getting married can they?'

Chapter Twenty-One

They'd had an Indian Summer, an unseasonably warm, sun-bloated autumn but now, on their wedding day, it was raining, slicing in wires onto the King's Road, sparking in the headlights, spitting on the tarmac, painting the pavements a dark gloss like mussel shells. People huddled in the bus stop with their backs to the weather wearing thin crumpled macs and clutching plastic bags over their heads like bonnets. Shoppers dashed across the road dodging the traffic. A businessman in a beige coat with bird droppings of rain on the shoulders strained stoically at a forty-five degree angle against the wind with his chin up high pretending the rain didn't exist. In the gutters grey water gurgled into the drains and to Alex they sounded like hungry stomachs.

Lydia's hand was as cold and damp as a corpse. It rested in his palm as he peered out of the doorway of the municipal swimming pool behind Chelsea Town Hall. She was shivering in a ridiculously thin blue dress which he'd remarked on. He wasn't so stupid about women, Sally had trained him. It must be her best frock. Even in their circumstances you'd wear your best for your wedding wouldn't you. Her hair went dark in the rain and stuck in wet kinking red coils down her back and across her face. He squeezed her hand. Fuck, what was Sally going to say about this? And his mum? Holy moly! They were going to go ape shit. A corner of him was pleased. A smile tugged at his lips. But that was childish, he told himself, got to think of it from their point of view. Old Sally, like some Jane Austen maiden, gagging for a husband and his mum just wanting the best for him as she saw it, no divorce or any of the other shit she'd gone through. A nice stable happy family. Was he having second thoughts? Too late, nothing he could do. He was in this too deep. He had to go ahead now. His stomach twisted and gurgled like the drains.

An old lady tramp with mediaeval-looking bindings on her legs trundled past pushing a trolley piled high with bundles of bedding and plastic bags. Must be horrible in the rain, where do you go when it's pissing it down like this, Alex wondered. A coach pulled up in front of her and out spilled swarms of kids in cutesy uniforms with knickerbockers. The old woman grumbled and muttered her way through this sudden obstruction while a nice young Sloane with highlights and a polka-dot skirt herded the sprogs in the direction of the swimming baths.

'What time is it?' asked Lydia. Her feet squelched as she stamped up and down. It was the second time she had asked that in about ten minutes so she must be nervous as well.

'They'll come,' said Alex and he hoped that they bloody would or maybe they wouldn't and that would save him.

'We could still ring Richard.'

'No!' he snapped in a sudden flash of bad temper and nervousness. Richard was too cool. Had she slept with him? He wished he'd never thought of it. She wanted him here yet she said she hadn't even told him they were getting married. Said she didn't want to until afterwards. Paranoia. She never did answer him properly that night when she'd turned him down. It didn't matter now. They were getting married, all that was in the past. Another life. It was different now. He was saving her and everything would be fine. It was a new chapter. He was going to look back on this day and see that this was the day when everything changed, this was the day when his life turned around. When he was famous he'd tell them about it in interviews. He didn't want Richard here making him feel small. He'd tried to explain to Lydia why and his reasons had got mangled and warped in the words. He didn't say that when his mind drifted he'd imagined her sleeping with Richard and the image had been half-nightmare, half-fantasy that he couldn't leave alone, that he kept on picking at it like a scab. He'd said that he didn't think Richard liked him, that sometimes he found him a bit superior and she'd given him a transparent kind of look and drifted over to the other side of the boat and started folding clothes and he'd felt relieved that she'd understood without him having to go into the details. At least that's what he'd thought at the time so it was annoying that she should bring it up again now. He had a bit of a stitch. He was nervous.

The drops ricocheted off the pavement. At ankle level there was a fog of spray. 'They'll come,' he said again.

'And who is the other man?'

'I told you. I don't know. He's called Morris. He's Steve's flatmate. I haven't met him.' She didn't ask any more questions. How did he know he was nervous, it's important for acting to analyse these things. He felt sick, not like car sick but as if he'd eaten something that wasn't ripe, his guts were cramped and they were scrunching tightly around each other. He was finding it hard to keep still. When this was over and final, no one would be able to stop them. He wouldn't be able to change his mind either. Probably this was the most stupid thing he'd ever done. Getting married to a complete stranger, someone he hardly knew. A Russian. And all because he fancied her so badly it made his prick sit up and beg if he even thought about it. Was that it? *I don't love you*, she'd said. But what if I do? And I'm rescuing you after all, so aren't I owed something? Too late, it wasn't in the rules of the game. Rules that he'd suggested. He was here, standing in front of the registry office with his appointment booked and unless Steve and his mate completely fucked up he'd be married in an hour's time. He was too far in. He couldn't back out now.

He looked down. Lydia was hunching her shoulders and trembling from the cold. He began to laugh hysterically. Fuck it! This wasn't real. Too crazy for that. He began to hum. '*I'm getting married in the morning, ding dong the bells are gonna chime!*' Where was that from? He couldn't remember the name of the film. Was it a black and white or was it later? One of those things they played at Christmas. He knew it so well. It was one of the most famous films in the world. How could he forget it?

Lydia was looking at him as if he'd cracked. Maybe he had. Who knows? She was still shivering, hardly surprising wearing that dress in bloody November. Age of chivalry's not dead, got to be the gentleman. He shrugged off the jacket of his best interview suit and draped it around her shoulders and he put his arms around her. Come on Steve, where the fuck are you? He pointed at the people by the bus stop. 'Bet none of them have guessed that we're about to get married. They probably think that we're school kids waiting for the coach after swimming.' Lydia smiled. Alex lifted her up so that her feet completely left the ground and began to swing her from side to side. '*We're singing in the rain, La de da de de da, What a glorious feeling, I'm happy again!*' That was definitely a black and white. Humphrey Bogart wasn't it?

Two motorbikes roared around the corner framed by arcs of opalescent spray. He looked Lydia in the eye and raised his eyebrows. Smug, knowing (and relieved), of course he'd known they wouldn't let him down. Still, they'd cut it tight. Three minutes to go by the town hall clock. Steve stopped beside them and flicked up his visor. He mouthed over the noise of the engine, 'Sorry we're late. I'll just park up,' and roared off again giving them a thumbs up sign.

'Told you they'd be here,' he said. He could feel his guts

twisting up again. Once they'd done it he wouldn't be able to undo it again. You could get divorced, maybe, but you couldn't get unmarried. He thought of his own mum and dad. Divorced twenty years and his father with a new family but they were still connected. That's how it would be, whatever happened, he'd be connected to Lydia for the rest of his life. What he was about to do was irreversible.

They met up inside, Steve and Morris with their leathers and helmets dripping. Morris had a large clump of mouse-brown dreadlocks, his wrists were bound with leather thongs and copper bracelets. Steve hadn't told Alex that Morris was a crusty. He loped forward bouncing gently on his knee joints to shake Lydia's hand. 'Hi,' he drawled, even his voice sounded stoned, 'you've got to be Lydia. Congratulations.'

'Shit, I thought you were never going to arrive,' said Alex.

'What's the matter,' said Steve, pulling off his gloves and laughing and slapping him on the shoulder, 'We're here aren't we? That's all that matters.'

He gave their names to a desiccated grey-haired woman in one of those cubby hole reception desks that you sometimes get in guest houses and seaside hotels. 'Carmichael and Gurova,' she repeated, as if it was a particularly nasty flavour of soup. 'You'll have to wait your turn, the last lot haven't come out yet,' and then she directed them around the corner to a line of wooden and vinyl chairs in a dimly lit corridor. Alex perched on the final centimetre of wood and leaning his elbows on his knees let his arms hang down inside his calves. He felt like he was back at boarding school, waiting to see the headmaster.

The room they got married in was papered with flock wallpaper. Maroon paisley patterns on a cream background. A vase of pink gladioli and white chrysanthemums had been placed on a heavy wooden table. The man who officiated was old; he had wispy grey hair, a black suit and a gloomy manner. How many times a day did he do this, Alex wondered, how many times that day had couples, all nervous and sweaty, come in from the rain and stood in front of those plastic coloured flowers? You think that you're unique, you've got your own mind, you're doing your own thing but you're not, it's just vanity. The room was a factory, a marriage factory. He and Lydia were the mid-afternoon slot. What had all the rest of them got married for? Because they fancied each other? Because the rest of the world said they couldn't be together unless they did? Security? Trying to get away from their families, trying to start a family of their own?

Lydia's hand fluttered on Alex's forearm. 'Are you sure?' she whispered.

He smiled at her, a huge warm smile like a break in the clouds, and then he bent down and kissed her forehead, inhaling. No, he felt sick but he loved her for asking. Stuff the rules, he did love her. She wasn't taking him for granted, anyone would be able to see that. Her hair smelt musty. 'Of course I am. Never been surer of anything.'

The ceremony flashed by so quickly that afterwards Alex couldn't recall much, just odd scenes and details like a foreign language film where you automatically filter out the noise and concentrate on the subtitles. He remembered nodding as the man spoke, the grey bristles of his moustache and his arthritic hands with thick curved nails manoeuvring papers for them to sign and scuttling like crab's claws across the desk. He remembered Steve and Morris sitting at the side of the room in their sodden leathers with their helmets on the empty chairs beside them. The noise as the rain rattled on the windows. Lydia handing her camera to Steve and carefully instructing him how to use it. The awkward way that Morris held the pen in his fist and the line of signatures all indecipherable scribbles apart from Lydia's round childlike hand, still not at home in Latin script. Then he kissed Lydia and with his hand on the small of her back he could feel the knuckles of her spine through her dress. God, her back, he had a thing about her back.

They tumbled around the corner to a nearby American

theme bar. Morris bought them all champagne. Alex felt like he was bouncing on the bubbles and Lydia was laughing with her tiny, overlapping teeth and she was so beautiful it made him weak. He couldn't believe he'd done it, he'd married her and his family didn't know and nobody had stopped them. Don't know what he'd imagined, something like Young Lochinvar with his mother screeching down the King's Road in the car that Sally bought her and stopping the ceremony in the room with flock wallpaper. *'I've just recovered from a fatal illness. He's my son and he's not marrying a foreigner!'*

'We've just got married!' he told the Australian girl behind the bar. He bent down and kissed Lydia again. 'We just got married,' he told her.

'I know,' she said, 'I was there, remember?'

'We've got to do something,' he said to the others, 'I mean you don't get married everyday. We should go somewhere, I don't know. What shall we do Lydia?'

'Maybe we could go to a restaurant?'

'No, no, it's got to be something bigger than that. You can go to a restaurant any day, we work in one for God's sake. What do you really want to do? Think of something wild.'

Lydia thought and then the small pink tip of her tongue appeared between her lips. 'Well,' she said hesitantly.

'Go on what is it? Anything, anything at all. It doesn't matter how wild it is.'

'Well I don't know how we could do it but I would like to see the sea.'

It was four o'clock. There were five other people in the bar; two schoolboys and three builders. The bottom half of the windows was covered in coloured transfers. The raindrops left pock marks on the glass. Cars swished past on the road outside. In the corner a juke box blinked red and yellow lights. For a minute they were all silent. Then Morris spoke, 'Yeah, right, we should go to the sea. What do you say Steve, why don't we take them on the bikes?'

'Okay, Okay,' said Steve, a bit nervously, making up his

mind as he said it, 'I'm on for that. It'll be fucking cold though. Have we got enough leathers?'

They went to Dorset. DORSET. That was Morris's idea as well. Alex was horrified. 'But I come from Dorset,' he'd protested. 'My mum lives there.'

'Well you don't have to see her. We're not going to see your mum. Your wife wants to see the sea, so we're taking her.' And then Alex grinned full throttle. He was a big boy now. He could go wherever he liked. He could go home with Lydia (his wife) and his mother didn't have to know about it. There was something very satisfactory about that.

They went back to the moorings, picked up some warm clothes and went over to Morris's boat to get dressed in leathers. Lydia borrowed some trousers and a jacket off Morris's girlfriend. They put on as many layers as they could until they could hardly walk. The rain stopped and the sky grew brighter. 'Maybe it's clearing from the west,' said Alex hopefully as he got on the bike behind Morris.

'We'll bring sleeping bags and firelighters. Two, two and a half hours I reckon. I'll take the coast road,' replied Morris.

Alex had never ridden on a motorbike. This wasn't cool. Everyone's meant to have been on a bike. It's one of those initiation, boy into man things. So, like when he lost his virginity (sixth form disco at a girls' school), he kept quiet. To calm his nerves he smoked a joint while they were pulling on their leathers in Morris's mother's beautifully decorated drawing room. The joint was a bad idea. He felt dizzy and staying on didn't look that easy. He grabbed on to the bar behind him with white knuckled fists and wobbled badly as Morris set off. Jesus, Morris only had to swerve and he'd be on the tarmac, skinned and squashed beneath the first lorry.

At the first set of traffic lights Morris flipped up his visor and shouted over the engine. 'It's probably better if you hold on to my waist. And lean with me as we go around the bends.'

Alex nodded and gingerly gripped a handful of leather on either side of Morris's jacket. It felt sexual, like he was making a gay pass at Morris. This is what girlfriends do, ride pillion with their hair out behind them, their arms around their man's waist and his machine between their legs but if that's what it took to stay on then he was doing it, he just hoped that Morris didn't think he was feeling him up. They were on the Hammersmith Flyover now. The freezing wind was sobering him up. His face was going numb, icy drafts penetrated through the cracks in his clothes. He ducked slightly behind Morris's shoulder. The force of the wind pushed him backwards towards the exhaust and roared around his helmet. His eyes were watering through the visor. The tarmac beneath his knees was a blur, they passed cars on either side of them. Alex peeked his head over Morris's shoulder, the speedometer read 110mph. 'Shit,' he thought, both happy and scared as he grabbed Morris's jacket a little bit tighter and laughed with a rush of fairground adrenalin.

It rained again, the drops had banged hard against the helmet and as the leathers grew damp the wind freeze-dried his skin. He huddled down behind Morris's warm body and tried to use it as a windshield. They came off the motorway and there was a region of roundabouts that went on and on and seemed to be almost interconnected so that the moment they swung out of one, cutting through the wash on the road, they were slowing down for the next.

At Poole the rain stopped. By Ringwood the sky was clear and the road was dry. There was enough moon to light the road to smooth tinfoil. Five miles outside of Dorchester they came through some woods that capped a hill and saw the pewter sea. Alex yelped with triumph but the sound was lost to the road. Ahead of them he saw Steve pointing to the moon-burnish that ran between the hills on their left. By the time they had reached Bridport the thrill had gone. He was colder than he could ever remember being, his bottom was numb, his arms were stiff and his ears squashed tight to his head and sore with the noise. At Chideock they turned off into a narrow lane and then they were there; the sea, heard not seen as it crashed in the darkness onto the pebble beach in front of them and to the right a steep hill with a pub on its flanks.

Alex clambered off the back of the bike, stiff, buzzing and sore. He started slapping his hands and rubbing his arms and legs to get the blood circulating. 'We made pretty good time,' said Morris taking off his helmet and letting his dreadlocks fall with a crack onto the back of his jacket.

'Let's get the drinks in,' urged Alex, 'I need to warm up.'

They stamped and shivered in front of the fire until after the second pint when they went outside to sit on the benches next to a brazier and listen to the sea. Lydia announced that she was going down to the beach to look at the waves. 'Just think,' said Steve as he arrived with a tray carrying their third round of drinks, 'grey rainy London.'

'Just think,' said Alex, 'I got married this afternoon!' They all raised their glasses to that and cheered and Alex watched the moon-cast halo on top of Lydia's head disappear behind the Chesil bank.

'So is it real then this thing?' asked Morris. He had an offhand way of speaking so that everything he said sounded like a passing comment of no particular urgency that he just thought he might voice anyhow.

'Do you think we'd get caught if we rolled a spliff out here?' asked Alex.

'Neah, there's nobody else out here to catch us. I've got some skunk if you want.' Alex began sticking together cigarette papers.

'Yeah Alex, is it real?' prompted Steve, the veins in his forehead bulging slightly.

Alex crumbled the dried pieces of skunk into the crease of the cigarette papers. He was prickly, defensive. What was between him and Lydia was, well, not anything you could stick an easy label on. It was still tender, unformed. These guys wouldn't understand and anyhow it wasn't any of their business. He didn't want them judging it, he wanted to shield it from them. 'Yeah it's real. I got married because I wanted to. Maybe we wouldn't have done it if Lydia was English but she was going to get deported.'

The skunk was strong. Good thing there was a wind to blow the smell away. They drank more beers and Alex had a whiskey chaser. The white walls of the pub seemed to curve up above Alex and threaten to crash over him like a wave. The sounds of their voices ebbed and flowed like the sound of the sea and it did, it really did sound like a shell. A car pulled into the car-park and its headlights shone on the foaming sea. Lydia was there suddenly and he'd forgotten that she'd gone. They got married today with Steve from university and his crusty friend. He told them again, 'we got married today.' He leaned forward, grabbed Lydia's arm with one hand and Steve's hand with the other. 'I love her,' he said unsteadily, 'I love you.' Lydia's face was white in the dark, so that was like a shell too. Morris was squinting at him. 'I don't know you,' he said pointing at Morris and cackling with laughter, 'but you've got great dreads and I could love you too.' Then they were walking along the beach and Lydia was on his arm. It was hard work because of the pebbles. He fell over and the pebbles were sticky with salt and he couldn't be bothered to get up so he rolled over and laughed at the sky and listened to the sound of his laugh echoing against the cliffs. They built a fire and the stones exploded in the heat. He lay on his sleeping bag. The fire was hot on his face and the cold sat on his back and the sky was covered in grey fishscales of cloud and it was a long, long, way above the pale dizzy cliffs. Lydia curled up against him and he watched the flames with his chin resting on the top of her head.

That was the last thing that Alex remembered of the day until the others woke him up. They drove back to London with Alex clutching grimly to Morris's waist with an acid cramp in his stomach and a dry mouth. When he got off the bike at the other end Alex thought he was going to fall over his legs were so stiff and bowed. The crocodile file of headlights on the Embankment blurred in front of him. He found himself swaying and he put his huge gloved hand on Lydia's shoulder to steady himself. 'Can we sleep at yours,' he slurred, 'I can't deal with my sister tonight.'

Chapter Twenty-Two

Lydia woke early and sat upright, the duvet falling to her lap. Her conical rose-tipped breasts puckered in protest at the cold. She twitched her nose and turned back the edge of the curtain. There had been a frost. There was a fringe of ice around the window frame. The tide was out and the first smoky light was creeping across the mud . . . A needle-legged bird stalked between the pontoons probing the frozen crust with its beak.

Alex was making a sound closer to a snuffle than a snore. He sprawled across the bed, his arm flung out against both pillows. His mouth was open, Lydia watched his breath rising from his pink gums and clean white teeth. She felt like a voyeur, watching him while he was so exposed and vulnerable. A spark of conscience, a crossed wire deep in her brain – should she have let him do it? How much trouble was this going to cause him? Then the connection re-established itself and her thought lines ran as they had before. He'd wanted to. It was his life and his decision. It was patronising to doubt his judgement. She pulled the duvet up under her chin. He'd gone straight to sleep last night, just switched off. Lydia had yearned jealously for a similar black-out but it hadn't come and she'd lain in the foetal position feeling the heat from his body curled around her back. She'd listened for nearly an hour to the night noises of the river thinking about what they'd done and the consequences it would have. I'm here now, she thought, I can stay. That was the aim, wasn't it?

She clambered nimbly over Alex's sleeping body and, taking a turquoise Chinese dressing gown from a hook on the back of the door, she wrapped it around herself and tied the sash in a tight knot. The boat was cold and rank. The coal-fired stove had nearly gone out, too many cigarettes had been smoked in too small a space and Richard had obviously eaten another Indian take-away for his dinner the night before. She stoked the fire, prodding it with a poker to push the cold ash into the tray. She emptied the tray into a metal bucket and carried it upstairs. Opening the doors she tiptoed across the thin white carpet of frost, her feet burning red with the cold. The sky was a chemical blue but in the east behind the veined silhouettes of the park trees the rising sun glowed like the embers in the stove. The city and the river groped from the night in different pallors of grey. In mid-stream two rubbish barges undulated at their anchors. Lydia poured the contents of the bucket over the side of the boat and watched the cloud of acrid ash billow up from the hissing mud. Then shivering wildly she hurried back inside the boat, hastily shutting the door behind her. Inside was a mess, there was junk every-where: open CD cases, beer bottles, dirty mugs and glasses, paper bags and tin-foil take-away trays, plates and torn-up cigarette papers and more full ashtrays. With the ash bucket in one hand she picked up a selection of mugs and plates. Downstairs she opened a window to let in some air and filled a basin with hot soapy water. She smiled to herself as she quietly emptied ashtrays and collected dirty crockery from around the boat. It was so odd, she thought, that she should be happy doing this but for the moment she had the boat to herself and she felt at peace.

Richard appeared just as she had finished her tidying up and was wiping down the draining board. He was dressed but he hadn't shaved yet and his face was sleep-creased and grouchy.

'I was just about to do that,' he grumbled and then added a little too quickly 'whose are the leathers?'

'His name is Morris,' said Lydia feeling her good mood evaporating.

'Is that who you've got in there?' He snarled, jerking his head towards her bedroom door.

Lydia turned her back to him and draped the washing-up cloth over the tap. Now what do I say, she thought, how do I answer this question?

'You could at least tell me if you're going to go off and shag someone else,' complained Richard from behind her. 'I know I don't have any ties on you but it's kind of polite to give me some advance warning if you're planning on bringing someone back here.'

She settled onto one of the kitchen chairs and tried to tug the hem of her dressing gown over her knees. 'I had to get married Richard,' she whispered, 'for my visa.'

'So? I don't see the connection.'

'Alex, the boy from next door, he offered.'

'Alex?' he said pointing at the door and miming the word with astonishment.

Lydia fretted at the ends of her dressing gown. She couldn't look at him. 'Yes,' she said.

Richard sat down on the other chair and leant his elbows on his thighs. 'But *why?*' he hissed.

'Because,' she began. She could just make out Alex's body through the crack of the open door. She didn't think that he had moved but she couldn't be sure. What if he was awake and listening? 'Because,' she carried on speaking as quietly as she could, 'he says that he loves me and he wants to help me out.'

Richard stared with incomprehension at the bedroom and shook his head. 'He's nuts.'

'He wanted to do it.'

'He's still nuts. Surely he can't believe that you love him?'

'No, he knows what my feelings are. He wanted to help me so he did what he could. He's courageous. There aren't many people who would go that far.'

'He's a fool,' said Richard damningly. 'Did you tell him about us?'

'I don't think he needs to know.'

'Oh right, so I just get kicked out of bed for the schoolboy next door!'

'Would you have married me?'

'Well I might have done, you never know, but I didn't exactly have the option did I?'

Lydia refilled their mugs from the teapot. 'You just said he was nuts.'

'Well he is, isn't he. And so are you. He'll drive you crazy in six months. I guarantee it. Now as much as I would love to sit around all morning and discuss your newly married bliss I've got to get to work. Give lover-boy my congratulations when he eventually wakes up.' He zipped himself into his leather jacket and retrieved his gloves and helmet.

'Richard,' she pleaded.

He stopped, 'yeah?'

'Don't say anything.'

'I'll see how I feel,' he grunted and then having gathered all his stuff he started up the stairs.

Chapter Twenty-Three

Alex was leaning on the CD case. The hard cases pressed ridges into his back. They were listening to Angelique Kidjo. Nobody had said anything for a while. Alex had the feeling that while the music played the links between him, Lydia and Richard were adjusting and rearranging themselves according to the new situation. Alex smiled. His new position was a stronger one. His marriage had already changed things. He felt more powerful now. People couldn't dismiss him so easily. When he'd told Richard he'd grunted and made a sarcastic comment about 'playing happy families'. But behind the sarcasm Alex sensed a new element of respect; respect mixed with jealousy. Not surprising, thought Alex. I'd be jealous as hell, even if there was nothing between them he must have fancied Lydia, who wouldn't? He rolled himself a cigarette. On the other side of the room Lydia (his wife!) was standing up and looking out of the window and into the *Beagle*. She held on to the window-sill with her finger tips. Richard was watching Lydia too but when he saw that Alex had noticed he dropped his eyes and Alex felt a small, possessive male beast stir with satisfied contentment in his belly. Look at her, like a mythical thing and she's my wife, he thought. Even the way she stands isn't like an English girl at all. She's someone from a story. An interloper. If he stood up and walked over to touch her she might evaporate.

She turned from the window towards him, 'Your sister's next door,' she said, 'you should go and tell her.'

'You haven't told your sister yet? Shit man, I shouldn't think she's going to be very pleased, is she?' gloated Richard.

Alex looked at the ground and a blush burnt his face. He was dreading telling Sally. He'd been trying not to think about it all day. He shifted his position against the bookcase and tried to ignore a piece of eczema prickling infuriatingly on the underside of his wrist. He didn't really want to move, he was still hungover from yesterday and tired because he'd spent the afternoon in bed with Lydia, but she was right he should go and tell Sally. He didn't want to but he should.

'Has she met Lydia before?' asked Richard.

Alex shook his head.

'Does she know anything about Lydia? Of course not. Silly question. How can she when you hardly know anything about Lydia yourself.'

Alex rose to the bait. 'I know a lot about Lydia, actually. I mean we've worked with each other for ages.'

'Ah yes. Two months.'

'Three.'

'Well don't worry. You've got a lifetime to get to know each other's little secrets and foibles.'

Alex stepped forward. 'You're just jealous Richard,' he began heatedly but he was interrupted by Lydia caressing his shoulder. He looked at her.

She was shaking her head slowly and he understood that she didn't want him to have a go at Richard. 'Your sister,' she reminded.

He nodded. 'Yep, I'm just going,' he said ruffling her hair. He bent over the CD case and braced both his hands against it. 'Okay Lydia. Listen. How does this sound? I go in and I don't even try and make smalltalk, I just tell her straight out. Right?'

'Do you want me to come too?'

'No. I think it's best if I break the news myself. My guess is that it's going to be quite a shock for her but once she's got over it she'll probably want to meet you. So I reckon if you stay here for the moment then when I think the moment's right I'll come around here and collect you. Is that all right?'

'That's fine. You know your sister best and if you think that's the best way then I'm sure you're right. Now go and get it over and done with.'

He took a deep breath and opened the door into a freezing fog. A thin, icy sheen of moisture covered the pontoons like grease. A blonde woman walked past dragging a reluctant Scotty dog on its lead down a path of salt and grit that had been laid to stop people slipping over. Alex tucked in his shirt, pulled up his trousers and wiped some stray hairs from his face. Using the rails like a pair of parallel bars he swung himself down the gangplank.

Sally was gossiping with her best friend Flavia. A bottle of wine and the remains of a pasta supper lay on the table between them. He hadn't accounted for Flavia. She was an unknown. Flavia gave a yelp of pleasure. Alex hesitated at the top of the stairs. 'Alex I haven't seen you for ages.' She enthused. 'So how did finals go? Were they horrible? Sally tells me that you want to be an actor. Will you still remember us all when you're famous?'

'What a lovely surprise,' joined in Sally sarcastically. 'We hardly see each other,' she explained to Flavia, 'he's the most perfect flatmate. It's like living with a ghost. I work all day and he works all night. Very occasionally we collide as I'm coming back from work and Alex is going out.'

'Rather like my boyfriend,' said Flavia.

Alex took a deep breath and holding his head up high

walked down the stairs as if he was descending from the gallery of a stately home. On the last step he rested his hand on the round ball that decorated the end of the banister and waited portentously for Flavia to stop gushing. He wondered whether he should join them at the table and then decided that would ruin the effect. He knew he had to tell them straightaway or he would lose his nerve and he'd look a right tit if he went back to Lydia and Richard and told them he hadn't done it.

Sally beckoned him over, 'Hey what's up with you? Come and join us.' She scraped back her chair and began to get up, 'I'll get you a glass. We were going to open another bottle anyway.'

'I can't be long, I'm having a drink with the guys next door,' he said not moving from the base of the staircase and wishing that they wouldn't be so friendly and welcoming because it made it harder to stick to his position and make his announcement.

He threw back his head and running his fingers through his hair, sighed dramatically. Come on Alex, just get it out. 'What I mean is that I came around because I've got something quite important to tell you.' The girls swivelled around and waited for what he had to say. He had to tell them now he'd started. The pressure of two pairs of eyes levered him into the announcement. 'You see,' he stopped again. Stupid to be so nervous he thought, she's only my sister. 'You see, I got married yesterday.' Impact. Applause. Sensation. Sally poked her head forwards, her eyes looked like they were going to pop from her head.

Flavia carefully farmed the cuticles on her nails and wished she wasn't there or more accurately wished they couldn't *see* that she was there. Beneath her bent head her whole body was straining to hear each word that was said, each nuance. She wanted to be there to hear what was going to happen next but at the same time she didn't want to get involved. Flavia hadn't noticed the boat noises before but now they'd suddenly become very loud, waves clapping, a squeak like a radar, old boat bones wailing in outrage and a hissing sound that in her fancy was the sound of her friend's mind reacting to the news.

Alex rolled on the balls of his feet and waited. Behind Sally's head he could see the corner of one of *Toadhall's* windows and just, *just*, hear the tickle beat of the Angelique Kidjo CD. Was Lydia thinking about him next door? Sally had hung old-fashioned prints of various cathedral towns around the yellow walls. The one above the table was of Durham, Alex tried to work out which of the buildings his college was now housed in. He wanted Sally to say something now. The pause was too long. He was impatient. He wanted a response. 'Well,' he said, 'aren't you going to say anything?' Sally had been sitting at an angle to the pine table, now she swung around to face it head on, put both her elbows on the edge and placed her wine glass precisely midway between her hands. Alex thought that he could do with the glass of wine she'd offered him earlier but if he asked for one now she'd get angry. She'd think he was being frivolous.

'Alex,' said Sally, smoothing her eyebrows out with her finger tips, 'have you completely lost your mind? Do you mind telling me what the hell you are talking about?' She said in small staccato hammer blows.

Alex stood holding his right wrist behind his back like he used to do when he was a schoolboy in front of a teacher. 'Like I say . . .'

'Well *who*?' cried Sally.

'Sally don't make it sound like I've married a hamster.' Wrong thing to say.

'For Christ's sake Alex can't you at least take this seriously. I'm sorry about this Flavia. I've got to find out what my idiotic brother has gone and done now.'

Now it was Alex's turn to be exasperated. 'Sally listen to me. This is a happy thing. You don't need to get angry about it. She's lovely and I know that you'll get on really well together. Her name is Lydia. She's your next-door neighbour, although you probably don't realise that, and she works with me at Russki's'

'The Russian girl?'

'Well there is more to her then that but yes, the Russian girl.'

'Well *now* it's all beginning to make a bit more sense. Don't tell me she needs a visa and so she's found the nearest stupid mug who's willing to marry her.'

'It's not like that Sally. It was my idea and actually Lydia was very against it and it took a lot to persuade her.'

'In that case why didn't you wait and do it in a church with your family like every other normal human being? Instead of just turning up like this and saying "I got pissed last night and I got married". Flavia, back me up here. How would you feel if your brother came home one day and announced out of the blue that he'd just got married to the next-door neighbour's lodger. You might just be a little bit angry, mightn't you? A teensy weensy bit upset possibly?'

Flavia made a vaguely sympathetic grunt.

'Sally, I love her,' protested Alex dramatically, 'and if you can't see that . . .'

'What did Mum say about this?'

'Actually, I haven't told her yet.'

Sally pushed back her chair and stood up shoving it out of the way, 'Alexander,' she blazed, 'You are so cruel and bloody thoughtless sometimes. You could have at least told her before you did it. When you think what Mum's been through recently how do you think she's going to feel now when you, her only son, rings up and tells her what you've just told me.'

I've been through it too, thought Alex crossly. 'I'll tell her in the morning,' he grumbled.

Sally held the phone out towards him at arms length. 'You're bloody well not going to tell her in the morning Alexander Carmichael. You're telling her now and you're not leaving this boat until you've done it!'

He turned away from Sally and Flavia but their eyes prodded his back. He could see Richard moving around next door. The phone was ringing on the other end of the line. Please God make her not be in, please, please, please. He could see her as she had been when she was ill, lying on her bed in the sitting room, arms straight down by her side and white lumps of dried mucus in the corners of her slack open mouth, breathing shallowly to control the pain. He could even smell the sickly overbreathed air of the room and the stench of the disinfectant she used on her stoma. She had to be happy for him, after all he'd done for her.

Then there was a click and his mother's controlled voice, 'Maiden Newton 20322.'

'Mum, it's me Alex.' He could hear Sally and Flavia breathing, waiting for every word he said and then judging it. He bent his head and hunched his body over the receiver.

'Darling how are you?'

'Well actually Mum I've got something to tell you. It's good news, at least I think it is.'

'Yes. What is it then?'

'Mum, I got married yesterday to this wonderful girl called Lydia.' There was a silence on the other end of the phone. 'Mum are you still there?'

'That was a bit sudden wasn't it?' said his mother icily.

'Lydia's Russian and she's been having a few problems with her visa so we had to do it in a hurry but that's not the reason we got married.'

'I see. So what is?'

'Because I love her Mum and I'm sure you will to.'

'I wouldn't be so sure about that darling.'

'How do you mean?'

'Sounds to me like she's taken you for a ride.'

Alex began trembling. He could feel the receiver shaking in his hands so he wedged it between his chin and his shoulder. 'It was my idea.'

'Marriage isn't a game you know Alex. It's a serious business.'

'I know that. That's why I did it. I love her.'

'So you've said already. Does she love you?'

'Mum can't you just be happy for me?'

'It is a little hard darling. This is hardly how I imagined your marriage to be.'

'Well I'm sorry but that's the way it is. It's my life. I'm hardly going to get married to suit my mother am I?'

'There's no need to get abusive.'

'I'm not getting abusive I just don't seem to be able to get any of you to understand that Lydia is not some scheming adventuress. She's the woman I love. I don't think there is any point in carrying on this conversation any longer as you obviously don't want to understand.'

'She's not pregnant is she?'

'Oh Mum for Christ's sake.'

Alex jabbed at the receiver button with his forefinger and cut the line. He listened to the tone, replaced the receiver and glared angrily at Sally and Flavia. Hope they're satisfied now, he thought. Then he stamped up the stairs and out onto the gangplank.

Chapter Twenty-Four

The offices of the Immigration Advisory Service were on the third floor of a squat tower block near Borough tube. Lydia waited on a semicircle of foam furniture next to a dusty yucca plant and a pile of thumbed and out-of-date women's magazines. She sat upright with a straight back, on her lap she held her handbag and inside it was her deporation order. The office was hot and the partition walls were very thin. Telephones rang all around her and close by a man was pleading angrily with someone. People scurried past her, hunched forward, balancing mugs of tea and files. A woman with a Hispanic accent and a lot of make-up offered Lydia tea and then came back twice: the first time to ask whether she took sugar and the second time to ask whether she took milk. Tea-making seemed to be her job. Lydia decided that she was a charity case, somebody who they had saved from deportation. She sipped daintily at her tea. It was too strong. I could make it better, she thought.

'Mrs Carmichael?' The voice had to repeat her new name twice before Lydia recognised it. She looked up slowly as she made the connection between the foreign name and herself.

This was the first time that she had really absorbed her change of name. For twenty-six years she had been Lydia Gurova and now she was another person; a woman with an English name. 'I'm Claire Lloyd. What can we do for you?' Lydia forced herself to concentrate on the woman standing in front of her. She was in her early thirties, with curly brown hair and a kindly, battling face. She wore a polyester jacket with shoulder pads and gilt buttons over a drawstring Indian cotton skirt. Lydia, who had a puritanical and conservative streak, found the combination of hippy and office woman ugly and ill-matched.

'Would you like to come to my office?' the woman said, indicating with a fistful of papers a corridor that ran off to the right of the dejected yucca plant.

As they walked down the corridor the woman made a speech about the Immigration Advisory Service being independent from government. Lydia sneered to herself. She was not going to be taken in, offices were never independent. She would listen to what this woman had to say and make her own mind up. The woman's office was tiny, a house of cards made from pale-blue padded partition walls. Above her desk was an Oxfam poster and a postcard that read 'Behind every successful woman there is normally a well adjusted cat.' Boxfiles lined the walls. The desk was covered in paper. Knee-high piles of more paper rose like tower blocks around the room and formed a row beneath the window-sill. The woman had big movements, when she walked she used the maximum width of her stride. It was the kind of generous expansiveness that made Lydia shrink. She distrusted her shabby little office and had little confidence in her ability to help her. Miss Lloyd or Mrs Lloyd – Lydia wished the woman hadn't introduced herself with a first name, she didn't want to have to be that familiar with an official – leaned forward, grabbed a large pile of papers from the spare chair and swivelling her body around added the pile to the end of the row by the window. Then with exaggerated caution she picked her way between the other obstacles on the floor until she reached her side of the desk.

Lydia slipped sideways into the space left by the papers. Through the window behind the woman's head she could see the black drip marks on the back of another office building. 'I got your address from the appeal form,' she said, taking the neatly folded deportation order from her handbag and handing it to the lady over her overcrowded desk. 'I am married to an Englishman. They are not allowed to do this.'

The woman glanced at the documents and wet her thumb and forefinger with her tongue as she turned the pages. 'How long have you been married?'

'A day,' said Lydia quietly. She held her chin up to the woman and looked at her defiantly.

Claire Lloyd swivelled her chair sideways and looked out of the window. 'That's not going to be much help to you I'm afraid.' She let her forefinger drop down onto the documents making a sound like someone breaking through the seal on a new jar of coffee. 'The grounds for appeal on this are restricted. You've got to prove that you weren't actually working when the police came into . . .' she trailed her finger down the page, 'Russki's Restaurant. If you could say that you were just helping for the night that might be acceptable, especially if the owner of the restaurant would be prepared to make a statement to support you.'

Lydia absorbed this information. She looked around her at the piles of paper. Each piece is probably about another person like me. She imagined the piles growing and growing and growing until they touched the polystyrene squares that covered the ceiling and then they would fall on top of her and Miss (or Mrs?) Lloyd and they would have to clamber out together through the papers until they reached the air. She sighed. 'Surely my marriage must make this unnecessary?' she said, weary and imperious.

Claire Lloyd also sighed. 'You could write to the Home Office separately,' she said patiently, 'and ask them for leave to remain on grounds of marriage but I doubt you'll get it. You see because you got married after your notice of deportation was served they're going to be suspicious and they'll probably discount you on the primary purpose test.'

'What is this?' asked Lydia.

She watched the woman prod the soil of a cactus plant. Hail began to rattle against the aluminium-framed window. 'The primary purpose test means that you have to prove to the Home Office that the primary purpose of your marriage is to live together with your husband for the rest of your lives. You can try but the timing is definitely going to count against you and unless you're pregnant I doubt you're going to have much luck.'

Lydia pursed her lips. 'And the appeal form, what should I do about that?'

The woman picked up the forms in her lap and handed them back to Lydia with a polite smile. 'Well I'd advise you not to appeal as I don't think you have much chance of winning it but obviously if you still felt like going ahead the Immigration Advisory Service would help you with the procedures and that can take anything up to three months. You are incidentally still allowed to claim income support during that time although there is a Bill going through parliament which will change that pretty soon.'

Lydia picked at the tatters of skin on her finger tips. Seriozha's office in Lenfilm was very different from this. He often used to tell the story of how when he first became a director they gave him an office and he'd told them that he 'couldn't think in a rabbit hutch'. His office was larger than her room and her mother's room put together. It was painted a pale green and it had a high moulded plaster ceiling and palatial windows blocked by large panelled shutters. A secretary worked in one corner and in the middle of the room was Seriozha's heavy old-fashioned wooden desk. He would get up and walk around the desk to greet you in front of it when you entered the room. Lydia remembered the acid watchful eyes of Natasha, his secretary, and how carefully they had to school their expressions because Natasha was a friend of Seriozha's wife. She remembered the vicious gossip and intrigue that bred in the canteens and echoed down the cold linoleum corridors, gossip that before the changes had the power to send you to the camps. She thought of the cramped flat that she shared with her mother and the fragile balance between them. In her imagination it was dark outside the windows of the flat and the glaring reflections in the windows seemed as solid as metal. She tore a strip of skin from the side of her nail and a small bead of blood broke the surface. She felt a thick wall of obstinacy forming inside her. She still wanted to stay in England, if they wanted to get rid of her they would have to try harder, she wasn't going to go yet.

She pushed back her chair and stuck her hand out over the desk to shake the woman's hand. 'Thank you Mrs Lloyd for your assistance. I shall be getting in touch with you in the near future.'

The woman's handshake was limp, she nodded sadly at Lydia and Lydia bristled, suspecting that the woman had already discounted her. As she turned to leave the room the woman sat down behind her and began punching buttons on her telephone.

Chapter Twenty-Five

Alex was working the afternoon shift, which left Lydia alone on the boat. She completed her appeal to the Home Office. Even if it did nothing else it would buy her time. But she still needed money. She promised herself that she wouldn't borrow from Alex. She should never have accepted Seriozha's money. It was a stupid thing to do. He had a hold on her now and he was capable of getting very ugly if she didn't pay him back. She wasn't going to make the same mistake again. Alex had offered to marry her; that was his gift and she was grateful but if she asked him for money that would be her debt. She didn't want to be obligated to him. She shrank from the idea of it. Borrow from anybody but not from your lover, she told herself. Then who?

She had to find work; but she couldn't drive, she couldn't type, her written English was poor and it had to be a place where they wouldn't ask for her details. She crouched over the kitchen table scanning the jobs page of the *Evening Standard* and curled her toes around the cross bar of her chair like a bird. The stove glowed gold and red in the corner while the rain pecked at the glass and the gloomy afternoon pressed in around the boat. She twisted the problem round and round as if she were wringing out a wet towel. She could sell photographs but that would take time and she needed money sooner than that. The woman at the Immigration office had said she could claim money from the government but Lydia didn't like the idea, dangerous to draw attention to herself. She remembered Igor's friend Max, he'd worked in a place where they didn't ask questions but she couldn't remember the name of the bar. It was on Kingsway that's all she knew.

She looked at her fingers; they were grey with newsprint. Oh money, she thought, slapping the paper petulantly down on the table. Her pride kicked against the idea. Wars, police, governments even love affairs were all worthy opponents but money was such an anonymous, everyday enemy, it was so ordinary. All over the world there were people worried sick about money. It had her trapped. Without money she couldn't pay the rent and she couldn't afford to process the films from her camera, she couldn't afford to live in England but nor, even if she'd wanted to, could she afford to go home. I won't borrow from him, she promised herself again, he probably doesn't have any money to spare but I won't even ask.

The phone rang and she let the answer phone pick it up. It was Seriozha. His deep voice was assured and commanding. He wanted to know when she was coming back. She stared at the black plastic machine. His voice fanned out across the room like an electro-magnetic field surrounding her. She listened to the click as he put down the phone. Silence flooded in to replace his growl. Lydia remained crouching on the chair staring dumbly at the squat little answer phone and then, quite slowly at first but with gathering force, she began to vibrate with anger and inside her furious fists hammered in frustration at her ribcage. 'Fuck You Seriozha' she said, very quietly and very deliberately. And then she got up, wiped the message from the machine, put on her overcoat and walked out into the rain.

She walked all the way to Kennington to the house she

had stayed in when she first arrived to see Sasha. He was the one person who would know for sure whether Seriozha was behind the raid on Russki's. The rain licked at her face and bit her nose and her clothes grew sodden with the wet but the anger stayed with her all the way, purring like a motor inside her. She snapped her feet onto the streaming pavements and stiffened her body to control the drive of her rage. The doctor who had been her neighbour answered the door. He squinted at her over his beard. 'It's Lydia,' she reminded him, 'you know. I used to live in the back room.'

'Ah yes,' he said, slowly and lugubriously licking his lower lip, 'if you're looking for Sasha he's in his room.' She dripped up the stairs and knocked on his door. Sasha was amazed. He looked at her with his eyebrows lifted right up to his hairline. Behind him Lydia could see a woman with long bleached blonde hair sitting primly on his brown velveteen sofa with her knees together and her hands resting on her thighs. 'Ly-ly-lydia,' he spluttered.

'I need some work.' She said breathlessly and slightly too fast. 'With no questions.'

Sasha glanced over his shoulder at his guest and fingered the black plastic door handle. 'There isn't anything,' he said, 'Russki's is the only place.'

So he knows about the police raid, thought Lydia as she drew a wet strand of hair behind her ear. It was dark in the corridor and now that she'd stopped moving she was growing cold.

Sasha barred the way between her and the warm well-lit room behind him. 'It's Seriozha isn't it?' she said.

Sasha fixed his eyes on a spot an inch or so above her head and repeated mechanically, 'There is nowhere else. Russki's is the only place.'

Rain, thought Lydia to herself, as she peered at the splatting streets from the shelter of Holborn tube station, is much worse than snow. She turned left down Kingsway under a plastic Father Christmas and a string of red and green light bulbs and at the first sandwich bar that she came to she asked the middle-aged woman behind the counter if a Polish man called Max worked there. 'Sorry, never heard of him' she said moving her eyes onto the next customer. Lydia backed out of the narrow little stall that smelt of wet wool and tea and toast and condensation and carried on down the street. Half an hour later she pushed open the smoked glass and aluminium door of a private bar called 'The Garden Bar'. Inside there was a narrow corridor guarded by a large stone-faced man in a dinner jacket who stood behind a waist-high black wooden desk. He had a bristling moustache and the pores in the skin on either side of his nose were as large as pin pricks. The cream walls had been painted to look like marble and hung with black and white photographs of old film stars. Two closed circuit televisions allowed the man to watch the street outside and the customers in the bar. For a second the left-hand screen was filled with the bluish image of a bald head. The man grunted at Lydia.

'Excuse me,' she started, 'I am looking for a Polish man called Max. Do you know if maybe he works here?'

The man softened slightly. 'He's in the bar,' he said, 'I'll get him if you want.'

'Please,' she said gratefully.

'Who shall I say?'

'Erm, tell him, tell him it's a friend of Igor's.'

Lydia waited hesitantly while he repeated this information into an intercom. Suddenly Lydia wanted to run out into the street. She shouldn't have come. The intercom and the cameras made her feel uneasy. Max wouldn't recognise her. They'd only met once. It was just that Igor had talked so much about him. He'd seemed like a hero. A man who had made his way in this new country. How could she ask advice from a man she barely knew? She shuffled her feet. She was wearing a little pair of ankle boots, a pair of jeans and a padded coat. They were the wrong clothes for this place. Hot air blew from a vent in the ceiling on to the black rubber doormat. Lydia stood to one side to allow room for a group of departing customers bulky with raincoats, briefcases and defensive umbrellas. A black taxi panted in the gutter.

Max appeared, running his fingers through his floppy blond hair. Two small and slightly splayed front teeth protruded over his bottom lip.

'Lydia? I couldn't work out who it was. What are you doing here?'

At least he recognised her. That was a good start. Beside him the bouncer was unapologetically rolling his eyes over her body and tugging at his moustache. Lydia tried to ignore him.

'I need work,' she said to Max in Russian.

Max lowered his voice and replied in Russian. 'What's wrong with Russki's?'

'I got picked up by the police.'

Max sucked at his teeth. 'You know,' he said watching her very carefully, 'that this is a hostess bar.'

Lydia didn't know but she nodded all the same. 'Does that mean prostitutes?' she asked gravely.

'Some of them yes, but not all. You don't have to be.'

Lydia swallowed, 'I don't understand,' she said.

'You serve the men their drinks. You persuade them to buy you drinks and you smile and you listen to them and if they like you they leave a big tip. It's not complicated. I don't know if there's work at the moment but I can ask the manager for you. I think there probably might be, one of the girls is pregnant so she's not going to be able to work for much longer.'

'And that's all there is. Just listening.'

'That depends on you,' he glanced around at the bouncer. 'Look I can't talk now. I've got to get back to the bar,' he took a piece of paper from behind the bouncer's desk, wrote down a number and handed it to her. 'Ring me. I'll put in a good word for you.'

She thanked him and stepped back into the street.

It was still raining. The drops fell so thickly they smeared Lydia's vision. Cars crowded down Kingsway under a barrage of rain. The clouds hung like smoked hanks of wool over the rooftops. The sound of water was everywhere: hissing under car tyres, rushing along the gutters and dripping from the road signs. Another raindrop caught on Lydia's eyelash. She blinked to dislodge it and then bending her head she pushed up the street against the rain towards the tube station. On the train she sat dumbly viewing the warped reflection of her small white face in the window, scarcely aware of her wet clothes or the other passengers around her while the idea of the hostess bar squatted inside her as a solid indigestible fact.

When she got back Alex was downstairs learning lines and cradling a mug of tea in his hands. 'I've emptied the loo,' he announced. Emptying the loo was the most unpleasant job on the boat. It was a bucket in a wooden commode upstairs and when it was full it had to be taken down the pontoons and tipped into a large drain. Normally Lydia did it because Richard had a habit of leaving it until the very last minute by which point the bucket was almost too heavy to carry and you had to be very careful not to let it slop over your clothes. '*And*,' he said proudly, 'I've talked to my mother and she's invited you to Dorset for Christmas.'

She smiled, relieved that he was too self-centred to ask where she'd been. 'She's not angry any longer then?' she said.

'Well not exactly but as it's Christmas . . . Please Lydia. I need you to come with me so that I can show them that, well that I haven't done something stupid. I mean they'll come around. I'm not really worried about that but they need to get to know you first.'

'Don't worry,' she said peeling off her wet clothes to warm herself in front of the stove, 'It'll be interesting for me. I have never been to an English Christmas.'

He reached out his hand and caressed the backs of her cold legs. 'Oh God, Lydia. I love you so much. I know you don't like me saying it but I can't help it.'

'I know,' she said stroking his cheek with the back of her hand and feeling a rush of tenderness for him, 'I know.'

With his other hand Alex picked up a copy of *Hamlet* that lay face-down on the table. 'Lydia,' he asked hesitantly, 'would you mind listening to my audition pieces? I've only got a week left and it's much easier if you've got someone to act it to.'

Lydia nodded and not being able to think of anything suitable to say she simply moved a chair in front of the stove and then crossed her legs and waited for him to begin. *Toadhall* was a small boat, there wasn't much room to move about in. Alex cleared a space between the armchair and the door to Lydia's bedroom by moving another chair and putting Richard's spare helmet and biking leathers on the bench that ran down one wall of the boat. Then with a deep breath and a quick nervous glance at Lydia he began to perform.

When he had finished Lydia lit a cigarette. She didn't understand what the piece was about. The language was too archaic for her and although she had seen the play in Russia many years ago she couldn't remember the details of it and it wasn't clear to her which part Alex was playing. This was disappointing. She wanted him to be very talented. She wanted to be able to cheer and clap and be amazed by his skill but this hadn't happened and now she was unsure how to respond. She knew how extraordinarily sensitive she was when she showed people her photographs and how she would pick up the smallest hesitation or note of criticism and brood morbidly on it afterwards. That's how Alex would be feeling now. She began scolding herself. Nobody is perfect straight away, that's why he's rehearsing. Think how terrible some of your early photographs were, think how terrible they sometimes are now, it doesn't make you less of a person. Every artform takes work, nothing happens overnight. He's trusted you with this, you mustn't let him down, you must think of a way for him to improve, you must help him to see some way to get better.

Alex was chewing his lip and anxiously waiting for her verdict. 'Well, what do you think?'

'It's difficult for me to understand the language.'

'Of course,' he said flatly. His shoulders dropped. He was disappointed. He moved the chair back into the space that he'd been acting in. His pride was hurt – she sensed it and she felt for him.

'Put it back,' she said. 'You must do it again Alex, but first, tell me in your own words what this man is feeling. What he is trying to say.'

Alex stopped moving furniture and loping forward he took one of her cigarettes from the packet on the table. He waved the cigarette casually in the air. She felt his sense of relief and relaxed, she had got through it, the moment of danger was over. 'Well Laertes is just about to go to university in Paris and Hamlet's been flirting with his sister and he's trying to give her some advice. Basically he's warning her not to take Hamlet too seriously and not to go to bed with him because he's a prince and he's not going to be allowed to marry anyone he wants to.'

'And have you ever given advice to your sister about men?'

'No way! I wouldn't have dared. The other way around more like. Just before I went to university Mum tried to give me a talk about sex and being responsible and all that and I was so embarrassed I nearly snapped her head off so she got Sally to have a go as well. I remember really resenting that. Sally's what, six years older than me and, I don't know, she's always been a bit of a bossy cow.

'I remember one time just after the divorce and we were coming up to London to meet Dad's new wife. I was pretty excited because we'd never been on a train without an adult before and Mum had explained to me, all very neutrally and unemotionally, that Dad had another family. I was pretty excited about that as well – I thought there would be lots of new kids to play with. Actually I can't stand my stepsisters they're both completely vacant bimbos but I didn't know that then. So I'm sitting there all excited about the train and Dad's new family and everything and Sally completely ruins it all. The train is just going around this big harbour on the coast when she blurts out, 'Alex you've got to promise me you'll behave yourself in London. You're not going to do anything embarrassing are you? 'Cos I've got to look after you and Mummy now.' He stopped speaking, unsure of himself, somehow he had got side-tracked, that hadn't been what he'd meant to say at all.

Lydia smiled and threw her cigarette into the heart of the coals. She could imagine him as a small boy. Click. The image was very clear. A snapshot of a twelve-year-old Alex, eyebrows clamped together, smarting with injustice on a train with the sea outside the window.

'Maybe you should pretend that you're Sally when you're acting that piece. Pretend it's not poetry or Shakespeare or anything in particular. Just imagine what she felt when she tried to tell you those things about sex; she would have been worried about her little brother, maybe she was a little embarrassed as well, maybe she was thinking of something that had happened to herself. Think like that. It doesn't matter that I don't understand all the words, I should be able to sense the meaning.' Alex nodded solemnly and picking up the book started the piece again.

Chapter Twenty-Six

This was what RADA students looked like. Two girls sat at a formica table by the door. One was bright blonde and the other had her hair tied back in a kind of Eastern European-style scarf. Alex could see a pair of high-heeled boots underneath the table. 'Hi!' they chorused with big, polished, white-toothed smiles. They were trying very hard to be welcoming – putting all their effort into it. An Asian bloke stood beside him looking cool and nonchalant, hands in his pocket, black leather jacket puffed up around his shoulders. He looks so relaxed, I bet he's good, thought Alex. With the same determined friendliness the girl with the scarf asked Alex what pieces he was doing. He turned his shoulder slightly against the man standing beside him. A hot panic swept through him. It was hard to speak, hard to force the words out of his gullet – the guy beside him was bound to have chosen the same pieces. The auditioners would be gorged by now. People must choose exactly the same pieces year after year. He muttered them surreptitiously under his breath. She wrote them down carefully in neat round letters with her fingers tightly gripping her plastic biro. 'Okay Alex!' she said in a sing song is-there-any-way-that-I-can-help-you voice, 'Julie will take you and Naseem up to the room. The others are already here, but not to worry because they're running a bit late at the moment. Okay? Either me or Julie will come and get you when they're ready. There's a vending machine in the corridor upstairs, but if you want to smoke I'm afraid you've got to go out into the street. Okay?'

The building smelt like a school; feet, linoleum, disinfectant. Alex felt cheated, he had expected something different, something more grandiose than shabby scuffed corridors that smelt of school. The room they waited in had a rush matting floor and a blackboard. Around the edge of the room there were chairs. Alex couldn't keep still. He milled around the room murmuring his lines under his breath. He was nervous but he was excited as well. He'd tried to explain it to Lydia that morning as he got dressed. 'This is my big moment,' he'd said, 'I've been waiting for this since my finals. This is my chance to prove myself. To show my mum and Sally and people like them that I'm really going to do this and I haven't just got my head in the clouds. God it feels like so much is happening at the moment. I really feel that it's all coming together. I mean I met you and now there's my audition. It's like it's falling into place. This is my dream, Lydia, this is the big one for me. You know the weird thing is, it's a bit like when we got married. I mean that I've got the same kind of feelings. I was so nervous then but I was excited as well,' and Lydia had smiled and listened to him go through his pieces once more.

Lydia was amazing like that, thought Alex leaning on the radiator of the RADA classroom, she was so easy to talk to and she always seemed to understand what you were going on about but even as he said this to himself there was a filament of his mind that disagreed. Precisely, it said, she always *seems* to understand.

He looked around him at the other people. The opposition. There was a Scottish girl with big teeth who kept on starting nervous conversations with people in a voice that was too loud. She won't be much good, decided Alex, too clumsy and awkward. Naseem sat in the corner looking completely self-contained with his right ankle balanced on his left knee as if he didn't give a fuck. He was the one to be worried about. A short curly-haired girl sat at one of the desks with an expression of terror on her face. Another one down, he thought with a twinge of guilt that he couldn't feel more sympathetic.

After a while a stubby, balding American boy came and sat down next to Alex. He introduced himself as David from Boston and said that he'd flown in that morning. Alex ran his fingernails up and down the old wrought-iron radiator and wondered how the jet lag would affect him. 'Do you want to go out for a cigarette?' he suggested.

'Yeah, that's a great idea' replied David, 'I'm so keyed up about this thing that I can't sit still.'

As they came back up the steps they could hear someone singing down one of the corridors. David smiled and tilted his head, 'Could be us next year.' Alex hearing him felt a hot, fluttering, thrill pass through him. It could be. Why not? Back in the room he pressed his nose against the window, the glass bloomed under his breath. They were in a modern building between Tottenham Court Road and Gower Street. On the other side of the road shining brass plaques gleamed from beside glossy doors with Regency fanlights over them, black wrought-iron railings led to basement flats and tradesmen's entrances. If I get accepted, thought Alex, all this would become familiar. I wouldn't notice the view, I would see it every day and these people could be my colleagues. Julie came in through the door and they all looked around. It was Naseem's turn first, he looked back into the room as he walked through the door and they all smiled nervously at him. Someone, Alex wasn't sure who, said 'Good luck'. After half an hour Julie came to collect the Scottish girl and then it was Alex's turn.

It was strange. The space was so big after the boat and the light was as bright and blank as a hospital. Nothing was familiar. No actors to react against and no Lydia to act for, just two strange men behind desks.

He breathed in and started to speak, rather too fast at first:-

My necessaries are embark'd. Farewell.
And sister, as the winds give benefit
And convoy is assistant, do not sleep,
But let me hear from you.

'Do you doubt that?' said one of the men at the desk, repeating Ophelia's line. She's Lydia, thought Alex and the whole speech seemed to rearrange itself in his head. Why hadn't he thought of it before? It's Lydia and Laertes is trying to warn her against someone like me.

For Hamlet, and the trifling of his favour,
Hold it a fashion and a toy in blood,
A violet in the youth of primy nature,
Forward, not permanent, sweet, not lasting,
The perfume and suppliance of a minute,
No more.

It's not like that, thought Alex protesting against Laertes, you're wrong, you think I'm going to leave her but you don't understand that I love her. Then the man behind the desk read Ophelia's part in a flat voice which unbalanced Alex. He started again and tried to ignore the men but he found that he couldn't lose the edge of irritation in his voice.

Perhaps he loves you now,
And now no soil nor cautel doth besmirch
The virtue of his will; but you must fear,
His greatness weigh'd, his will is not his own;
For he himself is subject to his birth;

He knew he was doing badly as he spoke. He was trying too hard. He felt like he'd lost control of the piece. Every word he said sounded wrong. He tried to act in a world inside his head. The words felt lumpy in his mouth and all the time the men just stared at him with awful neutral faces. When he'd finished he stood in front of them with his arms hanging limply by his side. The strip lighting buzzed over his head. He'd been sweating. His shirt was sticky under his armpits. He wiped his hands on his jeans and grinned vacantly. The men asked him questions about the plays he'd been in at university and the other schools he'd applied to. They were friendly but he was stupid, his brain didn't seem to work, there were big gaps between their questions and his answers. Eventually they told him to go and he walked through the door carrying the other-worldly feeling of the room with him.

He stepped out of the bus onto the pavement at Beaufort Street and breathed the cold vital air. He had the slightly punch-drunk feeling of coming around from a dream. It was over. He'd finished. He began to reassure himself: things like that always seem much worse at the time, it hadn't really been that bad. He'd done his best and anyhow it was over. He was drunk with relief. He began to grin and once he'd started he couldn't stop. He swung himself down the ramp and then clattered across the pontoon to *Toadhall* and burst through the door. Lydia was sitting in the armchair smoking a cigarette. There was music on which was unusual because Lydia didn't normally play music. 'God I'm glad I've got that behind me,' he said, snatching the cigarette out of her hand and taking a drag.

'How do you think you did?' she asked.

'Impossible to know. Can't tell. I'll just have to wait but you never know, I could get a second audition,' he said taking a puff from the cigarette and looking up to the ceiling. 'I *could*,' he insisted, 'I mean, you know, people do.'

'I've found a job,' she said timidly.

'Fantastic! Where?'

'In a bar.'

'That's brilliant. Which one?'

'I don't think you'd know it. It's over in Holborn.'

'What sort of place? What are the customers like?'

Lydia lit another cigarette. 'Oh, boring,' she said airily, 'businessmen mainly, but the pay's quite good.'

Alex drew a big arc in the air with his cigarette. 'It's all coming together,' he said. 'There must be something in the air.'

Chapter Twenty-Seven

On the morning of Christmas Eve Lydia woke early, stoked the fire and cleaned the boat. She padded around in her slippers and dressing gown wiping tables, collecting ashtrays and mugs; relaxed in the intimate privacy of the morning. Alex was asleep. The tide was high and the water undulated lazily around them. The windows were clouded with feathered etchings of ice. Upstairs she paused to look through the french windows at the soft blue-fogged morning. The bridge had been closed for repairs and it was now encased in spidery scaffolding. She watched the vanilla-coloured water crumple like silk as it squeezed through the arches. A seagull landed on the deck railing and hooked its claws around the metal tube. It scrutinized Lydia with eyes like chips of dark marble, cocked its head and jabbed its beak backwards and forwards very quickly. The bird appeared to be accusing Lydia of something. She turned away. A man stood by the window of *Gloriana*, the boat on the other side of *Toadhall* from the *Aku-Aku*. Lydia waved at him. He looked embarrassed, as if he'd been caught naked. I shouldn't have done that, thought Lydia, I've broken his peace like the bird broke mine. She picked up two mugs and an ashtray and carried them downstairs.

Richard's helmet and biking jacket were on the bench which meant that he'd spent the night in his bed. He often stayed away nowadays. Which was convenient, she mused, as it meant he couldn't ask her about rent – already one month behind but it'll be all right after Christmas when I start work. Max had promised hundreds of pounds a week. I won't do it for long she decided, I'll pay the rent first and once I've got a little saved up and enough money for Slava I'll go back to photography. Where did Richard go when he stayed the nights away? Jill. Sure to be, she's the most likely candidate, but I can't ask him because I'm his ex-lover so I'm the last person who's allowed to question him. And her husband? Is he a good man? Is he a kind man? I can't start feeling sorry for husbands. Too late for that now. He's a photographer, maybe I should try and get a job with him. Has Richard forgiven me? Maybe not, not completely. Maybe we pushed him into it, Alex and me.

Lydia dipped her hand once more into the washing up bowl. The water was almost black with dirt. She hadn't noticed it before because the bubbles from the washing up liquid had hidden it. She rinsed a plate and pulled the plug and waited for the dirty water to drain away. The bedroom door was closed. I wonder what Alex's dreams are like: manic she supposed. It's the way he lives. Our marriage is mad. No one else would have proposed like that, but then everything about him is crazy. She thought of Alex practising his lines over and over again, frantically searching for envelopes from drama schools, rushing back from work reporting record tips and pitched battles with Slava and Dimitri and telling her how much he loved her with such fervour that it was impossible to look at him. It's all a mission. I'm another challenge for Alex, he wants to dedicate himself to something. He's not just another lover, she thought uneasily, I can't be separate. I pretend to myself that our marriage is a convenience, but it isn't for him.

She wiped down the draining board. There was no more tidying up left to do. She sat on the chair by the fire, lit a cigarette and tried to reassure herself. He doesn't really love me, he just thinks he does. He doesn't know what love is, she told herself and then wondered rather uncomfortably whether she did either. I told him I didn't love him, she reminded herself but she knew that was immaterial, he'd already scribbled it out of his memory so he didn't have to deal with it. She thought of the phrases he constantly repeated. Everything's turning out right! It's all coming together! I love you. I love you. I love you! This will be true! This is going to happen! Statements so positive and brittle that Lydia felt the only way she could possibly react was to remain silent and try to damp the fires.

Later on in the morning Lydia agreed to go out with Alex to buy Christmas presents. The shops were seething with last-minute shoppers. There was panic in the air. People's eyes flickered frenziedly over the potential presents laid out in front of them. Tin thin music seeped like gas from ceiling speakers. Each shop window was filled with synthetic snow, cotton-wool snowmen, coloured bulbs, tinsel and silver Christmas trees. Alex rushed around the shops periodically stopping, picking up goods, turning them over in his hands and then rejecting them. 'No, that's too expensive. That's not her style. What do think Lydia? Do you think Mum would like that?'

'Should *I* buy presents for your family?' asked Lydia outside a book shop on the King's Road. Alex shook his head vehemently, 'No! Don't worry about it. It'll be fine.' Lydia frowned. Alex was too manic to think straight. He was probably saying what he thought she wanted to hear. It would be wiser to have a few small gifts, she decided and while Alex was frantically surveying the shelves of a cosmetics shop Lydia bought two bottles of aromatherapy bubble bath.

At Waterloo station Lydia began to catch some of the excitement of the festival. There was an air of anticipation.

People crowded shoulder to shoulder across the white marble concourse clasping polystyrene cups of coffee and craning their necks to watch the rapid clatter of the departure board. Lydia had an image of all the people of London being sucked out down the train lines leaving the empty shell of the city behind them.

There was a party atmosphere on the train; men and women wedged laden plastic bags between their feet while they loosened their waistbands and ties and swigged back cans of beer. Alex and Lydia found a space by the toilets. They perched on their bags, deafened by the wind and the wheels. By the time they reached Salisbury the train had emptied enough for them to find seats. Alex leant his elbows on the grey formica table and peered eagerly out into the dark fields and hedges.

'We'll go to church but first we'll open our stockings and then afterwards we'll open our presents and then we'll have a big Christmas dinner. You've never had plum pudding have you? You'll love it. It's the best. With loads of brandy butter. We'll probably just slump in front of the telly after that or if we've got enough energy we'll go for a walk. It's beautiful countryside you'll love it. I know you will. And I mean Mum and Sally might just be a bit funny tonight but it won't last for long. It's Mum's illness you see. It's made her more protective somehow that's all. She doesn't take life for granted any longer. She's been that bit too close to death to be able to do that. But sometimes she forgets that it affected us as well. Obviously not as much but it has all the same. I've always had big ideas and stuff but before Mum got sick they used to be just that: ideas. I mean I don't think I would have gone for the auditions this year if it hadn't been for Mum's illness and I certainly don't think we would have got married.'

Alex broke off and squeezed Lydia's hand. 'Life's too short. We don't have enough time for dreams. I really believe now that I've got to try them out and see if they work. That that's the most important thing. I mean when Mum was sick I was the one doing all the housework and all the cleaning and stuff and changing her colostomy bag, wiping her up, giving her the pills and driving her to hospital and everything. I was the adult but I actually felt like I was a child again and it got to the point when I thought that I was never going to leave home. So I suppose when I did it was like being shot out of a catapult.'

Lydia nodded but what Alex was describing was the opposite of the time she'd first looked after her mother. It had been before her father had come back from the camps so she'd only been six or seven but she'd been the adult then and her mother'd been the child. Looking back, Lydia knew that her mother had never recovered from that time and nor, really, had she. That had been the end of her childhood and she'd never got it back again.

Sally picked them up. She was standing under the platform lights when the train pulled in. Alex kissed her on both cheeks and Lydia hovered self-consciously behind him. 'You must be Lydia,' said Sally sticking out her hand like a sword, 'nice to meet you. Come on we'd better be getting back, Mum's in a real tizz about everything. You'll have to be gentle with her.' Sally looked directly at Lydia. The platform lights reflected in her gold button earrings. Headlights flared in the car-park and an engine started. 'This has all been a bit of a shock for her.' Sally turned on her heel and Alex and Lydia followed her over the walkway to the car-park.

There were no street lights in the village. Lydia pulled her suitcase out of the boot of the car and stood by the door of the cottage looking around her. Somewhere a dog was barking and the sound echoed against the clouded sky as if it were made of stone. It was both darker and colder than London. Alex squeezed her hand and then dropped it. Some sweat from his palm lingered on her knuckles and the night air brushed against it. Alex ducked his head as he stepped through the cottage door. His mother was standing just inside the threshold. Lydia watched him hug her ebulliently. A little dog rushed out yapping and leapt up Alex's legs while Marjory fretted around her son making anxious comments about his appearance.

'Come on, let's get inside, it's bloody cold out here,' urged Sally from the doorway. Alex stepped portentiously to one side and beckoned Lydia into the cottage. 'Mum,' he said proudly, 'I'd like you to meet Lydia.' Marjory stiffened and stepped forward to shake Lydia's hand. She wore a gold wedding band and a sapphire-and-diamond ring on her left hand. She had well used hands, the bones and veins were prominent and callused saddles of skin covered each knuckle. 'Come on in then,' she said and Lydia smiled demurely.

For dinner they sat around a small table beside the television and ate ham with bread and chutneys. Lydia sat with her back to the Christmas tree and every time she moved a shower of pine needles landed on her chair. She could feel Alex's mother scrutinising her through small blue eyes. She had a large nose and dark grey hair cut into a short bob. She wore a box-pleated lightweight tweed skirt and a round-necked wool sweater. Her clothes were unfashionable but well kept. They had never been thrown in a careless pile on the floor. She had an air of determination about her. A firm bargainer, decided Lydia.

'Alex tells me you are from Russia,' said Marjory carving the ham.

Lydia smiled politely, 'I come from St Petersburg.'

'Ah yes, that used to be called Leningrad didn't it? I went there once.'

'I'd forgotten about that, you went on that one week package tour didn't you?' interrupted Alex, his voice full of false jollity.

'Stunning art collections,' said Marjory, 'but the people all looked so grey and miserable and the food was absolutely filthy.'

'There have been lots of changes in Russia recently,' said Lydia.

'Is that enough for you Sally?' said Marjory handing her a plate. Sally said that was perfect and Marjory returned to her carving. 'Tell me Lydia,' she said, 'what is it exactly that you are doing in England?'

Alex glanced at Lydia and then answered for her, 'Lydia wants to be a photographer.'

'How interesting,' said Marjory icily and then turning to Alex, she continued talking with hardly a pause. 'Did I tell you darling that I bumped into Sarah Allen in Dorchester the other day and John's apparently got a very good new job in marketing.'

The room was small and it was difficult to squeeze between the different pieces of furniture. It was neat and tidy and the white walls were bare. A worn armchair and sofa faced a television and a meagre brick fireplace. On the mantelpiece was a row of framed photographs of Alex and Sally in their childhood. Behind the television was an electric sewing machine, a sewing chest and a rack of half made clothes pinned with pieces of tracing paper. Lydia looked down at the eager face of the terrier who waited under the table for scraps.

At the end of the meal Marjory gathered the plates in front of her. 'Sally,' she said imperiously, 'why don't you take Lydia and Jim for a quick trot around the back lane.'

Alex felt a tightening in his chest. He'd be in for it now. Sally had the dog lead in her hand and the terrier was leaping up in the air yelping with excitement. Alex got up heavily from his chair. The door closed. An uneasy silence occupied the cottage. 'I'll do the washing up Mum,' he said without enthusiasm and picking up a pile of plates from in front of his mother he trudged through to the kitchen and filled a scratched yellow plastic bowl with hot water. A moment later he heard his mother behind him.

'Do you like her then Mum?' asked Alex with studied

casualness as he lifted a plate dripping with bubbles from the bowl.

Marjory picked up a tea towel. 'She seems a nice enough girl,' she replied brusquely, 'but I can't quite see how either of you imagine you're going to be able to afford to eat. You want to be an actor and she wants to be a photographer. It strikes me you're both living in cloud cuckoo land. For a start where are you both going to live? Where are you going to have your marital home?' She was speaking very quickly. Alex knew that she would have carefully prepared and rehearsed this speech waiting for her opportunity to release it. 'Darling you're not a rich man and unless you change your ideas about what you want to do with your life you're never going to be a rich man. I hope you've made that quite clear to her. I don't know what her motives are but I'm sure that a waitress in a Russian restaurant doesn't earn very much money.

Bubbles sprayed in the air as Alex threw his washing up cloth into the water. 'Mum! You're hardly one to talk.' he snapped, 'You and dad weren't Romeo and Juliet! I *love* Lydia. Okay? Got that? Our marriage was my idea and I did it because she was about to be deported and I couldn't bear the thought of her going away. I still feel that way. I've never loved any girl in the way that I love Lydia and I honestly believe that I will love her forever. I don't expect you to love her too, I can't make you do that but if you respected me at all you would at least trust my judgement . . . Especially at Christmas.'

'Christmas,' snapped Marjory, 'has got nothing to do with it. This is your home and you are welcome here at any time of year. I'd even go so far as to say that any guest of yours is welcome here too. And as far as I am concerned Lydia is just that: a guest. Call me old fashioned but I cannot and will not accept that this is a proper marriage.'

Alex ran his tongue along his bottom row of teeth and rolled his eyes to the ceiling. What's the point, he thought, she's already made up her mind and she's not going to listen to anything I say. 'The law thinks it's a proper marriage,' he said sulkily and he began attacking the bottom of a saucepan with a scouring pad. Come on Sally. She was probably dawdling on purpose. I mean how long did it take to go for a walk for God's sake.

'The law's an ass,' remarked Marjory acerbically. 'Boys of your age fall in and out of love as if it were going out of fashion. If you're still in love in a year's time, in two year's time, in ten year's time then that's a proper marriage. If Lydia gets deported and you're prepared to live in Russia then that's a proper marriage. If you're both prepared to work all hours that God gives you in order to bring up a family then that's a marriage. All you've done at the moment is stand in front of a man in the Town Hall and, as you say, that might be good enough for the law but to my mind that's not a real marriage.

Chapter Twenty-Eight

Two days after New Year's Eve Alex left for work at six o'clock. He kissed Lydia goodbye and hugged her tightly. 'Angel, what would I do without you? I'll try not to wake you up when I come in,' he said dropping another kiss onto her forehead before climbing the stairs.

She waited until she could no longer hear his footsteps on the gangplank and then taking her diary from her coat pocket she opened it at the page with Max's number at the club. She stood in front of the stove with the telephone in her hand and her right foot resting against her calf like a stork. In front of her was a seat that ran down one side of the boat and on it lay one of Alex's tee-shirts and a stray sock. She hesitated. Alex would hate the idea of her working at a hostess bar and if Seriozha ever found out he'd go crazy. It wouldn't fit in with the image they have of ethereal Lydia at all, she thought. But it's my life and not their image and I need the money.

'So you are going to work for us. Oh good. There was a horrible girl who came in today. A real tart and I told Jim you were much sexier. I'll put you onto him now.' The telephone began playing an instrumental version of 'Penny Lane'. Then the line clicked, 'Nice to talk to you Lydia,' said a buttery voice. 'Max has told me all about you and I hear you want to join our team. When would you be available to start?'

'As soon as possible,' she said, extracting a cigarette from a packet on the table. She pushed it between her lips and wedging the receiver under her cheek she carried the telephone over to the little kitchen and lit the cigarette from a large box of cook's matches.

'Lovely job, lovely. Well what I suggest is that you come in early on your first day when the bar's nice and quiet and we'll get one of the girls to show you around. Then you can get a feel for the place. Now, dear, what clothes were you thinking of wearing?

'Erm. What would you advise?'

'Well we like our girls to look nice and smart. Nothing cheap or tacky. We're not that kind of establishment. Obviously no trousers, I'm sure that goes without saying, although you'd be surprised what some people think is suitable, you really would.' He gave a little laugh.

Lydia took a long drag of her cigarette. Oh dear, she thought, this may be worse than I thought. The boat rocked violently on the wash of a passing barge. Lydia held onto the sink. A cold sweat prickled across her forehead. She felt an acid gorge rise in her throat.

The man was saying that she should look nice and feminine. 'Tasteful makeup and be sure to show off your good points. Well I think that's all for now Lydia. I'll look forward to seeing you at four o'clock on Thursday.'

'Four o'clock on Thursday,' she repeated weakly and then putting down the telephone, turned hastily around to the basin and was sick.

She ran the tap when she'd finished retching and let the cold water splash across her face and the back of her neck. Then, badly shaken, she wiped herself dry with a dishcloth and sat down at the kitchen table. Had she eaten something bad? Was it the cigarette? Seasickness? Her period was late but that wasn't unusual, Lydia's period was often late. She went to the toilet to check that it hadn't arrived and stared despairingly at her unstained knickers. She pushed the idea from her mind. There was no point in worrying about it yet. Being sick once did not mean that you were pregnant. Better not to think about it at all or it would delay her period further.

She wore a fake Chanel suit with a very short skirt that she bought for ten pounds from the World's End Oxfam shop. Alex watched with interest as she got ready. 'You look fantastic,' he commented, 'you should wear make-up more often. So tell me again what this place is?'

Lydia blotted her lips with a piece of loo paper and then pouting in the mirror carefully applied another layer of postbox red lipstick using a small paintbrush. 'It's in Holborn. I'm going to be late,' she said, grabbing her coat and holding up her hand to stop him coming nearer to her, 'you can't kiss me or you'll rub it all off.'

'Good luck,' he shouted to her as she hurried up the stairs in her unfamiliar high heels, 'If I'm asleep when you get in wake me up and tell me how it's gone.'

Lydia was surprised how nervous she was. She sat on her hands on the bus so that she didn't rub her eyes and smear her mascara. At the club the bouncer recognised her. He was friendlier this time. He jerked his head to a door behind him, 'Jim's in the back with Marlena and Max.' She nodded, she was feeling nauseous again, the now-familiar cold sweat beginning to break out across her forehead. Praying fervently that she wouldn't be sick she pushed through the door into a bald concrete corridor lined with boxes. Max was leaning against the wall talking to a short man and a very tall and beautiful black girl. The girl was smoking a cigarette. The smell made Lydia's stomach buckle. Jim was scrawny and only just over five foot. His neck was shrunken and wrinkled like a gizzard and contrasted bizarrely with the luxuriant crop of grey hair that gushed from the top of his brown puckered head. 'Ahh, Lydia, Lydia, Lydia,' he said licking his tongue all over her name, 'you look *lovely*.' Max grinned and nodded vigorously at her from behind his back.

For two hours there were no customers and Lydia, Marlena and Max sat drinking orange juice on high stools lit by spotlights in the ceiling. Marlena was American. 'Chicago. I'm touring Europe. I've been here four months so far which is crazy in this godawful climate. I want to go to Spain next. I hear Barcelona's real nice.'

'And how long've you been working here?'

'Pretty much most of that time. It's cool. Have you worked in the sex industry before?'

Lydia shook her head.

'You should have said! It's like your first day at school isn't it? Don't worry about a thing. This place is cool. Some places are awful but here there's really not much to worry about. It's pretty much the top end of the market.' She patted Max's arm. 'Max here take's care of us. So if you get into any trouble then you just give him the nod and he'll come and sort you out.'

Max sucked at his orange juice through a straw, 'Don't you worry,' he said, 'I'll make sure that you're all right.'

Lydia licked her forefinger and rubbed it around the rim of her glass and tried not to think about what kind of trouble they might be referring to. Seriozha's face appeared in her mind. He looked very angry, his face had turned a purple red and a vein bulged from his forehead like a cord. She shook her head to lose the image. 'And we just have to talk?' she asked.

Marlena looked at her sharply, wondering whether she was being judged. 'Depends on you. Jim's line is that if you don't want to do tricks you don't have to do tricks. Which is okay but maybe a little optimistic. You know sometimes the pressure's pretty strong. You're not supposed to leave the bar when you're on shift but you can be pretty sure that the other girls will cover for you as long as you're not gone longer than an hour or so. You'll get into it. The money's good. These guys are all rich as fuck. They're business men you know and most of them come from abroad so they've got hotel rooms and stuff and they just want a bit of company. They're not poor.'

Lydia looked at Max. He was grinning. She pushed her glass towards him for more orange juice. The sick feeling was beginning again. Marlena chattered on, 'Heeeyyy, Lydia, you don't look so good. Am I making you scared? You just get them to buy you lots of drinks and you'll be fine. Lena's coming in later on and if you've got a customer who wants a turn then she's always glad of a bit of extra money and from time to time I don't mind obliging neither. We've had lots of girls like you. Max'll tell you. We had these two Croatian girls and they were just like you, all they ever did was hostess. Isn't that right Max?'

But Max wasn't listening, he'd slipped to the other side of the counter as a group of seven businessmen entered the bar. Marlena crossed her legs and eased the edge of her skirt up her thighs so that you could see her stocking tops. 'Here we go,' she hissed under her breath, 'just make 'em feel like they've got really big dicks and then they'll leave you a nice fat tip.'

They were from America, a group of computer programmers come to install a system for a company publishing academic journals. Lydia and Marlena brought them their drinks. One particularly tall man with a moustache was a Mormon. There was lots of joking about that.

'Sure he'll drink a whiskey!' said one of the others when it was obvious that the Mormon only wanted lemonade. Lydia felt sorry for him. She wished she was on his side of the table but, she reminded herself, she was being paid for this and she couldn't choose. She perched on a stool next to man with a red face and orange blonde-hair that curled over the stiff white collar of his shirt. Smoothing her skirt across her lap she cocked her head to one side and looked up at him through her eyelashes. 'You know I've always wanted to go to America. It's fascinated me all my life but I've never had the chance. Which part do you come from?'

'Me?' he said, 'I come from Texas. Now most people they move to Texas but I was born there and I'm proud of that.' It was the first time that he had been overseas he explained and he thought England was overcrowded and the English unfriendly but he was impressed by the buildings being so old. He had a wife he said he respected.

The man on the other side of Lydia was called Mark. He told her not to believe a word of what the old cowboy said. He himself had been abroad three times before but only on business. He didn't see the point of going abroad for holidays when there was so much of America to enjoy. Other groups of men came in and more girls arrived. Mark said he'd been married three times before and the last one had been a real bitch who'd tried to steal all his money. He wouldn't say that he was disillusioned exactly but he knew now that some women were just after one thing and that was cash. Lydia nodded and smiled and made encouraging noises.

'You're doing fine,' said Marlena as she ushered her over to a new group of men, 'but you don't have to be shy, girl. You can be a little bit more forceful 'cos you know you've got to get those drinks out of them!'

'Okay' said Lydia, 'I'll do my best.'

'That's the spirit!' said Marlena, and sent her off to a man named Will who was sweaty and so obese that the back of his neck bulged over, hiding his collar from view. He came from Scotland.

Lydia uncrossed and recrossed her legs. 'You know I've always wanted to go to Scotland. It's fascinated me all my life but I've never had the chance. Which part do you come from?' she pressed her hand on his great boulder of a knee to emphasize her desire. He said he came from Aberdeen and he'd never been to a bar like this before. Lydia didn't believe him, especially when he asked her whether she . . . you know? She left him in the hands of Lena, a painfully thin blonde with dry grey skin and almost pancake make-up. Lydia thought she looked too fragile, physically and mentally, to cope. Her eyes never stayed still, constantly flickering and leaping from object to object in the room. Lydia hesitated as she walked away; surely, she thought, she'll be crushed but the only other option was to service the fat Scotsman herself and she wasn't prepared to go that far. So I sacrifice Lena, she thought unhappily, and she left the room to snatch a few free minutes in the toilet.

The feeling of sickness was constant now. She pressed her face against the mirror above the sink. The glass was cool against her face. She splayed her hand across her stomach. It's all the smoke, she told herself but knew she was lying. 'I'll get a test tomorrow,' she whispered to the mirror, 'I promise.'

She forced herself out of the toilet and back into the bar. I'm not here, she told herself, I'm not here at all. I'm floating above this room. I'm watching it all happen beneath me. She squirmed and simpered to a group of Japanese academics who with much hilarity patted her knee, brushed against her breasts and left her a tip. Peter from South Africa told her that his wife was sleeping with his best friend and they thought he didn't know. Four men told her that they had fantasies about red heads and two said that Russian accents turned them on. One even said that he'd married a woman from Omsk through a dating agency and now they had a child. 'But she's a right bitch. All she wanted was the visa,' he snarled with a hatred that affected Lydia like a nerve being pulled in her tooth.

After that she found she couldn't float above the room any longer. She was back in the room and although she tried she couldn't escape again. She lost count of the men she talked to but she remembered the drinks she was given because she received a commission on those. Twenty-five glasses of acrid fizzy wine between four o'clock in the afternoon and one in the morning, almost all of which ended up in a chuck bucket that Max had behind the bar.

She sat numb and exhausted on the night bus. The river was reduced to a trickle in the middle of the channel. The boats slept side by side on the bank. Lydia was sick over the edge of the pontoons and the vomit splattered against the soft mud leaving little craters behind. She let herself onto *Toadhall*, washed her face in the basin, took off her clothes and left them in a pool in the bathroom. Alex was asleep and gently sucking the corner of the pillowcase. He'd told her to wake him up but Lydia recoiled from the idea of any contact with him at all. She slipped under the duvet and lay hugging her belly and balancing precariously on the edge of the bed so that not one inch of her body would touch him.

Chapter Twenty-Nine

It was a miserable day but, thought Alex, there is something luscious about being inside by a fire on a miserable day and knowing that you're warm and cozy and not like poor Lydia out *there* where the rain's hitting the windows like thrown fistfuls of gravel. Ten days exactly until his audition with Bristol Old Vic.

> And in the morn and liquid dew of youth
> Contagious blastments are most imminent.
> Be wary then; best safety lies in fear:
> Youth to itself rebels, though none else near.

Alex paced backwards and forwards in front of the fire muttering his words and making phantom gestures. Occasionally he referred to the copy of *Hamlet* that lay face-up on the table. The air in the boat smelt sour and toasted from the coal smoke. The raindrops landing on the window slowly gathered together to form rivulets that jumped across the glass as the boat rocked jerkily against the chopping waves.

There was a discreet double-pulsed knock on the door. Alex climbed the stairs, three steps at a time, and opened the door to two middle-aged men in suits and rain-coats.

'Mr Carmichael?' asked a balding man with a skimpy fringe of greased curly hair circling his pate. Alex swivelled his eyes from one man to the other suspiciously before agreeing that yes, he was Mr Carmichael.

'Is Mrs Carmichael available?' asked the bald man's squat ginger bearded companion.

'She's out,' replied Alex warily, 'can I ask who is calling?'

'My name's Douglas and this is my colleague Mr Young. We're from the Home Office and in Mrs Carmichael's absence we would like to ask you a few questions relating to your wife's application for permanent residency in Britain,' said the ginger-haired man.

Alex watched three fat raindrops slither off the bald man's skull. The wind nosed its way under their rain-coats which flapped like tails. 'I suppose you'd better come in then,' said Alex grudgingly, stepping back from the door.

They looked around, rotating their heads on their short squat necks and appraising the boat with a cold curiosity. Who do they think they are, thought Alex shuffling his feet, angry at their intrusion. Water dripped slowly from their coats onto the carpet. Alex regarded them, resting his weight on one hip with his arms tightly barricaded across his chest. He considered offering the two men cups of tea. It was, he knew, what his mother would have done but he decided against it. He hadn't asked for them to come barging in and he wasn't going to cooperate any more than he absolutely had to.

'Is this your own property Mr Carmichael?' asked Mr Young.

'No, it belongs to our landlord, Richard Fitzmaurice. He lives here as well.'

'I see. We'd like to have a look around, if that's all right with you.' Not at all right actually, thought Alex aggressively, and he wondered what they would do if he refused but the rebellion remained in his head. He shrugged and told them sarcastically to make themselves feel at home.

They walked down the stairs with Alex following close on their heels. Neither of them had been in a houseboat before. It was a change from the normal round of bedsits and flats that they visited and they were both pleased to be out of the rain. Mr Douglas sniffed and his beard twitched in a way that reminded Alex of a pet white mouse that a boy in his class had kept at school. 'Damp must be terrible,' he pronounced in a nasal voice.

'Actually we try and keep the water on the outside,' said Alex with a sneer. It was what Sally always said. Alex winced. It wasn't even funny when she said it.

'It's really quite snug in here,' commented Mr Young in a surprised voice. 'Now Mr Carmichael, can you show us your bedroom please?'

So you want to know where we have sex then? Alex nodded sullenly to the door below the stairs. Like I'm in a fucking zoo, he grumbled to himself. The two men squeezed into Lydia's cramped little bedroom. Through the open door Alex watched the bald Mr Young pick up and turn over two pots of face cream. Alex prickled. What a nerve. He'd like to kick the bastards out. How dare they touch her creams? He glared at them from the doorway, his arms battened across his chest. He listened to the small metallic chimes of colliding coat hangers. 'And where do you keep your clothes Mr Carmichael?' asked Mr Douglas.

Alex blushed, 'My sister lives on the next-door boat and I haven't moved all my things over yet.'

'So you don't actually live on this premises all the time?'

Alex knew that he had been caught out. 'Yes I do, actually,' he said defensively, 'I just haven't had the time, that's all.'

'I see,' said Mr Young knowingly. He brushed past Alex and opened the door by the stove.

'This is the bathroom?' Alex nodded. The man's voice echoed against the tiles.

'This shaving equipment, does that belong to you or to your landlord?'

'Actually it's Richard's,' said Alex. You stupid git Alex, what did you say that for?

'You er keep your shaving equipment next door?' said Mr Young brightly.

Alex rolled his eyes to the ceiling.

The ginger-haired Mr Douglas emerged from sniffing around the bedroom, he glanced at his colleague in the bathroom. 'Do you have any photographs of your wedding Mr Carmichael?' Alex took a packet of snapshots from the bookcase and sulkily handed them to Mr Douglas who carefully examined each one. 'Just the two witnesses then. Your family didn't attend the ceremony?'

'Well my mother lives in Dorset.'

'But she didn't come to your wedding. And your sister who lives next door?'

'She didn't actually know that I was getting married until afterwards. You see I knew that my family wouldn't really approve and so I didn't really want them to be there. It would have spoilt it. Lydia and I just wanted a private ceremony. I told them afterwards when it was too late for them to do anything about it.'

He knew how bad it sounded but what else could he say? Mr Young had emerged from the bathroom and was scrutinising him carefully. Mr Douglas handed him back the packet of photographs with a curt nod, 'What made you think that they wouldn't approve of your marriage?' 'They were prejudiced,' blurted out Alex, his eyes wet with tears of frustration. 'They didn't understand that I love Lydia and that she loves me. All they could see was that she's Russian. They automatically assumed that she wants something from me but it's not like that at all. They understand it better now. We all spent Christmas together.' There was a pause. 'We're planning to have a family,' blurted out Alex, 'I mean we want to do it all properly. I'm saving up so that we can have a flat of our own and we're going to bring up our children bilingually and we'll take them to Russia as well. It's not easy living like this you know, with everyone automatically assuming the worst. But I'm right, I know I am. Love is the most important thing in the end isn't it? That's what we've got to hang onto.'

Alex scuffed his big toe nail across the carpet. 'I know what you're thinking. 'What's going on around here? He keeps his clothes next door, blah di blah di blah but you've got to realise that I love her. I don't know what I would do if I lost her. I think I'd go crazy I really do. I just couldn't bear it.' There was an embarrassed silence. The officials digested Alex's emotional outburst. Alex gripped the back of a chair to steady himself and stared at the floor. How much of that was true and how much of that was acting, he wondered.

'But your wife's not actually pregnant at the moment Mr Carmichael?' asked Mr Young from the doorway of the bathroom.

'No, she's not actually pregnant right now. We're going to wait for a little bit first,' confirmed Alex.

Alex showed the men out and leaned on the door jamb watching them bustle away down the pontoons with the collars of their rain-coats pulled up to stop the rain rolling down their necks. He could see their heads turn as they talked to each other. What were they saying? He wanted to run after them and explain it all again, shake them by the shoulders and scream his love for Lydia in their faces. I should have lied more, he thought, I shouldn't have told them about Richard, I should've pretended that all his stuff was mine, they would never have found out. I should never have even mentioned Sally, what did they need to know about her for? The two men had now reached the Embankment. Alex could see their heads over the wall as they waited on the kerb to cross the road.

Chapter Thirty

After the men had gone Alex listened to the rain drumming on the roof of the boat and fed the stove with coal. Lydia would be back soon and what was he going to tell her? He'd fucked up badly and he knew it. If they rejected her appeal now he was going to feel awful. Hell he was meant to be an actor. He hunched over his knees and blew a smoke ring at the stove. Lydia's face undulated in the embers. There was a big lump of coal in the middle glowing so fiercely that his eyes danced with blue spots as he looked at it. What a fucking idiot, it was almost as if he'd said all the worst things on purpose. He heard her footsteps. Oh God what was he going to say?

'How did it go,' he yodelled up the stairs, 'what do they look like?'

She came down the stairs She looked tired. Her hair stuck to her face in little worms, the skin under her eyes was puffy. 'They made a mistake. The prints won't be ready for tomorrow. I'd better get ready for work or I'll be late.' Her voice was flat and drained. He couldn't tell her now.

'Let me run you a bath, then I can talk to you while you soak.'

She stood awkwardly with her feet turning inwards. 'Actually,' she said, 'do you mind but . . . well I quite like having baths on my own.'

After she'd gone he stayed by the fire and tried to carry on rehearsing his lines but his concentration had gone. It was dark by half past four but he didn't turn the lights on and when Sally got back at six he watched her through the windows. Flavia was with her and together they moved up and down her boat. Alex wondered if they were talking about him. He thought about the two men from the Home Office. Maybe Lydia didn't need to know about them at all. If he didn't tell her he wouldn't have to admit how stupid he'd been. It's too late now isn't it, he thought, I mean there's nothing that she can do about it is there?

He heard footsteps on the gangplank. He stood up. The door opened and he heard the sound of shrill laughter and then Richard's voice hushing and after a pause saying, 'It's okay, there's nobody here.'

Alex picked up his cigarette and the ashtray and quickly slipped into Lydia's bedroom. He sat on the end of the bed and took a drag. He could hear their voices above him but he couldn't make out the individual words. The woman, he realised with a prudish shock, was Jill. Alex scowled. That wasn't right. They were padding around above him. He tried not to think what they were doing but the more he tried to ignore them the more conscious he became of every sound. Richard came downstairs. Alex heard him run the basin tap in the bathroom and open the fridge, there was more giggling, Richard's low rumbling voice, little thuds on the floorboards and sentimental music.

Alex stared out of the window, the lights from the pontoons were reflecting off the mud like great big rolling fat blubbery thighs. He remembered Jill telling him about her husband at the cinema party in Dalston. They'd been married for twelve years, they were childhood sweethearts for Christ's sake. It upset him and made him angry. If only they knew he was here then they wouldn't be able to do anything but it was too late now. He couldn't go out now. How long would they be? He was going to have to sit it out and listen to them. His eyebrows knotted tightly together. He opened the window and rolled another cigarette smoking it into the cold muddy air. After a while Richard and Jill's laughter slowly petered out and, after an even longer while, he heard them whispering urgently on the stairs then bodies softly colliding with the kitchen table followed by the little smacking wet sounds of kissing and Jill's voice unnervingly close by, suggesting that they go to Richard's bedroom.

Alex flicked the glowing butt of his cigarette out of the window and heard it hiss as it hit the mud. He lay back on the bed. Jill's rising rhythmic cries swept through the boat. Alex clenched his hands by his side. She's pretending, he thought furiously, she doesn't have to be so loud, it's not necessary. Come on, come on, he kept on thinking, it's got to be now and when she eventually did climax his whole body went tense and rigid. He turned to face the window and breathed in the mud-filled vapours that were creeping in from outside. Now that they had stopped it was too quiet and Alex wished that some new noise would come and fill the silence.

He fell asleep as he was, fully clothed with his boots still on and his fingers gripping the duvet like a child with a teddy bear and he didn't stir when Lydia slipped in beside him at quarter past two. He woke the next morning full of the confused jumbled feeling of unremembered dreams, there'd definitely been a chase but it wasn't clear whether he'd been the hunter or the prey. He felt cranky and unrested, his eyes were full of gum and his head was heavy. The tide was in and the boat was shimmying in little jerking hip movements on glittering morning waves. Lydia was sitting at the kitchen table with a cup of tea. Her thin mottled pink-and-white legs protruded from her turquoise kimono.

He lumbered to the bathroom. When he came out Lydia had poured him a mug of tea. He sat down and scratched his chest. 'Has he gone?' he whispered, jerking his head in the direction of Richard's bedroom.

'Yes.' Lydia sounded puzzled.

'Did you know he was sleeping with Jill?'

Lydia looked very quickly at her lap and then back at him, 'No,' she said firmly, possibly more firmly than she needed to.

'I didn't know,' she repeated, 'but he has been away a lot recently and I suspected that he might be.'

'But she's married!' hissed Alex.

'Yes,' said Lydia in a peculiar voice, 'that's true. She is married.'

Chapter Thirty-One

Three days before his audition for Bristol Old Vic Alex went in to work the lunch shift. Slava was out and Dimitri was in the kitchen taunting Volodya. 'I will leave you here all alone,' he was saying, 'and then Slava will say, "come up to my office little Volodya," and he will stroke your bottom and there won't be any Uncle Dimitri to save you. Or maybe you would want me to, hey? Maybe you like boys too?'

'Stop it!' snapped Alex, 'leave him alone you fat bully.' Dimitri rounded on him. The slopes of his blackheaded nose glistened under the strip lights. 'The great defender!' he sneered, 'but you didn't say anything when they came for the Russian princess did you?'

Alex felt a cold finger jabbing at his neck. 'You don't know what you're talking about Dimitri,' he said evenly.

'You let Mother Russia claim her back just like that.'

'It was the Immigration Police, it had nothing to do with Mother Russia.'

Dimitri leant back on the stove and wiped both his hands across his big belly. Volodya stared at Alex. 'Who do you think told the good British policeman about the illegal immigrant working at Russki's? Eh?' jeered Dimitri. 'Why do you think we weren't working that night? Do you think it was a coincidence? Do you think kind Slava was giving us a free holiday? No, no somebody's husband wanted her home didn't they?'

Alex moved across the kitchen and began to swing his fist out behind him when Slava walked through the door. Alex stopped and gulped at Slava. One, two, three. He mustn't lose this job. Lydia, the money. One, two, three. He let his arm fall by his side and taking a deep breath walked out into the restaurant.

Saturday lunchtimes at Russki's were busy and the customers more hurried and demanding than on other days of the week. Teenagers, released from their school uniforms, questioned every item on their bills. Shoppers plundering the sales pulled things out of bags and wondered about the things they hadn't bought – maybe I could afford it, should I go back? – and then demanded their food instantly, there was no time to waste in eating. All afternoon Alex weaved between the tables of beckoning customers and every time he took an order or cleared the tables he heard Dimitri's spit-rich voice. '*Someone's husband.*' Two words whispered in his ears as he hurried around the restaurant. He remembered as well the strange way that Lydia had responded when he'd told her about Richard and Jill. '*Yes that's true. She is married.*' All afternoon these two memories danced round and round each other in his brain. He'd never thought that there might be someone in Russia, never even dreamed that she might be married. Why hadn't she told him? Maybe she was running away from him. He must want her back pretty badly to have her arrested for God's sake. He was scared of all the things he didn't know about her, scared of this shadow man in his shadow country that was trying to claw her back to the other side of Europe. He took the plates from the hatch. He tipped leftovers into the bin. A couple left. He wiped their table then a group of four came and he found more chairs and he laid it up for them. The room hummed and whirled around him. He'd have to ask her. It was the only thing that he could do but he was afraid of the answer.

He tried to forget about it as he walked home, she wouldn't have been able to keep something so big secret from him. Surely he would have known, he would have guessed. It struck him how, in fact, he knew very little about her life. She'd never talked about it and he'd never asked. After the audition he'd buy himself a book and get Lydia to start teaching him Russian. Maybe he could take a course. Between Boris's Sandwich Bar 'Hot Poppy Seed Cake, £1.00 a slice' and the Chelsea Antique Market a placard stood on the pavement advertising the *Evening Standard*. 'Communism rises again', 'Russian result stuns reformers'. The word *Russian* caught Alex's attention. It's her country, I've got to learn as much as I can about it. He bought a copy and opened it out as he walked down the street.

Internal wrangling among Russia's democrats has left the door to power open to extremists raising fears that the neo-Fascists could be unstoppable . . . A surge of popular support for the neo-Fascist Vladimir Zhirinovsky has left Russia in the same position as Weimar Germany before the rise of Hitler, a leading reformer claimed last night as democrats and neighbouring states expressed alarm at the results of Russia's first parliamentary elections since the revolution. With the extreme nationalist Liberal Democratic party heading for the largest share of the vote, Yegor Gaidar compared his country with Germany in the thirties and said 'Zhirinovsky means war. It would be enormously dangerous if there were the slightest chance of this man becoming president. Mr Zhirinovsky, who has virulent anti-Western views and wants to establish Russian domination over former Soviet territories . . .'

It was Lydia's day off but she wasn't on the boat when he got back. She arrived soon after him, lugging two bags of shopping from the supermarket across the gangplank. He kissed her hello. He had to ask her, he knew he had to do it but something held him back. He couldn't do it straight away. 'Have you seen the news?' he said, waving the paper in front of her as she heaved the bags onto the kitchen table.

Lydia snorted, 'Doesn't mean anything,' she said dismissively, 'politicians in Russia don't have any power anyhow.'

Alex was flattened. He'd been pleased that he'd bought the newspaper and both impressed and a little scared by the article. It had seemed dramatic and portentous.

'Let's go for a walk,' he said abruptly. Lydia was putting milk in the fridge, she straightened up and looked at him puzzled. 'We never do anything. We just sit here drinking bloody tea all day. Let's go out.'

'But it's nearly dark.'

'No it's not, there's another half hour at least. Come on. We can put the shopping away later, let's walk along to the Peace Pagoda.'

Alex took Lydia's hand as they walked over the bridge and he swung their arms between them as they walked past the rush-hour traffic standing bumper to bumper puffing fumes of frustration. He felt a surge of love for her. Why did he doubt her? Why couldn't he just leave it alone, it was only one of Dimitri's bitchy comments after all and what did it matter what she had done in Russia. They hadn't met then.

No, that wouldn't do. If she had a husband he had to know, and now that he had resolved to ask her he had to carry it through. It would be cowardly not to. His own life, his own feelings and experiences seemed very limited to him now. He'd been too arrogant, it should have occurred to him that she might be married. There had been an unspoken rule between them never to talk about her past. It was taboo. It tried to think how that had happened. Lydia had never said anything. Whenever somebody mentioned Russia she went silent and she never referred to her past life in any way. Why did I go along with it, wondered Alex. There must have been other boyfriends. It seemed unnatural to him now that he hadn't insisted on knowing more about them. Had she loved them? And this husband, if he existed, what did she feel about him? He looked sideways at her. He wished that he could tell what she was thinking but he really had no idea.

They crossed the road and walked down some steps to a footpath that ran along the river. A line of Dutch barges was moored on one side of them and on the other a wooden fence separated them from a wine warehouse and a wholesale DIY shop. Yellow ragwort plants and small lilac bushes sprouted from gaps in the embankment wall, a battered and padlocked postbox with 'ANTJE' painted on it was cemented to the top. Alex became preoccupied with the lives of the people in the barges. What was it like? How did you find out about them? How much did they cost? That would be real boat living. He could imagine them with their own barge, Lydia dressed in dungarees with a streak of tar on her cheek and maybe a black cat. They came to a modern mirrored office building, inside they could see men and women working on architect's boards.

Ask her if she's already married. Just say it.

They'd reached the stone gates to the park. A bright blue-and-green metal sign read 'Welcome to Wandsworth, The Brighter Borough' and on railings another sign read, 'Gates Shut 5pm'. Underneath the trees the shadows were thickening, the yellow sand path and the paler chips on the bark of the trees glowed in the fading light. A woman was attaching the lead to a dachshund just inside the gate but the dog wouldn't stay still. Joggers pushed past them. On the other side of the river lightbulbs were strung like beads between the trees. They walked in silence until they reached the pagoda. A large golden Buddha stared across the Thames. Alex looked at his watch, it was nearly ten to five. He stopped at the base of the white steps. The shadows were now creeping out from the trees into the open. He had to do it now. He breathed in, 'Lydia, I want to ask you something.'

She sat on the fourth step. 'What?'

He stood very stiffly in front of her and as he spoke he conducted himself with his hands. All afternoon he'd been running this over in his head, practising how to say this but he still found himself blushing. There was something very humiliating about having to ask her if she was already married but he had to know, he wouldn't have any peace until he knew.

'Dimitri said something to me this morning.' He looked at her but in the thickening dusk he couldn't read her expression. 'He said that when the police came to Russki's to arrest you that they had been tipped off by someone in Russia and that Slava had given him and Volodya the night off on purpose. He hinted that it was your husband.' Alex paused and looked at his hands. 'Please Lydia, you've got to tell me the truth. I need to know. Are you married to someone else?'

She gave a cynical half-laugh and leant forward. There was a hole in the knee of her jeans and she worried at a thread on the edge of it. When she eventually spoke Alex knew that she was picking her words very carefully.

'I didn't know that Slava had given them the night off,' she said, 'but I did know that somebody had told the police. I had a lover before I came here. Seriozha. I wasn't married, but he was, to somebody else. He was my boss at work you see. It wasn't a comfortable situation. He lent me some money when I came here and he made me promise that I would come back. But even when I made the promise I knew that I wanted to break it. I just said it to please him. Getting away from him was one of the reasons I came here. He knew where I worked. I'm sure it was him. He rang the other day to ask when I was coming back but I didn't pick up the phone.'

Someone's husband, not hers, someone else's. Alex walked up the steps and bent down and kissed her. 'Thank you. I love you so much,' he said, 'I've been going crazy all day. I just . . . My imagination went wild.' He looked up across the rapidly darkening river. 'It brought home to me how little I know about your life.'

Lydia stood up beside him and they began to make their way through the darkness to the park gates. Alex gently stroked her hair as they walked.

'I know,' said Lydia soothingly, 'I understand. It's hard for you.'

They left the park just as the warden was closing the gates. His white Ford Escort van was parked on the pavement with its headlights on. He smiled at them, 'Just in time,' he said as he let them through and Alex knew he was smiling because he realised that they were lovers and that made Alex smile too.

They retraced their steps past the warehouses and the barges and over the river. At the top of the bridge they stopped and leant on the railings. The boats floated and winked from the edge of the black oily river. 'Which one's us then?' asked Alex, 'Can you tell?'

Lydia counted in from the bridge. 'There,' she said, 'you can see the deckchair.' Alex followed her pointing finger. The lights were on in the *Beagle*. 'Sally's in.'

'Does that still upset you?' asked Lydia.

He looked down. The river was further below them than he had realised and it made him slightly dizzy. He noticed the way the stream separated and flowed in ribbons around the feet of the bridge. 'Yes,' he replied, 'it does. But I've got to live my own life. I just wish they'd understand. I really do. I mean I think Christmas changed things a little but I still feel that they haven't accepted you completely and that really bothers me. I suppose in the end you're more important to me than they are. I mean I love you, you are the woman of my dreams.' He waited for her to respond but she said nothing. It was as if the river beneath them had hypnotised her. 'Lydia you do love me too don't you? I'm not just making a fool of myself am I?'

She sighed and pushed away from the railing. 'Nobody's ever talked to me in the way that you've just done,' she said. The wind shifted direction, blowing her hair in her face. She pulled it away from her mouth. 'I've always longed for someone to do that but it's odd you know, I can't respond. I can't tell you the things that you want to hear. The words just won't come out.'

Alex didn't understand. He hesitated, then deciding it wasn't negative, caught her arm. 'Come on,' he said smiling nervously and pulling her along the pavement, 'I'm starving. Let's get some food in.'

The notice arrived by registered post. Lydia was the only person up to sign for it and as Alex didn't wake for another hour she'd already had time to compose herself. When he lumbered sodden with sleep from their tiny bedroom she was sitting at the table fully dressed with the piece of paper on her lap. He had a pee and washed his face and when he sat down opposite her she pushed it across the table towards him. The letter was on Home Office paper. He hadn't woken up properly. He was still dopey and stupid. He unfolded it slowly. The language was official and terse. Lydia was to be deported, her appeal to remain had been rejected on the grounds that her marriage failed the primary purpose test. She would be escorted by immigration officials on a flight to St Petersburg on the nineteenth January. The day after next.

He heard the double-pulse of his blood beating in his ear drums. Dum dum, dum dum, dum dum, dum dum, dum dum. The air thickened to jelly around him. 'They, they . . .'

Lydia's eyes were on him. She combed her fingers through her hair and then with her elbows sticking out from her body she splayed her hands across her belly. 'They can do what they want Alex. My time has run out. There is no point in me carrying on.'

Why the fuck was she so calm? She wanted to leave? NO. NO.

'You tried Alex, I'm grateful, you did your best.'

NO!

He closed his eyes, the back of his eyelids glowed a scorching white. Quite slowly he banged his forehead on the table and swore. That was the start of it. He pushed back his chair so that it toppled over onto the floor and thumped his fist on the bathroom door leaving a dent in the painted plywood panelling. That dent was satisfying, a crater with the white paint cracked around the rim of it. The blow had jarred his elbow, shock vibrations ran down his arm. It hurt but not enough. He wanted it clear and clean. He powered his fist into the door once more. He felt the resistance of the plywood and then free air as he went through it. His knuckles burnt and the splinters cut into his skin. Arms around him. Funny little thin arms that he could break out of like a rubber band. And again at the plywood. Proper pain and real blood not just fantasising now. Screaming echoing around the boat. His hers, high low. More arms and these he couldn't bust out of, like his family holding him so tightly that he couldn't breathe. A tight choking security. THWACK! Heard the noise like a kung fu movie and suddenly he was staring, very clearly, at Richard's face furious, green eyed and freckled and there was a break and the time stood still with burning, stinging cheeks and Lydia staring at him with real red fear in her eyes.

Chapter Thirty-Two

The stove hadn't yet warmed the boat up, the air was still damp and a soft velvet sheen of condensation covered the windows. Alex stood in shock and chewed at his thumb knuckle. He covered his face with his hand. It's all over, he thought and he felt a guilty sense of relief. It's all over and now my life will return to normal. He sat down. The notice of deportation lay on the table. He poked at it with his skinny forefinger.

'I've got to go to work,' said Richard. He made it sound like a question. He had his hands on his hips and he sounded cross.

'Go!' insisted Alex, 'I'm fine.' Richard looked at Lydia. She gave him a tiny nod and he went back to his bedroom to get dressed.

Alex listened to Richard's heavy biking boots tramp across the gangplank; he was glad that he had gone. He wished that it hadn't been Richard who had brought him under control. He bowed his head and picked at his nails. 'It's my fault Lydia.'

'Alex what are you talking about?'

'It is. You see these men came from the Home Office. They wanted to see how we lived and stuff. But every single time they asked me a question I completely fucked it up. It was awful I just couldn't seem to say anything right. I mean they asked if the shaving gear in the bathroom was mine and I told them that it was Richard's and mine was next door at Sally's. And the thing was I messed up so badly I just couldn't face telling you.' He sniffed. 'So you see it is my fault.'

He got up and knelt before her and placed his hands on her knees. He was only wearing a pair of boxer shorts and the coarse sisal carpet pressed painfully into his flesh. The coals shifted in the stove. He looked up into her face. What was she thinking? He'd never met anyone as difficult to read as Lydia. 'What are we going to do?' he asked. He laid his head on her lap and breathed in the scent of her. Her thighs, tightly contained in jeans, touched his cheeks. He began to cry in small, rhythmic, sobs. It seemed to him that he had thrown everything at Lydia and him and now they – that mysterious, cruel and faceless *They* – were trying to split them apart.

Lydia stroked his hair and after a while his sobs began to slow down. 'You can make another appeal for me,' she was saying.

He felt as if there were a cord joining his shoulder blades and it strained and ached. He was suddenly exhausted. He burrowed his face further in between her legs. 'Why can't I come with you?' he demanded angrily.

There was a silence. 'You wouldn't like . . .'

Alex's lips began to twitch into a smile.

He sat upright and clearing his hair from his face, retied it in its ponytail. 'That's it! I'm coming with you. They can't stop me doing that can they?'

'But Alex what about the audition?'

'Stuff the audition. Love's the most important thing. That's what I've always said. I'm coming and that's final.'

'What about money?' protested Lydia.

'I've got some money saved up and I've got a credit card –

I don't know how I'd pay it back but there's not much they can do about it if I'm in bloody Russia is there?'

Now that he had a plan Alex was excited. He swung into action rushing breathlessly around London making arrangements. Lydia told him about a Russian travel agent in South Kensington who booked him onto her flight and for a substantial fee got him an 'express visa'. He bought some thick winter boots from an outward-bound shop on Kensington High Street, a guidebook to Moscow and St Petersburg and a Russian dictionary and grammer book from a bookshop on the other side of the road. Then he took the tube to Sloane Square where he bought long johns, woolly socks and thermal vests from Peter Jones and then he walked up the King's Road to an Oxfam shop in the World's End where he found some gloves, a scarf, a pair of tweed trousers and an overcoat. That night he taught himself how to count and in shaky baby script he practised the Russian alphabet on any piece of paper that came to hand. He hunched over his knees at the kitchen table tracing letters and rang Steve, wedging the telephone between his ear and his shoulder. 'Yeah, it's Alex. Fine, how are you? Actually I'm going to live in Russia, that's why I'm calling. That's right, with Lydia. She's being deported so I don't really have much of a choice. You should come out and visit us. Yeah, Okay, you take care of yourself too.'

'Shit that's brave of you man,' said Steve. Alex could hear that he was impressed and slightly envious. He rang other friends and each time he got a similar reaction. The only people he didn't phone were his family. He knew that this was cowardice and every time he thought about it he felt terrible. He could see Sally through the windows of the boat but he still couldn't face her. He kept putting it off. Lydia mentioned it twice and he said he'd go around to Sally's later on but he knew that he couldn't do it. He'd leave them a letter. It was easier, and after the way they'd treated Lydia it would serve them right.

After he'd finished his phone calls he turned his attention to Lydia and while she cooked them supper he chain smoked cigarettes and bombarded her with questions. How cold will it be now? Where's your mother's flat? And you've never moved out? How much do you think I would get paid for English teaching? Was your mother born in St Petersburg too? How often do you go to Moscow? How long does it take? What shall I pack? Have you told your mother when we're arriving? So she doesn't know about me at all? How will she take it? Will I be able to use traveller's cheques? Do you think you can buy Marmite? How about English books? Teach me how to count. What's the Russian for 'hello'? How do I say 'I don't understand'?

The next morning Alex woke to the sound of Lydia rattling the grate of the coal stove. Lead waves thumped up against the side of the boat. Lydia squatted in front of the fire prodding the remaining red coals with an iron poker. When she had finished she continued to squat, rocking backwards and forwards on her heels and tapping the poker meditatively on the concrete base of the stove. She was on her own, wrapped in her own world and Alex couldn't remember ever catching her in such a private moment. It made him uncomfortable but he couldn't take his eyes away. It was like being a voyeur watching someone getting undressed. He got out of bed and coming up behind her he brushed her hair over one shoulder and gently caressed her neck. He wanted to explain again how happy he was that he was coming too and it didn't matter how many difficulties there were he would still love her but he had already said it too many times before. I'm beginning to sound like a stuck record, he told himself and he crouched down behind her and rocked gently to and fro in time with her as she tapped the poker on the concrete.

They spent the whole day preparing for their departure. Lydia folded her belongings into three old fashioned hard plastic suitcases of the kind that Alex's grandmother used to have. As she filled each case up she put it outside her bedroom. Once Sally had left for work Alex spread his belongings out across the *Beagle's* varnished floorboards and began to build piles. A pile of things to take with him, a pile of things to leave with Sally, a pile of things to take to Oxfam and a pile of things to give to Steve. Next, he packed the pile of things that he was taking with him into a large purple and black rucksack but there wasn't enough room so he had to take it all out again refold everything and divide them into two more piles: one for things that were absolutely essential and another for things that weren't quite so essential but that he would like to take if he had room.

They held a farewell party in the Water Rat in Milmans Street. Jill came with her husband Barry and so did Steve and Morris and Richard. After closing time they all crammed into the sitting room of *Toadhall* and smoked and drank whiskey until four in the morning.

When the three members of the Aliens Deportation Unit arrived from Scotland Yard at ten thirty the next day the boat reeked of stale alcohol and ash and the sitting room was filled with the sleeping bodies of Jill and Barry. Richard appeared at the top of the stairs looking very bleary, peered at them huddling on the doormat and disappeared into the loo. Alex followed him up the stairs. 'I'm her husband and I'm coming with her,' he said defiantly.

Jill lifted her head from the blankets to see what was going on. Alex didn't like seeing her with Barry. It made him feel uncomfortable knowing that she was sleeping with Richard and for some obscure reason it also made him feel guilty. He wished that they weren't there this morning of all mornings. He had more important things to think about and the fact that he felt bad about Jill's infidelity annoyed him.

'And where is your wife?' asked a red-haired policemen while his colleagues, like the Home Office officials before them, stared curiously around the boat.

Lydia came up the stairs at the same moment as Richard

tried to emerge from the loo. There were too many people and not enough room. Alex, Lydia, the two policemen and the policewoman shuffled further into the sitting room until they were virtually standing on Jill and Barry's heads. 'Can my husband travel with us to the airport?' asked Lydia. Her accent had grown much more pronounced.

The red-haired policeman looked Alex up and down and having evidently decided that he was harmless, agreed. 'Right,' he said brusquely, 'let's get this over and done with, Mrs Carmichael. A car's waiting for you on the Embankment.' Lydia put on a wool overcoat and followed the man out onto the pontoons carrying two suitcases. Alex loaded himself up with his rucksack, a bag of cameras and Lydia's portfolio. The remaining policeman and woman looked at each other briefly. The woman made a minute nod with her head and they bent down and picked up the last suitcases.

Lydia sat in the back seat of the police car between Alex and one of the policemen The rain hissed up from the wheels of the car and the wipers squeaked rhythmically across the windscreen. Occasionally the radio crackled and emitted a muffled voice. Did they enjoy their job? wondered Alex. He stared out through the rain-beaded window at the white London houses. Large placards outside the Earls Court Exhibition centre were advertising the Caravan and Outdoor Leisure Show and Olympia Show Jumping. This evening he would be in Russia and all of this would just be a memory thousands of miles away. An electric thrill of anticipation ran through him, he slipped his hand sideways into Lydia's lap and finding her hand squeezed it tightly.

Heathrow was like a market, everywhere Alex looked there was commotion and movement. Floor cleaners with buckets and barriers, airline staff in synthetic uniforms, businessmen, families and slick Europeans looking like they had been dipped in varnish milled around the rows of check in desks. Orange-and-black monitors hung from the ceiling and flickered with constantly changing information. The shops were decorated for Valentine's Day and their windows were full of red plastic hearts, roses and unhealthy-looking cherubs.

It was just before Valentine's Day when I arrived, remembered Lydia. She felt curiously detached and unemotional. She was feeling sick again. She'd grown used to it now. It reminded her that the child was real and not just something in her mind.

They stood around the trolley. 'It's time to say good bye for the moment,' said the red-haired policeman to Alex, 'your wife has to go through a separate channel.'

Lydia looked pale and distant. She hardly seemed to be aware of where she was. Alex looped his arms around her, 'Well that won't stop us will it? See you in a second darling!'

Lydia smiled wanly back and then surrounded by policemen she was escorted through an unmarked door in a white plastic wall.

When Alex boarded the plane he scanned the heads of the seated passengers for Lydia's red hair. He couldn't see her and as he stood looking a traffic jam of passengers developed in the aisle behind him. He apologised to the man beside him, squeezed into his seat and sitting up so that he could see over the backs of the chairs he scrutinised the faces as they boarded the plane. When all the passengers seemed to have boarded and Alex had a stitch from worrying, the blonde-haired policewoman came into view followed by Lydia herself. Alex waved energetically with his arm stretched up above his head as if he were trying to get attention from a teacher in class. Lydia gave a modest wave in return.

The businessman beside Alex looked up from his inflight magazine and followed the direction of Alex's gaze.

'That's my wife,' explained Alex, 'we're going to live in Russia.'

'Is she Russian?' asked the man as he did up his seat belt. Alex leant back into his seat.

'Yes,' he said nodding energetically and proudly, 'she comes from St Petersburg.'

'Right,' said the man with understanding, 'a visa marriage.'

Chapter Thirty-Three

The blonde policewoman flew all the way with Lydia. As if, thought Lydia sourly, I'm going to try and escape while we're in the air. Once the plane was airborne the woman took a wildlife magazine from a blue sports bag and read each article in turn, carefully following the print with her forefinger. The plane was full. Alex tried to change places by pleading emotionally with a steward. He blocked the aisle and braced his arms against the overhead luggage lockers. The steward was unimpressed by Alex's story. He hears it every week, thought Lydia. 'If I let you do it then everyone will want to,' he said with the patient voice that people use with children when they are asking troublesome questions. Alex rolled his eyes and returned to his seat, his rounded shoulders and dipping head telling the steward how close he was to causing a scene and how lucky the steward was that he had decided against it.

Lydia was relieved, she didn't want Alex to sit beside her, she wanted to be on her own. Her breasts were aching painfully and the smell of the air conditioning was making her feel ill. Last night, when they had eventually got to bed, Lydia had lain on her side watching Alex twitch in his dreams but she hadn't been able to close her eyes herself. How was Seriozha going to react when he found out about Alex? She'd rolled onto her back and let her eyes bore into the ceiling. Please, please, let there not be a fight. She hadn't been able to lie still, she'd turned back onto her side. The duvet had shifted and a draught had snaked under it. She'd stared at Alex's back; the coils of his hair and the skin on his shoulder stretched tightly across his bones. He was going to Russia and he was going because of her. She'd been pretending to herself that she wasn't responsible. It was his decision: he'd wanted to come. But she knew that was a lie. She may not have asked for anything from Alex but she had to answer for the things that she'd accepted. He was coming to Russia and it was, at least partly, her fault. She shifted her position again. She was pregnant with his child. She'd had two abortions. She told herself she should do the same again. How could she possibly bring up a child? Suddenly she fiercely resented Alex. She wished that he'd never offered to marry her and she'd just been deported. She didn't want to tell him about the child; that would give him one more claim over her. If she had an abortion he would never know it had existed.

It was four o'clock when they landed. Outside the dusk glowed on the snow-covered marches. A damp vicious wind flicked shards of ice into their faces from the concrete runway. Lydia and the policewoman were the first to leave the aeroplane. Their roles had changed: Lydia was now escorting the foreign policewoman in her own country. They waited on the runway in the blue bitter cold for Alex to come stumbling down the steps and then Lydia led the little party to the arrivals building where she explained the situation in Russian first to an immigration official and then to customs. Both officials were young men and they both looked at her with sympathy as she bent her head to fill in a series of forms, each one accompanied by three or four pastel-coloured carbon copies.

It's probably not sympathy, thought Lydia cynically as she signed her name in her own script for the first time in a year, it's probably lust. Lydia didn't care. She was feeling overwhelmed by her return to Russia. Weariness, relief, resignation and fear jostled for attention inside her. Her life had changed, she told herself, nobody could take her year in London away from her, but she still couldn't shake off a dreary sensation that she was being handed back her uniform and slotted back into a place that she thought she'd escaped.

It wasn't a pure emotion. Lydia's never were. Another part of her smiled with nostalgic fondness at the familiar leer of young officials, the cloying beige-coloured paint that covered the walls and the impersonal probing stares of the other Russian passengers as they passed Lydia's little group (the Europeans looked the other way). She would never have noticed these details before but now she was seeing the fine texture of Russia in a way that only someone who is returning from exile can. I'm seeing Russia through a Westerner's eyes, thought Lydia. But then she looked at Alex who was scanning the room, swivelling his head from side to side trying to absorb everything at once and she realised only a Russian would have the precision of perception she was experiencing now.

She completed the last of the forms and handed it back to the young customs official. He had a very narrow face with flyaway mouse-coloured hair and long translucent eyelashes. He blinked at her, cold and appraising. 'You can go,' he said, flicking his hand dismissively. He took no notice of either the policewoman (a person in uniform!) or Alex. It was as if they were merely Lydia's shadows, they might just as well have not existed. The immigration official had been the same, he hadn't even bothered to look at the visa that Alex had spent so much money on.

They pushed a trolley loaded with their luggage through

into the arrivals hall. Predatory taxi drivers and men with names on cardboard signs circled around them. The policewoman said an awkward and constrained goodbye. The plane was simply turning around and she would be flying back with it to London in two hours' time. She shook Lydia's hand and for one almost hallucinogenic moment Lydia thought she was going to curtsey to her. 'Good luck,' she said.

Lydia breathed in the smell of wet boots, linoleum, black tobacco and glycerine soap. She felt responsible for this rather stiff woman whose name she still didn't know. 'Will you be all right?' she asked.

The woman shook her head making her police cap wobble dangerously. 'I'll be fine,' she said, backing nervously away from Lydia. She held up the blue sports bag as proof, 'I've got my magazine.'

Lydia continued to act as tour guide. Alex found the businessman who had sat next to him on the flight. He shook Lydia's hand and said he was pleased to meet her. He said it with a knowing smirk. Lydia got the same expression from the taxi driver. They knew nothing about her or her life, how dare they judge her because she was married to an Englishman. Fuck them! That made her smile to herself. She had sworn in English, she would never swear in Russian even if it was only in her head.

She turned in her seat to face Alex who was sitting in the back with the businessman. His nose was pressed against the window. Lydia couldn't imagine what he found so interesting, all she could see in the darkness that surrounded the car were some advertising hoardings – in English – and a line of meagre-looking silver birch trees. Despite her apprehensions about Alex coming to Russia, now she found she was pleased that he was there. He was concrete proof that she had lived in London. It was only his presence that made this homecoming bearable, without him the sensation of being pushed back into her place would have been too much. How did it all appear to him? She wished she could hear his impressions. She remembered how chaotic London had seemed when she first arrived and how difficult it had been to discern a pattern. What, for instance, would Alex think of their flat? He often used to complain about the lack of space in *Toadhall*. How was he going to cope with sleeping in the sitting room surrounded by all her mother's furniture and pieces of bric-à-brac? He was going to be like that English expression about bulls in china shops: too big, too clumsy. Would her mother be back from work when they arrived at the flat? Lydia began chewing at her little fingernail. Please, please, please don't let her get hysterical. It was a lot of changes to digest all together; her daughter home unexpectedly, her daughter married and to a foreigner at that (Lydia wouldn't tell her that she was pregnant, she didn't need to know). She remembered how Alex's mother had responded and she felt a surge of sympathy for the woman.

The taxi drove through the archway into the long rectangular courtyard and stopped by the door to the staircase. Lydia looked up as she got out of the front seat. The lights were off. Her mother wasn't home yet, but it was five o'clock so it wouldn't be long. Alex and the taxi driver built a pile of luggage just inside the door. The sounds of banging saucepans and dripping water echoed around the walls. A television was playing somewhere. The taxi driver shook both their hands. He wished Alex good luck. Lydia obviously didn't need it. She was Russian.

Lydia's key didn't work, which meant that yet again Lydia's mother had changed the lock. After Lydia's father had died the locks had been changed every few months. Olga used to maintain that she could hear 'them' trying to get in during the night but Lydia hadn't heard her mother mention the phantom intruders for seven or eight years and she thought her mother had forgotten about them. They sat despondently on their suitcases outside the burgundy plastic padded door.

'Maybe there was a burglary?' Alex looked concerned. His face was all crushed up. Lydia guessed that the cold dark stairwell with its one swinging light-bulb was making him nervous. She leant on the window-sill. It was a double window but the glass in both of them was loose and cold air whistled through like breath coming through the gap in someone's teeth. There was a muddy puddle on the stone floor of the landing where the rain had got in. The courtyard was deserted apart from a line of battered cars. 'We should keep our voices down,' she said, 'if word gets around that there is a foreigner living here then we really will have a burglary.'

Chapter Thirty-Four

Lydia's mother stalled on the top step of the landing and stared at her daughter. She was wearing a small beige felt hat the shape of an upturned saucer, her brown wool winter coat and a pair of rubber-soled bootees. She was carrying a sharp-edged handbag and a string perhaps bag containing two large jars of pickled tomatoes. Nobody said anything. The only sound was the breathy whistle of wind through the cracks in the window. Men's voices passed by the bottom of the stair-case. Alex shuffled his feet and looked embarrassed.

Olga blinked, snapped open her handbag and bringing out a fistful of keys marched to the door. 'I told you that you would come back. They always do,' she said as if she were continuing a conversation with a third person. There were two doors. Olga opened them both, hung her coat on a wooden hanger, placed her hat carefully on the window-sill beside a tray of seedlings and changed from her bootees into a pair of worn, high-heeled slippers.

Lydia stood by the open door and briefly closed her eyes. Her mother had obviously decided not to forgive her for going away. Thank God they were speaking in Russian. At least that meant that Alex couldn't understand. 'Mama,' she said through the gap in the doors, 'I'd like you to meet my husband.'

Olga quivered. Her eyelashes fluttered with confusion.

'Well bring him in then,' she said in a voice close to the edge of panic and then she turned and bustled away down the narrow corridor, the heels of her slippers clacking on the grey scrubbed floorboards.

Lydia turned to Alex. 'Welcome to my home,' she said wearily. Did she really mean it? How much welcome would anyone find in the dark narrow hall lined with packing cases? The worn wallpaper and the hanging wires. Every surface scratched from scrubbing. Boxes of bottles and jars washed and ready to be returned to the shops for their deposits, piles of newspaper tied together neatly with string. The icons cut from magazines, the glass and china animals and the crockery covered with squares of old sheet to protect it from dust and cockroaches. Nothing new, nothing modern, everything mean, scrubbed and shabby.

Alex looked concerned, 'Is she all right?' Why couldn't her mother just be pleased to see her? Why did they have to go through this play act? Lydia knew in advance exactly how it was meant to go. Olga was pretending to ignore her, Lydia would now have to plead and beg forgiveness from her which Olga would eventually and graciously grant. Lydia waggled her head from side to side to express the mixed-up nature of the situation. 'She will be,' she said, 'but now she's being cross with me for going away. Let's bring the bags inside and I'll try and calm her down.'

They piled the suitcases underneath a table in the sitting room. The table was covered with a faded yellow cloth that had once been a bedspread. On top of this was a large old-fashioned formica television. Lydia crouched down and arranged their belongings so that everything was hidden from sight by the table cloth. 'The sofa folds out into a bed,' she explained, 'and that's where we'll be sleeping,' and, because she suspected what Alex's expression would be in reaction to this news and because she didn't actually want to see it, she carried on arranging her cameras.

When Lydia couldn't delay any longer she led Alex through to the kitchen and installed him by the table on a spindly metal chair. Her mother was standing with her back to the room glaring at a large metal kettle on the stove. Lydia put her hand on her mother's tense, angry back, 'Sit down Mama, I'll make the tea.'

'What language does he speak?'

'I think he speaks a little French.'

'What, no German, no Italian and obviously no Russian. So not only is he virtually a schoolboy but he's ignorant as well. So this is what kept you so long. This ridiculous boy. What does this boy of yours do? Look at him. Why does he have long hair? Does he think he's a girl or something? Seriozha's not going to like this. He's not going to like this at all. At least he's a man. He's been very kind to me you know while you've been gallivanting around the West doing whatever it was you were doing. Yes, he's been very thoughtful. Sometimes he comes to see me now. He's a busy man but sometimes he finds the time and he even brings me food from his dacha. Yes he does. He brought me pickled mushrooms the other day and they were very nice too. Very nice indeed.'

Lydia could hear the agitation building up in her mother's voice. She knew the signs, if she wasn't careful her mother would have one of her hysterical fits. She knew that Alex was looking at her but for the time being she tried to ignore him. The kettle screamed as it came to the boil. Lydia moved quickly, with one hand she turned off the gas and with the other she gripped her mother's shoulder, wheeled her around and pushed her quite violently into a chair. 'Sit down Mama!' she ordered sharply, 'now breathe.' Her mother looked at her with a face as startled as if she'd just woken up. She took a large open-mouthed gulp of air then her shoulders and her entire ribcage seemed to slump. Lydia wondered if she was going to cry. She patted her mother's shoulder, 'It's all right Mama, it's all right,' she cooed.

Olga's chin sank into the sagging folds of her neck, 'I told you that you'd come back,' she said petulantly.

Lydia carried on patting her mother's shoulder. Out of the corner of her eye she could see Alex looking confused and alarmed. He dug into his pocket for his tobacco and began rolling a cigarette. Oh God, thought Lydia, another thing to explain. 'We can't smoke in here,' she said quietly, 'why don't we take our tea out on to the landing and leave her to calm down.'

'But you said we couldn't talk on the landing.'

Lydia could hear the frustration grating through his voice. Breathe, Lydia told herself, echoing the command she had just made to her mother. 'It'll be all right if we don't speak too loudly,' she said carefully filtering her voice so that he would-n't hear how harassed she was feeling, 'I just don't want every-one to know that you're English.'

Chapter Thirty-Five

Alex had never felt so needy in his life. When Lydia moved from a room he instinctively got up. On the second evening he spent in Russia he found himself following her to the loo. It was only when she turned around and, smiling at him, gently locked the door in his face that he realised what he had done. He stared at the locked door and blushed deep red with shame before shuffling back to the sitting room in the ridiculously small slippers that they had given him (and that he knew without being told had belonged to Lydia's dead father). Today was the day of the Old Vic auditions, he'd have been coming out about now. One day soon RADA would be writing to him telling him whether they wanted him back for a second audition.

Lydia's mother sat like a toad inside the door of the sitting room and glared at him as he entered. Alex resisted the temptation to stick his tongue out at her and sat down on the sofa to watch an incomprehensible talking head on the television. His mother-in-law was a monster. It was incredible to think that she had managed to spawn such a beautiful daughter. She had two modes, either she was cold and brusque or she lost her temper. And she disapproved of Alex – she glared at him in disbelief as if he was a freak and when Lydia's back was turned she mimed cutting off his ponytail with a pair of scissors. Alex avoided her as much as he could. In the mornings he huddled into the depths of the sofa bed and only emerged when he was certain that she had left for work. In the evening it was harder but for the most part they maintained a silent truce, moving around each other like bristling dogs while Alex willed her to retreat to her narrow bedroom beyond the sitting room.

One morning a week later Alex stood in his boxer shorts by the window in the sitting room. Each window had two panes of glass. It was like double glazing except that there was a gap of about six inches between the inner and outer panes. There was no fridge in the flat and his mother-in-law kept milk and butter between the two layers of glass. Alex hated this, it made him feel padded from the outside world as if the flat was contained in a sealed vacuum. He opened the small top window to let some air in. It was hot and stuffy. Lydia had explained that all the flats were heated together and they had no control over the temperature of the radiators. Alex watched a man in a padded jacket and a fur hat trying to push his car out of the muddy snow, putting his shoulder to the back bumper; *one, two, three, heave.* He heard Lydia's light footsteps entering the room behind him.

'I'm going out to buy food,' she said.

He turned around and stretched for his jeans that lay across the back of the sofa bed. 'Wait, I'll come with you.' He despised the note of panic that he could hear in his voice.

'I'll only be standing in a queue.'

'I'm coming, all right?' he snapped. He knew that she was trying to get away from him. He knew that he was crowding her. She never said anything, she never told him that he was, but that just made him resent it even more. What the fuck was he meant to do? He couldn't help it. It wasn't his fault that he couldn't speak Russian and even the bloody alphabet was different so he couldn't take the metro because he didn't know what station to get out at. And if he did go out where was he meant to go to? Knowing his luck he'd get lost. It was asking for trouble just to wander around. Obvious target. Foreigner looking stupid. And there was this ex-lover of hers. She hadn't said anything about him but then Lydia never did say much and he wasn't stupid, he'd heard her mother mention his name.

Then there was money. Where was that going to come from? They had to get a place of their own soon or he'd go crazy. He'd kept enough for a flight home. He hadn't told her that – showed a lack of faith – but he didn't want to break into that, you never knew, something might happen. He had to get a job but how the hell did you start when you didn't speak Russian in the first place? He couldn't even read the newspaper for ads (and anyhow which newspaper, they sold hundreds outside the metro station?). Lydia said she would ask around for him. It was a typical example of how helpless he was. He couldn't do anything without Lydia. Alex buttoned up his flies and pulled his rucksack out from under the television table to find a clean pair of socks. Even the Red Army man in the photograph looked like he was in a vacuum as he stared out from inside the glass cabinet with his stern expression. You didn't smile for cameras in those days did you?

Lydia stood in the doorway. There was such an air of quietness about her. It was as if she breathed some sort of cool paralysis out from her skin. She almost smelt of stillness. Alex rootled more frantically in his rucksack. He scrabbled through the clothes with his nails like a dog digging in the dust, pulling out the bigger items and flinging them on the floor. What was he looking for? Socks. She must be getting impatient. He knew that but the truth of it was that although he'd insisted that he did, he didn't *actually* want to go out. He just didn't want to stay in the flat without her. It was shaming how scared he was of the city. He was an adult for God's sake. Scared of the flat, scared of the street. It was only Lydia who made one better than the other.

The staircase was like a cave. Alex didn't like touching the sides because he imagined they'd be slimy. He made himself do it once and there was nothing odd about them at all, just normal plaster and gloss paint but even after his experiment he couldn't rid himself of the impression that there was something oozing from the walls. The pavements were coated with thick, bumpy and treacherous ice. After a few painful falls Alex had learnt to walk as if he were skiing: sliding each foot along the ice and only picking them up when he changed direction.

Lydia showed him around the area. They came through the arch to a canal which was covered with ice and disconsolate waddling ducks. On the other side of the canal was a dollar bar called the Seagull. As Lydia was pointing it out to him a navy-blue Mercedes drew up outside and two men in felt hats and overcoats like men from spy films got out of the car and disappeared down the steps. Alex asked Lydia whether they were mafia. He'd heard that St Petersburg was a gangster city, apparently the murder rate was soaring. Lydia said they were probably Westerners. At one end of the canal was a big church. Lydia told him it was built on the spot where one of the Tsars was assassinated. It erupted into the sky in a conglomeration of carved and painted snow-shaded onion domes. It was the only building that he'd seen that was typically Russian. This was the Russia of Alex's imagination, he'd expected hundreds of buildings like this: huge, bulbous and fantastical, glowering over the white Russian steppes. Lydia laughed when he said this. 'You've been reading too many books. That's like Russian schoolchildren thinking that London is a foggy city because they've all been taught Dickens. We're a long way from the steppe. Anyhow St Petersburg's not Russian. It's St Petersburg. It's different.'

Beside the church there was a little park where a prostitute stood dressed like a woman from one of Sally's aerobics videos with a short quilted jacket, a tiny leotard and thick, shiny, tan tights. In the opposite direction was Nevsky Prospect. Lydia pointed out the General Post Office. 'You can make international phone calls there. If you want to,' she said.

Alex pressed his lips together. 'Another day,' and they pushed on through the crowds of people shoving and spilling out into the road on and off the trolley buses or stopping to look at the books and cigarettes and newspapers and bad paintings from flimsy trestle-table stalls that lined the walls. Buffeted constantly by bodies padded with thick winter coats, Alex became convinced that people were knocking into him on purpose. It was the same in shops. They pressed up against him in the queues and Alex tightened his fist around his money, clutching it deep in his coat pocket and looking around him for the reassurance of Lydia's flame-red hair.

235

She slipped out of the door one day with her mother so that when Alex got up he discovered he was alone in the flat. He was furious. She'd obviously gone to see her lover. If it was anything else she would have told him where she was going. The old rotting images of Lydia having sex with Richard slithered back into his mind. What was this man, Seriozha, like? Alex already knew that he was older. He'd been her boss. The thought made him squirm. He was probably rich as well. He imagined a fight like they used to have at school, with a circle of boys cheering. Alex would humiliate him. Smash his face in and then let him limp off to hide. And the boys would cheer and cheer and cheer and lift him up on to their shoulders. Stop it Alex. Stop it now. Stop fantasising. Live in the real world. For once. Lydia can do what she likes, it's her own life and there's nothing you can do about it.

All morning he prowled the perimeters of the flat and brooded. It was his own fault. He'd been the one who'd insisted on coming to Russia. He tried to remember whether she'd even suggested it. But no she hadn't, it had all been his doing. He shook the windows as if they were bars. And over and over again he wondered, and tried not to think about it, and wondered again whether he had got a second audition. However much he turned his back on it, the suggestion, the idea, the question kept peeking out from behind his thoughts. And that, fuck it, wasn't her fault either. He could remember that, he could remember her asking him about the audition exactly. It was like a knifeblade of a memory. He could hear her accent, see the kitchen in the boat, the smell of the stove, the grain of the late afternoon light. He'd told her that it didn't matter, he'd said that she was more important to him. He sighed and continuing his perimeter patrol reached the hallway and sat down on the chair by the tray of seedlings inside the front door and willed it to open, willed her to be behind it with her key poised on the lock. He hated himself for being so reliant on her. That was her fault, that really was, no one else was to blame there. He wouldn't have gone the whole way across Europe to this gloomy watery city for anyone else but Lydia.

By eleven o'clock he had managed to rationalise it all. It was simple and understandable. The reason he was so angry with her leaving the flat in such an underhand way was that he was worried about her. He didn't know when to expect her back. What if something happened? He wouldn't be able to help her, he wouldn't know where she was. His conscience disagreed. He wasn't afraid of what would happen to Lydia. He couldn't imagine a situation in which she wouldn't know exactly what to do. He wasn't afraid for Lydia, he was jealous. But Alex managed to ignore his conscience and continue to tell himself that he was worried, that it was stupid and danger-ous of her and he'd tell her when she eventually got back (and when was that going to be?). He rehearsed it to the photo of the man in Red Army uniform. He'd be concerned and indig-nant and really quite cross. He would make sure that he didn't lose control but he would point out quite firmly, in strong language if he needed to, how thoughtless she'd been and that because he loved her he'd been worried.

She came back after lunch. He was sitting on the sofa

guiltily trying to summon the courage to call his mother and Sally and let them know that he was all right. They'd be furious, rightly so, he wouldn't blame them if they never forgave him. Just leaving a letter like that had been cowardly and cruel. If only he'd faced them. Why hadn't he realised how they would feel? The longer he left it now the harder it became. Then he heard Lydia's key in the door. He heard it immediately even though he thought (he'd told himself) that he'd given up listening. He hurried up the hallway fuelled with indignation. There was no excuse for sneaking off like that. If there was nothing between her and Seriozha she would have told him. Then there was Lydia, framed by the doorway, glowing with news. He could see it beaming from the cold flush of pink on her cheekbones.

'Could you teach English?' she asked as she hung up her coat, fastening the buttons so that it wouldn't slip off the hanger. A job! The reason for the question was so obvious that he couldn't be cross, he was denied the opportunity and that made him feel a fool. Slipping her feet into little slippers she bustled and tapped into the kitchen with Alex lumbering after her. She filled the kettle from the tap. 'I've been to see a language school on Vasilievsky Island. All the classes are in the evenings, but they say they're looking for teachers and they pay in dollars!'

Chapter Thirty-Six

Lingva Language School was in the back of a courtyard on the Seventh Line one block away from the metro station. The setting sun still soused the top floors of the surrounding buildings but in the bottom of the courtyard it was dusk. Alex, with Lydia walking briskly in front of him, entered the courtyard under an arch. The buildings to the right were caged in scaffolding and all around them were planks, piles of bricks and building equipment, wearing a skull-cap of crystalline snow. The round eye of a cement mixer watched Lydia lead Alex through a doorway in the far right-hand corner. Somebody had written the word 'office' in felt-tip pen on a new chipboard panel and underneath it drawn an arrow. Lydia pointed up the stairs, 'It's up there. Will you be all right?'

'I'll just be myself.'

'I didn't mean the interview. I meant getting back.'

'I think so. One stop on the green line. As long as I can get to Nevsky Prospect I'll be all right. I can recognise the way from there.'

'Good luck,' she said and she kissed him gently on the nose and turned back into the courtyard.

Alex started up the staircase on his own. Dark green floral wallpaper peeled from the old walls and in many places floorboards were missing, exposing pipes that lay in thick beds of mouse-grey dust. Now that Lydia had gone he suddenly felt very nervous. He climbed the steps two at a time and in his head ran through what he would say to them and how he would explain that he'd never taught English before. In the office a harried woman with a face scrubbed clean of make-up sat at a small school desk piled high with bundles of paper tied in elastic bands. Alex hesitated at the doorway. She was on the telephone but she acknowledged him and, still talking to the person on the other end of the line, pointed down the corridor. Alex didn't understand. She covered the mouthpiece of the receiver with her hand. 'Your class is in the room at the end of the corridor.'

Alex gulped. She was obviously mistaking him for somebody else. 'I'm Alex Carmichael. I've come for an interview.'

The woman looked exasperated, 'No, you're teaching. Go to the end and turn right. They're waiting for you,' she said impatiently before returning to her phone call.

Six people sat around an oval table in a room with orange paisley wallpaper, a naked light bulb and a blackboard with no chalk or rubber. They all turned to look at him as he walked through the door. They'd obviously been waiting for him for quite some time. It was like walking onto a stage. He felt slightly sick, he could feel himself sweating. It was the suddenness of it that was the worst thing. He'd had no time to prepare himself. There was a middle-aged man opposite him next to a plump blonde girl. He took a deep breath. 'Hello,' he said, 'I'm your new teacher and my name is Alex.' They looked at him with their mouths open like fish. Nobody said anything. 'I'm from Dorset which is in the south west of England and I want to be an actor. What do you all do?' Still nobody said anything. The light faltered and the large green-painted metal pipes that ran along the wainscot rattled loudly. Alex could hear the muffled voice of a teacher in a room nearby. Still there was silence. The students all looked at their hands and shuffled their notebooks on the table. Anything rather than face Alex. It was awful, like acting to an empty room. Alex recognised the symptoms. There'd been a visiting preacher who'd come to the village church when Alex was thirteen. The preacher had tried to get them to clap and join in but the Dorset congregation, not used to audience participation, had sat stolidly in a humiliated silence. Alex remembered seething with embarrassment. He'd elbowed Sally and hissed at her to do something, wishing that someone would start but knowing that he didn't have the courage himself.

The blonde girl reminded him of Sally. They'd be about the same age and she had the same capable air of bustling bossiness. She'd bought a new notebook for the lesson and written her name on the cover. It sat square on the table in front of her with a pen positioned carefully along its top edge. There was a spare chair next to her. Alex put out his hand to shake hers. 'What is your name?' he asked.

'My name is Irina,' she said blushing.

'What is the name of the man next door to you?'

She looked at him indignantly. Just like Sally would have done. 'I do not know him,' she said.

'Ask – in English.'

She sniffed and turned in her seat, 'Excuse me, what is your name please?'

The man's name was Sergei. Alex shook his hand and got him to ask his neighbour's name and so it went on. There were two students, a businessman and a waiter. Sergei was an engineer and Irina was a doctor. You'd probably get the same mixture in an evening class in London, thought Alex, and he found it comforting to think that people who'd lived such different lives from him should be in some way familiar.

After the first hour he taught two more lessons. It was just past nine o'clock in the evening when he finished. The harried woman was still in the office. A plate with a bright pink cake on it was balanced on a file in front of her.

'No problems?' she asked, chasing a piece of cake with a fork.

'Well I've never taught before so the first lesson was fairly scary but I think I did okay.'

'Good. And you can come back tomorrow. These courses are for six weeks.'

'Ye—ye-es' stuttered Alex.

'We pay you $7 per lesson.'

'Brilliant.'

The woman smiled. 'You want cake.' Alex grinned and loping across the room took a corner off the cake which tasted as if it had been flavoured with boiled sweets. He left the building whistling.

The sky was clear and it was very dark outside. The street lights left dim thumbprints of light on the pavement. Around the metro station a string of light bulbs lit up a row of stalls hooded with tarpaulin. The temperature was dropping fast. The air was as hard as sandpaper against his tongue and a cutting wind looped around his neck and flapped loudly under the covers of the stalls. Alex hurried up the stairs into the hot sour fug of the Metro station. He was exhilarated. He managed it. He'd taught three lessons. Just like that. And now he was taking the metro back to the flat on his own. He was triumphant. He'd conquered some of his dependency on Lydia.

He pushed his token into the barrier and let the escalator take him down to the gilt and marble platform while in his mind he replayed the lessons. Teaching had been like acting but he'd had to involve himself with his audience more than he'd ever done on stage. He'd had to think who he was talking to and change his performance because of them. He remembered how at the RADA audition he'd felt like he was disappearing into himself as if he were acting in his own world. That's what a lot of my life's been like, he thought, acting in my own world and not interacting with the people around me. He remembered his mother's illness: I was off on my own fantasy number even then, he thought shamefacedly. I was playing the perfect, self-sacrificing child, the ideal nurse and I've been doing the prodigal son ever since.

He got out at Gostinny Dvor station and emerged from the exit onto Nevsky Prospect exactly opposite the General Post Office. He stood leaning against the wind with his eyes watering and the late-night pedestrians swirling around him. The lights were on so it must still be open. Come on Alex, he said to himself, you'd better get this over and done with, the longer you leave it the worse it will get. He folded his arms across his chest, squeezing his hands under his armpits to keep them warm, and dashed across the road to the post office. He had to wait for half an hour and then the huge toad of a woman from the International Calls desk directed him to a wooden booth that smelt of farts and overbreathed air and reminded him strongly of the phone box at school.

He was only allowed one phone call so he rang his mother. She wasn't in. That seemed very cruel after he had summoned the courage to call her. He wanted very badly to talk to her, to hear what she'd been doing, to know what the weather had been like and what was growing in the garden. He listened to her voice on the answer phone message compressing his face so that he wouldn't cry.

'Mum. It's me Alex. I'm ringing from St Petersburg. I just want you to know that I'm fine. Everything's okay. In fact you would have been proud of me today because I got a job as an English teacher. I'll write you a letter tomorrow. When I've got some money together I'll come home for a bit of a holiday. I miss you. I love you lots.' He moved to put the phone down but then brought it back to his ear and added hurriedly, 'Mum, I want to say how sorry I am that I just left you a letter and I didn't talk to you before I left. I think I was frightened that you'd be furious. You would have been but I'm sorry all the same. I'll ring you again soon. I hope you're still well and everything's okay. I can't think what else to say Mum, send love to Sally, I'll ring you.'

Chapter Thirty-Seven

Every evening after they had eaten a silent strained meal with Olga, Lydia and Alex retreated to the landing to smoke cigarettes. 'I bumped into Andrei today,' said Lydia one night as she touched the flame of the lighter to the end of her cigarette. 'He works at Lenfilm. He was standing on the bridge over the Fontanka. I didn't see him. I almost walked straight into him. He's having a party on Saturday and he's invited us to come.' She was looking out of the window. Her white reflection stared at him from the dark glass.

'You were seeing Seriozha.'

'I wasn't. I was walking up Nevsky.'

He grabbed her by the shoulders and turned her around. She was so small, it was disturbingly easy to do. He tried to look into her eyes. Someone had once told him that you couldn't lie while a person stared into your eyes. She stared back at him, unblinking, her pupils wide and unfocused. It was like looking into two pieces of topaz. And the longer he stared at them the more inorganic they seemed. How could he believe her? How could he know for sure? Sometimes he found her face as unreadable as a stranger's in the street.

He broke the gaze and walked to the other side of the landing. He was being stupid. She was another human being, separate from him, he couldn't control her. Besides it would be good to meet other people, healthy for them to get out. 'What sort of people are they?' he asked turning back again and watching her face while she thought how to answer his question. 'I was beginning to think that you didn't have any mates at all,' he added. He meant it as a joke but the words came out sharp-edged and heavy.

Lydia didn't seem to notice. 'It's true,' she said easily, 'I don't have many friends.' Alex was cross with himself for letting the comment slip out in that way. Anybody else would have been hurt but Lydia was so casual about it. Her reaction unnerved him. Nobody admitted that they didn't have many friends, that was tantamount to saying you were a social failure but Lydia made it sound no more significant than the fact that she was wearing a blue jumper.

'It's snowing,' she said. Alex brushed aside his thoughts and hurried over to the window. He leant on the sill beside her and watched the flakes floating like ash through the dark sky. They sauntered in what seemed like slow motion past the window, in no hurry at all to get to the ground, just slowly spiralling down through space. A puff of wind shunted them sideways until they were moving horizontally and then the gust died away and the snowflakes slowly twisted towards the ground again. Alex looked down. The courtyard below was lost in the black shadows of the buildings.

The party was by the port on Vasilievsky Island. Leaving the warm stink of the metro behind them they picked their way across a large area of wasteland. Alex could see the cranes of the harbour like huge mechanical animals sticking up into the grey sky to the left of them. On the remaining three sides the wasteland was surrounded by squat, dirty-yellow-coloured blocks of flats. The new fall of snow clothed and padded the rubble landscape. Twice Alex put his foot down on what appeared to be solid ground and found it rocking dangerously underneath him. Men and women were spattered across the scene. At their feet lay plastic sheets bearing small piles of potatoes, second-hand tools or engine parts. Others stood with no obvious purpose, black marks on the white snow, breathing clouds of steam, stamping their feet and flapping their arms against their coats. They came to life only when someone approached them or passed close by and then they would thrust mittened fists gripping vodka bottles or packets of cigarettes out into the air with their arms straight. Alex stood to one side as Lydia bargained for two bottles of vodka from a purple-faced old man on the edge of the wasteland and then he followed her, kicking through the salted orange-and-grey sludge on the road to the flats.

Alex stood in the doorway as Lydia's friends fluttered and pecked and squawked around her. Eventually she extended her arm behind her and said his name and something which he presumed was 'and this is my husband'. They looked at him with polite interest. Six or seven faces crammed into a tiny hallway. Was Seriozha one of them? A man said 'Pleased to meet you' in English, the upturned faces nodded and a woman tried to echo the man's words in an accent so thick that it was incomprehensible. Lydia and he were stripped of their coats, provided with slippers and ushered into the main room. Two large curtainless windows looked out over the docks and the steel-coloured lustred sea that was swallowing the winter sun. A small plastic chandelier dangled like a tassel from the centre of the ceiling giving out a sharp bright light that cut the shadows into solid slices. A table covered with a white cloth and bottles, plates, dishes of food and glasses filled most of the room. The wallpaper was patterned with silver ferns and along one wall there was a bookcase. Alex noticed four James Bond books amongst the hardbacked Russian titles. Next to the bookcase was a glass cabinet.

Andrei was a small dark-haired man with red-shaded cheekbones. He pointed to the benches, 'Sit, sit!' he said and then taking a shot glass and a tumbler from the cabinet he filled one with fruit juice and the other with vodka. The rest of the party piled in, shuffling up the two benches, jostling elbows as they came and splashing vodka from the cluster of bottles in the centre of the table into their glasses. Andrei stared at the cornice and composed his face into a faraway and mystic expression. 'Welcome to Russia!' he cried and swinging back his arm in a triumphal arc he downed the glass of vodka in one.

There was a pause. Everybody's eyes were on Alex. He understood what they wanted but he hesitated. The thought of vodka made him heave. He'd avoided it since being sick after drinking too much of it with Jasper one night at university. Lydia was on the other side of the table to him. 'They want you to drink,' she said in her cool, clear voice. Shit, he wasn't going to let her down, he could down vodka, of course he could. He took a breath and keeping his eyes on her gulped the vodka and then they all cheered and laughed and thumped the table while he choked and spluttered on the neat alcohol jagging in his throat.

Andrei's wife was called Sonya. She had dark square-cut hair and olivey skin. Lydia had told him that she was an eye specialist for a German clinic. She leant across the table and piled rollmop herrings and pickled beetroot onto a plate for him as if he were a child. Everybody was speaking. The language washed around Alex like the sound of water. He looked around the table and tried to fix the faces of the guests in his mind. What else could you do when you couldn't talk to anybody? There was an elegant intellectual-looking lady at the end of the table with long grey hair swept up on top of her head. Lydia was sitting opposite him between a man with short grey hair that stuck straight up like the bristles of a shaving brush and a man with round brown eyes and hair that although greying was cut as if he were a ten-year-old schoolboy. Alex reckoned he was attached to the large bleached blonde at the end of the table.

The woman next to Alex wore a powerful vanillary scent and a lot of make-up. Her hair was bleached and hairsprayed to flick up at the ends like a child's drawing of a woman's hair. Alex decided that when she was young she was probably quite attractive but she was looking rather worn now. She didn't take any notice of Alex at first. Instead she stared fixedly across the table at Lydia in a way that made Alex uneasy. A blonde-haired little girl ran into the room wearing a glittery ersatz sailor suit and earrings made of looped gold chains. She tugged at the sleeve of the woman's crocheted jumper and squeaked something in a demanding petulant voice. The woman ignored the little girl and carried on staring at Lydia. Without looking she stretched for and found a vodka bottle and filled up her glass. The little girl tugged again and repeated her demand. Alex noticed that the woman's mascara had smeared under her left eye. There was something sad about the woman. Alex wished that he could talk to her and make her feel better. The girl tugged at her mother for a third time and this time she responded and in a bored brush-off voice she sent the girl around the table to the man with hair cut like a shaving brush who with his large slightly purple face somehow reminded Alex of a badger.

'So you married her?' drawled the woman. In English. Alex was taken by surprise. He hadn't realised that she spoke English. It took him a moment to respond. It was dusk outside. The sea had turned black and the sky was darkening fast. In the port floodlights shone on the long necks of the cranes and across the blank concrete docks. The wasteland that they had walked across earlier was disappearing and now only the metro station marked with a glowing blue M was clear.

'Do you mean Lydia?' he said smiling at the woman affably. He was glad that she spoke English. Now there was somebody else that he could talk to.

She turned her head to face him and leant it on her hands as if it was too heavy to hold upright. She nodded without removing her head from its resting place. 'You married her?' she repeated.

'Yes,' he said, remembering to speak clearly and slowly so that she would understand what he was saying, 'I'm her husband.'

'Yes,' she said echoing him, 'and he's my husband.'

The repetition confused him. He wished that he was sitting with Lydia so that she could translate for him and tell him what was happening. Through the open weave of the woman's jumper he could clearly see her black lacy bra and the cut of her cleavage. Her accent was strong but it didn't mask the desolation in her voice. Alex regretted being so friendly to her. He wished he could get away but the table was pushed right up against the window and he was stuck. He shook his head. 'I'm sorry but I don't understand.'

She repeated the trick of blindly stretching for the vodka bottle and this time she filled up his glass as well as her own. She sipped without taking her eyes from his face. In spite of all her make-up there was a feeling of nakedness about this woman. She was thrusting the pain of her life in Alex's face and he couldn't avoid it. Alex began to feel slightly panicky. Something had decomposed inside her. This is what you became when you craved love, when you begged for it even from someone who despised you. He saw their reflection in the window: she was bending so close to his ear that she appeared to be sucking liquid from it. She wanted something from Alex but he didn't know what it was. She hesitated for a moment and then looked down at her glass. Alex felt a thin sweat of relief prickle across his forehead.

'You don't know,' she sighed and looked up again. 'My husband and your wife are lovers. Is that clear enough for you?' His vision darkened as if someone had pressed their thumbs into his eyeballs. *That* was Seriozha. The badger-faced man was listening carefully to something his daughter was saying. Lydia had her back to him. She was talking to the man on the other side of her. Seriozha was old. There was an air of power about him, of coercion. One of his hands was resting on the table. It was large and heavy and Alex could see the thick black hairs growing along the backs of his fingers. The idea was revolting. He couldn't imagine it. He didn't want to imagine it. 'He was her boss at Lenfilm,' hissed the woman in his ear. He could smell the vodka from her mouth and the cloying scent of her cosmetics.

'I know,' he said very quietly. He looked at his glass. He'd emptied it without realising it.

'Don't worry, she wasn't trying to improve her position at work. That would be too sordid for her. He's an attractive man. Maybe you don't think so but I'll tell you that he is and many women have thought so but not her. No, that wasn't the reason. For a long time I couldn't understand it. It was a mystery to me what she saw in him. And then I realised that she didn't, he meant nothing to her, she didn't care, it meant nothing to her at all. That's why she let it happen. Have you discovered yet that your wife doesn't have a heart?'

Alex turned away from the woman. He didn't want to hear any more. He picked up his fork and speared a potato on the edge of his plate. Then he felt a hand on his crotch expertly pressing and curling around the base of his zip and his (to his huge shame) stiffening cock. His head sprang up and he looked at the woman with his eyes wide apart and wary. Her lipstick had creased into a little red worm in the corner of her mouth.

Her lips slinked into a smile that bordered on a gloat. 'Have you discovered that about her yet?' she asked again.

'I've got to go,' said Alex in panic, an angry blush fast rising up his neck and getting up abruptly he pushed out past her and searched the tiny hallway until he found the loo. He stood inside leaning on the door and refused to touch his traitorous cock until it had completely deflated. No, no, no, he said to himself, I'm not going to. Then he had a pee and after washing his face in the sink returned to the sitting room and sat down next to Andrei.

'Hello,' he said in a bright, false conversational mode. 'All this food is incredible, thank you very much for inviting me.'

Chapter Thirty-Eight

The day after the party was not a good day. Everyone was in a bad mood. Lydia was feeling particularly withdrawn and lethargic. The child growing inside her seemed to be sucking her energy and diverting it away from her mother and Alex. Olga was in a scrubbing mood. The flat was perfectly clean but Olga was taking revenge on them for coming back so late after the party and waking her up. She inched slowly and reproachfully up the corridor on an orange plastic knee rest, banging at the wainscot with a scrubbing brush that she fuelled from a block of yellow soap and water from a metal bucket. Whenever she saw Lydia she shot her a martyred look and then bowed her head and scrubbed furiously. Alex meanwhile cowered on the sofa with a terrible hangover and got Lydia to tell him again and again and again that Andrei and Sonya had not *really* minded him being sick over their bathroom door.

In the afternoon they escaped the flat and went for a walk around the back of Gostinny Dvor towards Ploschad Mira. The moment they were away from the crowds on Nevsky Alex started questioning her. 'What did Seriozha say to you?'

'Nothing.'

'I don't believe you.'

'Don't be paranoid. He wouldn't say anything in front of his wife and daughter would he?'

Alex gripped her arm tightly, his fingernails digging deeply into the soft veins and flesh of the crook of her elbow. 'Don't lie to me Lydia,' he shouted, his voice clanging against the buildings and the iced-over canal. A couple crossing the Lion Bridge turned to look at them. Lydia put her hand on her stomach; the child probably had a head by now. She, on the other hand, had lost weight, she could see her ribs and her hips pushed against her skin in two knobs of bone.

She heard Seriozha's voice in her ears. 'So? We're quits,' he'd said, 'we're both married now, but look at them? They're losers, nothing has to change, people like that don't matter.' Then his wife had come in and told them with a leer that Alex was being ill in the bathroom. Seriozha had offered to give them both a lift in his new car. Lydia had refused. He'd helped her into her overcoat. 'You owe me money,' he'd growled. She'd pushed her right hand into the arm of the coat, intensely aware of the bulk of him looming over her. 'I'll pay it,' she'd said tremulously. He was threatening her and she knew it. As she'd tried to do up the buttons of her coat she could feel her fingers fluttering with fear. She'd turned her back on him and said goodbye to Andrei and Sonya and dragged Alex into the metal lift. Once inside the graffitied metal box she'd slipped her hand over her stomach again. The gesture was becoming a nervous habit.

Lydia stopped walking and smoothed a semi-circle of snow with her foot. 'I'm not lying Alex, Seriozha said nothing. He asked me if he could see me and I said no and then he asked if you were really my husband and I said yes and then he asked me for the money that he gave me and I said that I would repay him. That was the entire conversation.'

'And what did he say to that?'

'He didn't have a chance. We were interrupted by his wife coming to tell us that you were being sick.'

'At least something good came out of it,' he muttered sulkily.

The following day she rang Andrei to thank him and to arrange to see a flat that he'd talked about. Alex was standing in the sitting room with his nose pressed against the window and she knew that when he moved away there would be a little greasy smudge on the glass. There was a line of them, at exactly the same height across all the windows in the flat. Outside it was snowing hard. The flakes obscured the court-yard like grain on an old photograph. Alex's back silhouetted against the dreary white sky. On the table were some lesson plans that he'd been working on. He'd become terribly restless. He found it hard to stay still for longer than a few minutes and he didn't sleep at nights. Lydia felt him beside her twisting and turning, trying to find a comfortable position, trying to get easy, trying to dissolve into uncon-sciousness. Alex, who used to sleep like a baby.

She'd done nothing about the baby: she hadn't told anyone and she hadn't organised an abortion. She couldn't yet bring herself to tell either Alex or her mother. She felt very calm and fatalistic, as if she were in a trance.

'Andrei's going to show us around a flat that's for rent. He told me about it at the party. I said we'd meet him there at twelve,' she told him. Alex covered his face with his hands. He was acting again, she thought crossly. This wasn't real emotion, it was sham. 'I can't face him,' groaned Alex, 'I won't be able to look at him.'

Lydia tried hard not to be irritated. It's pure egotism to make so much of it, she thought, as if the whole party had been about him when it hadn't, not at all. Alex vomiting on the bathroom door had seemed a minor event at the time. Minor, she thought guiltily, because you were so conscious of Seriozha.

The flat was on Vasilievsky Ostrov, on the Fifth Line

between the Neva and Bolshoi Prospect opposite the covered market. It was still snowing very heavily. All the normal street sounds were muffled and warped by the snow. On the other side of the street a caravan was selling beer. A queue of old men stood beside it, all clutching their glass jars ready to be filled while the snow settled on their hats and their shoulders. Lydia looked up at the number on the enamel plate above a set of double wooden doors large enough to drive a truck through. The ground floor had once been a German chemists and the cracked yellow plaster on the outside of the building still bore the legend 'Schmidt u. so. Apotheke' in Latin script. Snowflakes settled on her face and spotted her vision with fuzzy grey patches. At that point a smaller door cut out of the right hand side of the big one opened and Andrei poked his head out into the street like a mouse.

'Andrei,' gushed Alex floundering in apologies, 'I'm really, really, sorry for what happened the other night. I'm so embarrassed about it I almost didn't come today, I didn't know how I would be able to face you.'

Andrei looked startled and twitched his nose. Lydia smiled to herself, he wasn't used to onslaughts of this kind. A snowflake fell on his nose and he twitched it again, 'Maybe some of the vodka was bad,' he said kindly.

The flat was on the sixth floor and they reached it by an old-fashioned clanking cage lift. Andrei opened the door and Lydia stepped over a raised threshold into a dark corridor that smelt of yeast and dust and old newspapers. A faded red velvet curtain hung across the corridor on a brass rail which squeaked when Andrei drew it to one side. Because it was the attic the door was short and one corner of it had been cut off to accommodate the slope of the roof. Alex had to stoop and dip his head to get through it. His big feet echoed on the floorboards.

'Wow!' she heard him breathe and she smiled because although she hadn't said anything that was what she felt too.

The flat was built around an L-shaped corner of the

block. The foot was occupied by a loo and a small kitchen and a long narrow living room made up the stem.

'There's a public bath on the next block, but you've got to look at the view,' said Andrei, his feet stamping up clouds of dust as he bustled from one part of the flat to another, nervous with the responsibility of the deal. I wonder what he's going to get from this, thought Lydia as she followed him into the kitchen and peered through the window at Nikolsky church, painted fresh pink and white and veiled by trees. On the street below a woman in a red overcoat manoeuvred a pram over the tram rails. Maybe that's me in the future, she thought.

The snow mesmerised her. She looked down through the spiralling flakes. When she was twelve her grandfather had given her a kaleidoscope for Woman's Day. It had been her favourite toy. She'd spent hours with her eye pressed against the hole bewitched by the changing shapes and colours. She'd named it 'Nadia' after a famous gymnast and she'd sewn a little bag for it with a shoulder strap so that she could carry it around with her. At mealtimes she used to lay it on the table to the right of her plate and quite often she would go to bed with both hands curled around the cardboard tube as if it were a telescope.

This is a spy's flat, thought Lydia, living here would be like being a bird watching the animals on the plain below, so far away they're like ants. Lydia wished that she could be there the following day so that she could see if the woman in the red coat crossed the road at the same time. It suddenly seemed very important. Was the woman crossing the road for a particular reason? Had something happened to make her go out in this weather or was it simply her daily habit and the snow didn't matter to her? And the child? Was it a boy or a girl? Was it asleep or was it the child's crying that had driven the woman out of doors?

She moved away and drifted into the main room. Here she could see out on either side of the building. One window looked onto the market and the old men queuing outside the beer stall and on the other side there was a vista of black-and-white roofs like a jumble of cards spread out towards the distant spider-web thin cranes of the port.

'Look at that!' exclaimed Alex and Lydia jumped because she had been so absorbed in her fantasies of watching the outside world like a princess from her room in a tower that she'd forgotten about Alex and his voice, in English, startled her. She was irritated. Earlier she had been pleased that he liked the flat, but now it was different. She was possessive about it. She liked the taste of the smell when she opened her mouth. It was quiet and contemplative. The light's different, she thought, it would be like living in an aquarium. Dirty windows, she teased herself, or maybe it's so high that the air's grown thin with altitude. Alex would've been dashing about and gushing and saying 'Wow!' whatever the flat looked like, thought Lydia. He wants to please Andrei, he wants him to like him, he'll do anything. She watched the two men circling the flat fastening on one good feature after another. The sloping ceiling was romantic, the main room was 'really enormous' and it was so nice not to have furniture because it meant you had so much space.

Lydia looked out of the window. Down on the street the beer stall had run out. The tail of the queue curled around into a tight black cluster. After a minute a large man in a white apron appeared from the back of the stall. The cluster converged on him. He threw up his hands and one little black coat separated out from the knot and moved away heading in the direction of the river. The man took off his white apron and walked towards the metro and after he had gone the remainder of the cluster dispersed.

Lydia straightened up. 'Who does it belong to?' she asked.

Andrei turned around to Lydia grinning. He thinks he's already rented it out to us, thought Lydia. 'It's a colleague of Sonya's. They've erm, gone to Israel. If you see what I mean. You would pay rent to his parents.'

'How much?'

'It's really good value when you consider how close to the centre you are. In fact it's amazing, it's only $150 a month.'

A despondent weight dropped through Lydia passing from her head through her chest to her stomach. She drew the figures 1, 5, 0 with her finger in the dust on the windowsill. Where would she find $150 a month? She could do translation, she could teach English as well, Alex's school paid dollars.

'Lydia,' said Andrei patiently, 'you'd be very lucky to find something cheaper than this.'

'Even with no bathroom and no furniture?'

'Some people are paying thousands of dollars a month.'

'What if their son comes back?'

'Why would he come back from Israel to Russia?'

Chapter Thirty-Nine

Alex went off to his lessons and Lydia took the metro home. As she walked up the staircase she thought about the flat. In the summer it would catch the breeze. You might even be able to get out onto the roof. She imagined her child crawling across the floorboards through squares of sunshine. She was so absorbed in her dreams that she didn't immediately notice Seriozha standing by the window but even when she did she pretended that she hadn't. It was as if he were a bad part of her dream and if she turned her back on him she might be able to edit him out. She inserted her key into the lock.

'Are you trying to ignore me?' he demanded, taking a step closer to her.

She kept her back to him. 'I said I didn't want to see you,' she said quietly.

'What about me? What about what I want?' He gripped her wrist. Her fingers still held the key in the lock. 'I'd like a cup of tea,' he said in a deep bullying voice. She could feel his breath on her neck. She nodded in acquiescence and she opened the door without looking at him or saying a word. They took their coats off in silence, Lydia took off her boots and put on slippers. It was quarter to five. Lydia calculated that her mother would arrive back from work in half an hour at the least but if she stopped to do any shopping it would be longer.

In silence she led him through to the kitchen and Seriozha sat down heavily on a chair at the table. Lydia, with her head still demurely bent, filled the kettle. When she looked up she saw the two glistening tracks running down Seriosha reddened face. His eyelids were sagging with tears. Lydia had been bracing herself for violence but she was totally unprepared for tears. She stood looking at him with the tap running and the kettle in her hand. He thumped the table with his big fist and her mother's sheet-covered crockery chattered nervously.

'You said you loved me,' he choked. Lydia felt guilty and base, she turned the tap off and lit a match for the stove. 'Well?' he demanded his voice sticky with phlegm and tears. She put the flame to the gas and turned to face him.

'I did then,' she said. His wet slippery eyes held on to her face pleading with her to give him some sign of hope. 'Sometimes feelings change,' she added cautiously. Looking at him like a large and dishevelled lion weeping at her mother's kitchen table, she believed her lie. I did love him, she thought, but I took his feelings too lightly and I have treated him badly, I should have told him about all this a long time ago. Tentatively, she laid her hand on his huge shoulders to comfort him.

He roared and threw up his head. With his eyes blazing he demanded, 'And do you love him?'

Her mind thumbed rapidly through the possible answers and their possible responses. She spooned tea into the teapot. 'I'm having his baby,' she said. Seriozha's face froze for two seconds then it spasmed and he jumped from his seat and grabbed her by the shoulders and shook her violently. She dropped the teaspoon and heard it tinkle as it hit the floor.

His face had crumpled, as if someone had squeezed it up

in their fist, tears streamed down his cheeks. 'No,' he cried and it sounded to Lydia as if the word had been forced out from his lungs under great pressure.

She was terrified but the more frightened she was the clearer and calmer her mind became. She could see every object in the room sharply and distinctly, from their reflections in the window to the yellow plastic rubbish bucket under the sink. She could hear the dripping tap and the hissing from the stove. She could smell the gas and the bucket of potatoes. Her mind was on emergency alert. She could feel it discarding her body, shrinking to a nugget the size of the child inside her. She let her body go limp in his grasp.

He lifted a hand and smacked it across her temple throwing her across the room and into the side of the door. She slipped to the floor, bringing her knees up in front of her to protect her stomach. Her head rang and there was a sharp pain where his hand had caught the bridge of her nose. She tried to get her mind to float above her like she had done in the hostess bar but it wouldn't leave. It cowered inside her and watched and waited for his next blow. At that moment she hated him. Hated him more than she had ever hated anyone before. Hate tasted acrid and stung in her mouth and nose like smoke.

He stood over her and spat on her. The hot liquid burnt on her skin as it dribbled down her forehead. '*Whore!*' he raged. 'You said you were going to have *my* child. You said you loved me.' He was still wearing his heavy outside boots. He drew back his right foot and kicked her hard in the thighs.

She clung to the side of the cupboard and concentrated on keeping her legs in front of her belly. Please let it be over soon, she prayed, please let it be over soon. He kicked her in the ribs and he kicked her face. Each time, her muscles flinched and tightened against the impact and the room flashed with a white light. She watched the material of his trousers change shape as he drew back his foot to kick her again, this time against the fingers that were so tightly gripping her knees to her stomach. The pain was terrible, like scorching wires biting her hands.

The kettle reached the boil and began to scream from the stove. Lydia's stomach convulsed as she saw his foot aim once more. The big rounded toe of his boot crunched into her mouth. She tasted leather and mud at the back of her throat and as she yelped she felt hot metallic blood flood across her tongue. The sound of the kettle seemed unbearably loud. It screamed and screamed. Seriozha spat on her once more. She heard the sound and then felt it splash on her cheek like hot bird shit. 'You can keep the money,' he said and through the hysterical screaming of the kettle she heard his feet crunch down the corridor and the front door slam behind him.

Chapter Forty

She remembered her kaleidoscope. That's how the air pulsed. There was a woman wasn't there? In a red coat pushing a pram across the tram tracks. Then her mother was there and she started screaming and screaming but that might have been the kettle. There was blood. Lots of it. It was drying now and going sticky. In some places it was cracking and black. Lydia unzipped her trousers and squeezed her hand into her knickers. There was no blood there. That was okay. The other blood didn't matter. She moved her hand to her stomach. In the last few days she had begun to feel a hard lump. Her mother was still there trying to fuss at her with a wet towel. Lydia struggled away but everything hurt. Her legs hurt and her mouth hurt, she could feel jagged broken teeth with her tongue. Her hands were the most painful of all. Her knuckles were swelling up forcing her fingers apart. They looked like somebody else's fingers: fat and tight and blue. And now she was walking but it was like being drunk. She wasn't sure if she could stay upright. The corridor was swinging crazily around her. Her mother was still there. Then she was lying on her bed with her arms on her chest like Lenin in his tomb.

Somebody once told her that he exploded because of the gases in his stomach and the Lenin you saw was pure wax. Hands were pulling a blanket over her. Her thighs and her shins throbbed. Each throb hit a drumskin of pain.

She saw her reflection in the glass doors of the cabinet holding a candle in front of her like teenage Russian girls do to find out who they will marry. When she looked for the image of her suitor above her right shoulder she saw the black and white photograph of her father dressed in his Red Army uniform for National Service. Her father shook his head and turned away from her. She was happy when his reflection dissolved, she smiled and she realised that she had been holding her breath but now she could breath easily again. Something made her lean forward and she noticed that all the china and glass ornaments were in fact people she knew. There was a girl that she had been to school with, there was Alex and Andrei, her mother, Seriozha and his daughter, Alex's sister Sally. Everyone was there, all dressed like old fashioned *babbas* and *mushiks* in aprons and boots and long, belted shirts and surrounded by painted rocks and silver birch trees.

The dream disintegrated and the kaleidoscope turned to show her face flattened and paralysed into an icon. Slowly it became encrusted in silver and in the dream she became terribly afraid. Alex was lying beside her encased in red granite. His face was covered in wax and he had developed a little beard like Lenin but she knew (and in her dream she was the only one that knew) that he wasn't actually dead. There was no point in saying anything because nobody would believe her. Lydia wanted to weep but when she tried she remembered that she was an icon and her tears wouldn't move.

The kaleidoscope turned again. Her baby was sitting in the middle of a clearing in a forest. In the clearing the sun was shining and the baby was playing with flowers in the grass. Lydia became angry because the image was too idyllic and sentimental to be real. This couldn't happen she told herself and as she was berating herself she became aware of something watching the child from amongst the dark pine trees. She snatched the baby and ran panting through the woods with the danger chasing her. When she got to the dacha she put the baby on the floor and covered it with an old-fashioned tin bath. Almost immediately there was a knock on the door. She opened it to a story-book wolf with a Party official's voice who told her that he knew who her father was and he had information suggesting that she was hiding an illicit baby in the house. Lydia denied the charge but the wolf grabbed her arm and started rocking her backwards and forwards. Then Lydia woke up sweating with fear to find Alex kneeling beside her where the wolf had been seconds earlier.

It gave her a shock when she touched him. He was actually there. His head didn't dissolve as she put her hand on it. She looked around the room. Everything around her glowed and sweated. Individual objects pulsed with dark and light like eclipsed moons or the colours and shapes you see when you close your eyes. Her vision had the bright jewelled texture of condensation. She felt the cool tickling touch of Alex and his breath on her stomach as if someone else was describing them to her. They were removed from her, separated from her body by a gap. Somewhere else and more real to her was the pain. But even the pain and the throbbing were just another layer that felt quite different and separate from the dark pod inside her that contained her baby, her new life. Her core, the only absolute and undefiled element of the shifting vague, twilit universe. She thought that it had been real to her before but now she realised that had been an illusion. She was only partially aware of the world around her. The foetus demanded her energy and she retreated deep inside herself, clinging to her womb.

Alex and her mother fluttered on the periphery of her attention. Alex became very angry. His face muscles contorted with agitation, his lips opening so that she could see the wet intimate interior of his mouth. She felt as though she were watching him through a windscreen and all she had to do was turn her head away from him and he would be gone.

Chapter Forty-One

At first Alex went crazy. He howled. He banged his head against the back of the door. He turned round and round in circles with his arms flapping wildly in the air. He wanted to break something but he didn't know what. His blood thundered in his eardrums like a gale.

'Bastard!' he screamed and then added, 'I'll kill him. I'll kill him. I'll kill him,' in whispered, chanting sobs as he sank to his knees in front of Lydia. She was lying lengthways on the sofa, a pale blue blanket wrapped around her body like a shroud. Her grotesquely swollen hands rested on her thighs. Her skin was greasy white and her mouth was huge and pulped and blood encrusted like a burst plum. She was facing him but she couldn't see him. Her eyes were focused somewhere else. His hands paddled desperately in the air above her but he didn't dare touch her. He jumped up, 'A doctor. Lydia we must get you a doctor.' He turned and shouted at her mother, 'We've got to get a doctor!'

Lydia swivelled her head very slightly on the pillow. 'No doctor. I don't need. No blood.'

'What are you talking about? There's fucking blood everywhere. You need medical attention.

'No doctor,' she repeated faintly and turned her head to the ceiling. He had to obey her. That was the thing about Lydia, she knew her own mind. Alex sighed. He began to cry with frustration. He felt like a baby. He hadn't been able to stop some psycho ex-boyfriend from beating Lydia up and now he couldn't even take care of her. Her mother had taken the black and white photograph of her father out of the cabinet and placed it on the table in front of her. She looked up at Alex. Her mouth was slightly open, she dropped her eyes to the photograph and then got up and switched on the television. Alex screamed. 'Fucking hell. How the fuck can you turn the television at a time like this Look at the state she's in. Is that all you're going to do. Sit there and watch fucking telly?' Olga sat down again and ignored him. He strode across the room and taking hold of her shoulders shouted at her face. She looked at him as if she was an idiot. There was nothing there. It was as if it had all been knocked out of her. It was like holding a shell. He shook her violently to try and get some reaction and then terrified that he might lose control, he dropped her and stormed out of the flat to smoke a cigarette in the soothing darkness of the landing . . .

Later Lydia sat up and accepted bread and jam and sweet tea. She wouldn't look at him. She didn't want him there. He held his breath and closed his eyes for a second. This is all such shit, he thought, but it scared him all the same and he began to doubt whether there'd ever been any closeness between them. Maybe the whole thing had been a fucking fantasy. He darted forward to plead with her and then changing his mind, quickly retreated. 'Let me make the bed?' he asked gently. She still wouldn't look at him. He stepped forward again and lifted her chin with a crooked forefinger. Her eyes slithered away to the side. Then very shakily she stood up and went to the bathroom. She's blaming me for this, thought Alex as he tucked the sheets into the corner of the sofa bed, she doesn't think it's just Seriozha, she thinks it's all the men in her life.

When Lydia came back Alex stepped out of her way and without a word she got undressed. He winced as she uncovered the huge blue and yellow bruises on her shins and thighs. She got naked under the covers and lay in the foetus position cradling her belly and staring fixedly into the glass cabinet. Alex switched off the light and joined her but unlike Lydia he left on his tee-shirt and boxer shorts and lay very straight and still at the far edge of the bed. Moonlight shone in through the windows like the blue glare of a television. Alex concentrated on the ceiling. His made his eyes follow a crack that ran like a life line from the right hand corner to the centre of the room where it branched in two. He couldn't tell whether Lydia was asleep or not. He listened to her breathing. It seemed that the whole room contracted slightly with each inhalation she made. There were other noises; voices echoing under the arch, a baby crying in a nearby flat and a light scratching that might have been mice or might have been cockroaches or might have been his imagination.

The night passed very, very slowly. There was an ornamental steel clock in the glass cabinet with a hammer that chimed every quarter of an hour. Alex counted them one by one like drops from a leaking tap. At quarter past two he slipped from the bed and, pulling out his rucksack from under the television table, found his guidebook to St Petersburg. He padded down the corridor to the kitchen. The cockroaches scuttled under the surfaces as he switched on the harsh strip light. He made himself a cup of tea, sat down at the table and consulted the guidebook. Lenfilm was listed with an address near Gorkovskaya metro station. Alex clenched his fists. A faint blue light clouded his vision. I'll be there before the bastard gets to work, he said to himself, and then opened both the windows and leaning out of the window smoked a cigarette into the freezing air to celebrate his decision. The metal moon shadows shivered in the courtyard below and the nicotine tasted sharp and crystalline in the hard frost. He closed the windows, circled his hands around the glass of tea to warm them and at some point fell asleep on the table.

At seven thirty Olga woke him by shaking his shoulder. He looked at her, startled and confused. During the night he'd knocked his tea over. The glass lay on its side and poking out of it like a tongue was a pool of spilt tea ringed by a brown line of evaporation. He'd fallen asleep on his book and the spine had left a long red indentation on his cheek. Olga pointed to the kettle, she was asking him whether he wanted another glass of tea. Alex shook his head and picking up his book hurried along the corridor to get dressed.

There was an acid tablet of fear fizzing inside his stomach all the way to Lenfilm. It had frozen hard overnight and the snow at the edges of the road crunched under foot; the cold clung to his skin. It was rush hour and people pushed, close packed into the trains. Alex clung to an aluminium pole. At Gorkovskaya there was a long, long escalator separated by a line of bronze and plastic Olympian torches. The people coming in the opposite direction stared straight in front of them as if they were on a production line. Alex felt they were hypnotising him into a dream or a film. He didn't want the escalator ever to end because in his mind's eye Seriozha was standing at the top waiting for him.

He remembered the police raid on the party in Dalston. At the time he'd thought he was rescuing Lydia, saving her, whisking her away from danger. He cringed with shame at the thought of it. It was so childish; the stuff of fairy stories. Was that what their marriage had been about? Was that what he was acting out now? Another fairy story; the avenging lover? He stopped at the top of the escalators. He could just turn around and go back again. He would never have to justify it to anyone. He would be the only one who knew. His stomach buckled and twisted with fear. Seriozha was a big man. He saw Lydia's swollen face in front of him. Who am I doing this for, he wondered.

Alex rubbed his hand on the moving hand rest. He remembered Seriozha's wife: '*he meant nothing to her, she didn't care, it meant nothing to her at all. That's why she let it happen. Have you discovered yet that your wife doesn't have a heart?*' The escalator fell away from him in a long cascade. It seemed to ripple like a waterfall of people. At the bottom a middle-aged woman in uniform sat in a booth and watched the passengers come and go.

He turned and walked through the barrier. Outside there was a liquor stall and a caravan selling flowers, beer and plastic cups of tea. To the right was a park. Alex bought a cup of tea. His gloves slipped on the plastic, the vapour breathed over him and the tea burnt his lips. He sat on a bench by the park. The number of layers he was wearing made him chumsy and stiff. He watched the people pouring out of the doors of the metro, down the steps and past him into the street that ran towards Lenfilm. He felt as if he had just stepped out of a powerful current. This is moronic, he thought, if I do this, if I go and pick a fight with Seriozha I'll be making myself just as much as of a git as he is.

He looked around him, it was a raw white day. In the park the wind played at the baubles hanging from the plane trees and an Alsatian was barking at a girl to throw it a stick. A taxi drew up at the kerb and let out an old lady laden with shopping bags. Something shifted inside Alex's mind. There's no point in me being here, he thought despondently. I should-n't have come in the first place, it's her fucked up country, I should leave her to it and get on with my own life. That's probably what she wants. He sat for a moment, with his elbows leaning on his knees, then he drank the rest of his tea in one gulp, discarded the empty cup in a metal bin and clambered laboriously up the steps back into the metro.

Chapter Forty-Two

When Lydia woke up her swollen upper lip was pressing hard against the base of her nostril and her eyes were weepy and crusted. She moved her right hand towards her face and a sharp, electric pain flashed across her knuckles. When she sat up a distorted face stared back at her from the glass of the cabinet. It was like looking in a trick mirror. That's not me, thought Lydia indignantly, that's not how I look at all.

She got out of bed and walked naked to the kitchen. The bruises on her shins ached. Her toe nails scratched on the worn wooden floorboards and as she walked she let her hand drag along the corridor wall. She peered out of the window at the empty courtyard. The paths between the staircase doors and the main arch onto the street were marked by dirty lines in the snow. She filled the kettle and jumped slightly as the tap sprayed cold water over her breasts. She'd been concentrating on her bruises: an external sensation took her by surprise.

She lit the stove and felt a strange quickening just below her tummy button. A fluttering. She stopped with the kettle in mid-air and her hand above the gas flame. The baby, she thought, I'm miscarrying. This is it. This is the beginning.

She put down the kettle and waited for the pain to start. She pushed her forefinger inside herself. There was no sign of blood. She stood, stiff with anticipation, and watched the courtyard through the slightly warped glass of the double window. An old lady shuffled along one of the paths like a little black starling and disappeared under the arch. I imagined it, decided Lydia, my body's playing tricks on me. Indigestion. I'm getting paranoid. Then the sensation came back; like a bird's wing fluttering against the inside of her belly. She lifted a battered hand and gently brushed it from her tummy button to her pubic hair. It's kicking, she realised and her blood sang with a rush of happiness; it's telling me that it's alive.

She sat at the table, drank her tea and stroked her hand meditatively round and round her belly in interlocking circles and figures of eight.

She stopped abruptly. Where's Alex? But no sooner has she asked herself than she knew instinctively where he had gone. In her mind's eye she saw Seriozha's trousers creasing as he lifted his foot ready to kick. 'Oh please no. He'll beat him to a pulp.' She whispered the words aloud and in English. The sound of her voice using a foreign language in the mute flat was strangely disturbing. She left her glass of tea on the table and ran down the corridor. The sofa bed was unmade. There was a puddle of clothes on the floor: the clothes that she had been wearing when Seriozha had attacked her. She couldn't wear those. She hurriedly pulled her suitcase out from under the television table and struggled painfully into a pair of jeans. A green V-neck and a black polo neck lay neatly folded at the top of the suitcase. It didn't matter which one she wore, it was completely unimportant. She stood staring at the suitcase in a panic of indecision. She remembered a proverb her grandmother used to tell her about a crow flying through the sky and approaching a pine tree.

There were no other obstacles in the sky and all the crow had to do was fly either to the left or to the right of the pine tree but it couldn't decide which way to go. 'Shall I go to the left or to the right. Left or right? Left or right?' All the time the pine tree was getting closer and closer but still the crow couldn't decide. 'Left or right? Left or right?' Bang! Lydia's grandmother would clap her arthritic hands and then let one drift slowly away to show the crow falling out of the sky as it hit the tree.

Lydia snatched the V-neck, pulled it gingerly over her head and dialled Seriozha's number. The moment he answered she slammed down the receiver as if it had stung her. His voice echoed in her ears. She stared at the grey plastic telephone and her teeth began to chatter. She shook her head to get rid of the sound of his voice and then went out onto the landing for cigarette to calm herself down. I shouldn't do this, she told herself, it's bad for the baby. I'll give up tomorrow. She struck a match against the side of the box and the phosphorous head flew off and hissed as it landed on the window sill. Five other matches broke or fizzled out. Finally she lit the cigarette and pecked at it in short staccato sucks. Alex please come back, she prayed, please come back.

She heard someone coming up the stairs. Alex? No, it was the woman from two floors above. Lydia turned towards the window so that the woman wouldn't see her damaged face. Alex was coming through the arch. Relief washed over her. His shoulders were hunched and but he was walking quite easily and he didn't appear to be wounded. The sound of the outside door banging shut spiralled up the stairwell followed by the slow trudge of his footsteps. She stood very still waiting for his face to come into view. A tear toppled over the rim of her right eye and trickled slowly down her face.

He bent his head and stared at his feet as they climbed each step. His hands were thrust deep in his pockets.

'What happened?' she mumbled as he reached the

landing. Her swollen lip made speaking unwieldy. She swallowed the saliva that was gathering in a reservoir between her bottom lip and her teeth.

He was startled. He hadn't noticed her standing there. 'What are you doing out here? You should be . . . Lydia why are you crying?'

She sniffed. 'I was worried about you. What happened?'

'Nothing. I wimped out.'

More tears crept down her face. 'Thank God Alex. I've been standing here torturing myself. Imagining what he might be doing to you.' She sobbed and hugging him around the waist, pressed her wet face into his coat.

'I don't understand you,' he said with bewilderment, 'I never know how you're going to react.' He put his arm around her shoulder, 'Come on, let's get you inside. I'll make a cup of tea.'

She pulled away from him abruptly. 'I don't want to spend any more time in there,' she said tearfully, 'Why can't we go out for a walk?'

'Are you sure you're up to it?'

'I'm fine,' she said sharply.

He took off his hat and ran his fingers through his flattened hair. 'You'd better put on a coat then.'

Lydia put on her outdoor clothes, locked the door and took his hand to walk down the stairs. He flinched as she touched him. He was frowning as he held open the door for her to step into the bright snow-light. I've damaged him, she thought, I've pushed him so badly off balance that he even questions why I want to hold his hand.

They walked along beside the canal. The curly wrought iron fence made fantastic patterns against the ice. The sky was low and white and the air was very still. It's going to snow, thought Lydia.

A woman in a fur coat passed them and then looked pityingly back at Lydia.

'She thinks it's me,' grumbled Alex sullenly.

'It doesn't matter. She's wrong.'

'It does matter. I don't like people thinking I'm some fucking psycho who gets his kicks from beating women up. Besides if I hadn't been around that fucker wouldn't have done it would he?'

They'd reached the bridge over the river to Vasilievsky Ostrov. Lydia leant over the railing. Cars hissed past them throwing arcs of grey granulated ice into the air. 'He probably would have done eventually,' she said, 'I never admitted it to myself but I was always aware that he was capable of getting really violent. I think he beats his wife up from time to time.' Alex leant on the railing beside her. Below them blocks of ice were jostling against each other and colliding with the stone supports of the bridge as the current swept them down to the Gulf of Finland.

'What did you see in him in the first place?'

'Not much really, but he was my boss and it seemed easier to go along with it. He was good company sometimes and he had a wife which meant that there was no danger of him getting too seriously involved.'

'He could have left his wife.'

'He wouldn't have done. Seriozha sees himself as an honourable man.'

'The most fucking perverted idea of honour I've ever heard of. I don't call beating women up very honourable and anyhow if he wasn't prepared to leave his wife he had absolutely no right to be possessive about you.'

'Yes I know but that wasn't the way that Seriozha saw it. Anyway, he was angry that I'd married you but that wasn't what set him off.'

'Well what was it then?'

Lydia said nothing for a moment and then she turned towards him. 'Give me your hand,' she said. Alex straightened up and, pushing his fingers under his hat, scratched his head. 'Lydia what are you talking about?'

She swallowed. She was frightened of what she was about

to do. She looked straight at him. She wouldn't let herself dip her eyes. 'Give me your hand,' she repeated. She took off her gloves and unbuttoned her coat. Tentatively he put his right hand forward. Lydia held it by the wrist, took off his glove and then pressed his fingers through the opening of her coat and under her clothes. His hand was cold on the skin of her belly. She felt herself trembling with nerves. 'Do you feel anything?' she asked. Alex's eyes widened. He glanced down at her stomach and then back to her face. He looked terrified. 'You're . . .?'

She nodded.

Frantically he patted his hand across her stomach. 'Shit Lydia, what are we going to do?'

Using the railing as a support she pushed herself up onto her toes and kissed his nose. 'I want you to go back to England,' she said.

He pulled his hand away and shook his head vehemently. 'I'm not going to desert you Lydia.'

'You won't be,' she said, 'you will come back to St Petersburg many times and I will visit you with the baby in England and when you are in your first play we will come and sit in the first row. You must go to drama school and try to fulfil your ambitions otherwise you'll just become bitter and angry with me and I will feel trapped by you. I want to stay here with your child and bring it up. I've had abortions before. I could have another one now. It's not too late yet but I'm not going to. I decided that this morning when I realised where you'd gone.' She looked away from him. She couldn't bear to hold his gaze any longer. The cold air stung on the tears that once again were dripping from her eyelashes. She gazed up the river and fixed her eyes on the thin gold spire of the Peter and Paul fortress; a crack of warmth in the cold, grey day. 'I've never told you that I love you because I don't; not in the way that you wanted me to but you have taught me something very important. You've shown me how to really give to someone, how to be absolutely open to them. You've shown me how to love someone and that's how I'll love your son. I haven't been straight with you before. I've never told you how I felt. There didn't seem any point. I've got a policy of not sharing anything with anyone unless I have to. I've always told myself never to ask anything of the people around me and if they chose to involve themselves in my life that's their decision. I suppose I've now realised that my silence has allowed people to invent whatever Lydia they want. I *am* responsible for that. I mean I never talked to Seriozha about what I felt or about anything that was going on in my life and look what happened there.'

He touched her cheek with the crook of his forefinger, 'I've never seen you cry before,' he said quietly.

'No, well you wouldn't,' she replied.

'You say you haven't been straight with me but I don't think I have either. I was thinking this morning when I decided that I wouldn't go to Seriozha, I was thinking that I'd just imposed my own imagination onto you without ever really checking whether you shared my dreams.'

'You were just such an incredible thing to happen to me. You were like this magic creature that flew into my life and after the summer with Mum I was so desperate to start living that I fell for you completely. But in a way it wasn't really to do with you, I know this sounds awful but it could have been anyone. I wanted to feel. I *wanted* to fall in love. All it needed was a trigger and that was you. You were so exotic and mysterious. I'd never met anyone like you before and you were in trouble so I had all these stupid romantic visions and I thought I could rescue you and whisk you away like some fucking white knight on his charger.'

'You're demeaning it Alex. What you did was a big and generous thing. I *was* in trouble and you helped me when I really needed somebody. What I should have done is told you how I felt and then at least you would have known what was going on in my head and maybe you wouldn't have got so carried away.'

'I wouldn't be so sure about that Lydia. I don't know if I would have listened. Anyhow you did try: don't you remember? When I asked you to marry me you spelt it out.'

'Do you regret it?'

He stepped behind her, she felt the warmth of his body as he wrapped his arms around her and rested his chin on the top of her head. 'I regret hurting Mum and Sally, but that's my fault. I could have handled that a lot better. I just didn't think enough about how they would react. That's all I regret though. I don't regret meeting you for a second: or getting married for that matter. I mean you are still the most amazing thing that's ever happened to me. It's just that what's between us isn't quite what I thought it was. I've changed Lydia. I can't quite explain what it is but it's as if everything in my life is more solid now: more real. It's like I've got a handle on stuff now that was all just ideas before.'

'And the child? How do you feel about that?'

His hot breath parted her hair as he sighed. He squeezed her even more tightly before a yelp from Lydia reminded him of her bruises 'It's a big one Lydia. I can't quite get my head around it yet. If you really want to do it then I'll try and help you out with any cash I earn or whatever but to tell you the truth when you said that you wanted me to go back to England and try for drama school again my heart leapt. It sounds cowardly but the idea of being a father scares me completely shitless. I don't feel ready for that yet, I mean I'm not really sure if I've stopped being a kid myself.'

'Alex do you remember saying to me that if we got married it would be between us? It would be *our* marriage. It would have nothing to do with my government or your government. It would be what we wanted it to be. Well you were right. That's exactly what's happening here. It won't be easy. I know that but I'll manage and my mother will help me and somehow or other I'll make sure that our child will have more contact with you than I had with my father.'

'Or I with mine,' whispered Alex.

Lydia turned around in his arms and gripped tightly onto the lapels of his coat. 'This is our child,' she said fiercely, 'and it's not going to have parents with shadow lives. That's the most important thing.'

A selection of other books from Sceptre

SAM GOLOD
    – Sophia Creswell   0 340 666404 £6.99 ☐

TRICK OF THE LIGHT
    – Jill Dawson   0 340 653833 £6.99 ☐

THE HOUSEHUNTER
    – Henry Sutton   0 340 717319 £6.99 ☐

SINGLING OUT THE COUPLES
    – Stella Duffy   0 340 715618 £6.99 ☐

WILD WAYS
    – Jill Dawson & Margo Daly, eds   0 340 69517X £6.99 ☐

All Sceptre books are available from your local bookshop or news-agent, or can be ordered direct from the publisher. Just tick the titles you want and fill in the form below. Prices and availability subject to change without notice.

Hodder & Stoughton Books, Cash Sales Department, Bookpoint, 39 Milton Park, Abingdon, OXON, OX14 4TD, UK. E-mail address: order@bookpoint.co.uk. If you have a credit card you may order by telephone – (01235) 400414.

Please enclose a cheque or postal order made payable to Bookpoint Ltd to the value of the cover price and allow the following for postage and packing:

UK & BFPO – £1.00 for the first book, 50p for the second book, and 30p for each additional book ordered up to a maximum charge of £3.00. OVERSEAS & EIRE – £2.00 for the first book, £1.00 for the second book and 50p for each additional book.

Name_____

Address _____

_____

_____

If you would prefer to pay by credit card, please complete:

Please debit my Visa/Access/Diner's Card/American Express (delete as applicable) card no:

☐☐☐☐☐☐☐☐☐☐☐☐☐☐☐☐

Signature_____

Expiry Date_____

If you would NOT like to receive further information on our products please tick the box. ☐